CW00684127

HEAT

1.
VISION

The Messerschmitt lurched, an engine blossoming into flames. One wingtip thumbing out the moon, it carved an arc of light through the night sky, silhouetting the granite tors of the moor below against a second sunset.

"der fluch!" cried the pilot, struggling with the controls.

His passenger rocked in his seat, pressing his eyes shut. What was the curse? All he had been told was that they carried an important historical artefact which must be taken far away. They were losing the war and it wouldn't be safe when the fight was over.

They had been flying low, hoping to avoid detection by radar, and there was no room for error. With a sudden suck of air the pilot ejected, leaving behind the stricken plane and the smell of burnt powder. He twisted back beneath his parachute and saw the aircraft fall away beneath him. There was no second ejector seat. His yell was lost on the empty sky, whipped away by the wind and sung between stunted oaks, rattled down abandoned mineshafts or swept over the bare rocks of the higher tors. His passenger didn't hear it as he raced gravity to the earth.

The plane landed in a skid, trailing a meteor tail of fire. Night animals scattered at the intrusion, fleeing into burrows or taking flight clumsily, croaking a warning. It slowed and ground to a halt, hot metal crackling and beginning to hiss as water seeped in. The moor is like a great green sponge, pockmarked with bogs and running with fast underground rivers. A downed plane was not new to it. With a slow gentleness it welcomed metal and flesh back to the earth, oily water creeping over fuselage and wings until at last the bog closed completely over the plane. All that was left was a long graze in the earth, and that would heal in time.

Gemma stirred sleepily, brushing a strand of brown hair from her face. It wasn't light yet, but it sounded like a fox had pulled over the bin again.

"Bloody things," she muttered, reaching for her alarm clock. Five past six. Far too early. The noise came again, louder this time. She wondered briefly if the local foxes had developed a type of Morse Code and the one outside was broadcasting to his friends that he had found some out of date ham and a used nappy. The knocking happened a third time. She sighed. No, it was even worse than that; someone was knocking on her door.

"Hello-" she began, but the door she had opened a crack was pushed open wide and a body bundled in before she could say any more. There was only one person capable of such enthusiasm at this time of the morning. "Adrian," she said.

"Good morning. I brought you some coffee." he handed her the takeaway cup.

"Don't you think I get enough coffee at work?" she said, taking a sip.

"I don't know. Can you get enough coffee?"

She took another swig. "Probably not. What do you want?"

"I want to be a good friend and take you away somewhere nice."

Gemma raised an eyebrow. She knew all about Adrian's definition of nice. He was the kind of friend who would drag you around a ruined church for four hours because he had to keep stopping to feel the vibrations. He was the kind of friend who would disguise a weekend of cheesy ghost hunting as a spa break. He was the kind of friend who would promise that there definitely weren't going to be any vigils, mediums or angel card readings involved whilst failing to mention that you were booked in for a beginners lesson on divination.

"That work thing I just mentioned? I have it today. And tomorrow, and the day after that."

"Call in sick."

"I think I've used up all my sick days for the rest of my life. See this flat? Each month I need to give a man money so that I can continue to live here. Do you know how I make that money?"

"Yes, yes," Adrian brushed her sarcasm aside. "But I'm talking about fresh air, green hills and, sod it, pub lunches *and* pub dinners."

Gemma took another gulp of coffee. "I'm listening."

An hour later the city was disappearing past the car window, the coffee shop was left believing that Gemma's Grandmother had died, and Adrian was grinning like a chlld who'd got at the liqueurs.

"Go on then," said Gemma, "You can tell me where we're going now. It's unlikely I'll jump out of the car at this speed."

Adrian sat with one hand on the steering wheel, the other holding a can of energy drink upright on his thigh. Warm air from the open sunroof was blowing his fringe back from oversized sunglasses.

"Dartmoor."

Gemma allowed herself to settle in her seat a little more. Dartmoor sounded safe. As far as she knew, it was full of ponies and places selling cream tea and the kind of fudge that you give as a gift to people you don't know properly. The car rattled rhythmically beneath her, making her mind slow. It had been a while since she had been in Adrian's old Beetle and she was reminded afresh just how close to the road his lowering had made it.

"Ok." She let her eyes close, her body too used to caffeine to let a strong coffee get in the way of sleep.

The car slowed down as Adrian took an exit off the motorway and turned down a series of rapidly narrowing roads. Gemma woke with her face pressed to the window and an uncomfortable notion that she had been dribbling.

"Are we there?" she slurred.

"Not quite," said Adrian, "I'm just dropping in on a friend."

"Do they know we're coming?"

"She will soon." He turned the car down a small side road and bumped almost immediately up onto a steep, gravel driveway. It had the grey and green look of neglect, with established crops of weeds spreading from the corners.

"I take it she likes her privacy."

The road beyond the driveway narrowed and shortly afterwards petered out into a muddy track. A tall conifer hedge shielded the house on two sides and there were no neighbours in sight.

"You could say that."

Gemma followed Adrian to the front door. Years ago it must have been white, but sustained neglect had left it speckled with moss and yellow fungus. The two glass panels were papered over from the inside with pages of old newspaper, a deposit of dust and dead flies gathering in the space between. Glancing side to side, she saw that all the ground floor windows had been covered up in the same way.

He knocked sharply.

"Someone actually lives here?" Gemma asked.

"It keeps people away," Adrian murmured, giving the door a gentle push. It moved slightly. He knocked again. A few more seconds passed without a response so he pushed harder, this time setting all his weight against the wood. The door groaned slowly open.

Gemma stepped back in shock. The inside of the house assaulted her eyes with colour, different in every way to the rotting exterior. The hallway was brightly lit and painted lime green from floor to ceiling, which was painted black but crisscrossed with string upon string of fairy lights, glinting like netted stars.

Adrian beckoned her inside.

She hesitated. If the set up outside was meant to keep people out, wouldn't she be angry they were intruding? He grabbed her arm and pulled. She stumbled after him.

"Hello," he called. There was still no answer. He tried again. "Elaine!" But there was no sign of anyone inside the house.

Gemma followed him nervously, checking back over her shoulder. She crept close behind as he looked in on an immaculately tidy, but empty, kitchen. She glimpsed a darkened living room, filled with the dim suggestions of book shelves and cluttered tables. "What kind of person leaves their door open like that?"

"Someone who never has unexpected guests," Adrian replied.

"She'll be over the moon that we've dropped by then."

Adrian smiled. "She certainly will."

"I'm in the studio!" called a clear voice from somewhere ahead.

Adrian and Gemma followed the sound into a large room stacked with canvasses. The paintings were piled in teetering heaps against all four walls, some ripped and dusty with age. Any surface not hidden by art was covered by paint of every colour; the walls swam with patterns and snatches of murals vying for space. Away to one side was a low coffee table with three chairs. Through the very centre of the room ran the stump of a bisecting wall that once had split it in two, but was now pulled down. The unwanted masonry had been painted and piled in a rough circle around an enormous easel. Elaine stood in front of it.

"Welcome," she said, turning from her work. Her clothes were splattered with nearly as much paint as the walls.

"I was driving by so I thought I'd drop in and see you. I'd like you to meet-"

But Elaine cut Adrian off with a raised hand.

As if seized by sudden inspiration, she turned back to her canvas and began painting in wild strokes which rocked the easel. Minutes passed as she worked.

Gemma watched in fascination. The woman's hand moved from her palette to the easel without any sign of her gaze moving from the painting, but she didn't make any mistakes.

"Have we come at a bad time?" He asked.

12

Elaine jerked back to face him, as if surprised by his presence.

Adrian opened his mouth to apologise but she put her finger to her lips to stop him.

"There's a girl with you," she said.

He shifted uncomfortably. "I didn't think you'd mind me bringing a friend."

"I don't. What's your name young lady?"

Gemma's eyes flicked sideways to Adrian, who nodded encouragingly. She introduced herself.

"Of course," Elaine nodded. She felt for the canvas with a paint smeared hand and Gemma realized that the woman was completely blind. Elaine raked at her hair impatiently and wiped a line of silver paint through it. The streak shone damply against the dark brown tangle, already laced with strands of early grey. Momentarily inspired again she returned to the painting, abandoning the brush to knead the paint into the canvas with her bare hands. "This one is for you Gemma," she said.

Adrian walked with loud, exaggerated steps over to examine the other paintings that were stacked against the wall. Years ago he had asked Elaine how she painted each image so perfectly, without her eyesight to guide her hand. She had explained that she saw very well, thank you, just not the things of this world.

"Patience," Elaine told him kindly, "one day you'll have your own." She turned back to Gemma. "Did Adrian tell you I see visions?"

"No, he didn't." She shot Adrian a dark look, knowing Elaine couldn't see it.

"It might have put you off I suppose. Some people get worried over it; they think I'll be able to gaze straight into their soul." She laughed and tossed her hair over her shoulder. "I do see things, but most of them are things that anyone else could if they didn't block them out. The difference is I can't. I can't stop seeing them or explain them away as my eyes playing tricks on me. What I see isn't always very nice. But I paint them all." She stepped to one side and beckoned Gemma forward.

"That's very... interesting," she said, attempting to shuffle back behind Adrian. He pushed her firmly forward. Once she was within reach Elaine took her by the shoulder and pulled her close to the painting.

Adrian followed.

A single figure filled the canvas, painted from the waist upwards. White, gold and silver swept in feathery strokes around a torso silhouetted against a blinding background of white light. The painting was beautiful, but not complete. The chest was still sketched as a spider web of rough lines, and it seemed Elaine hadn't yet decided on the design of clothing. Only half of the face was close to finished, but already framed by waves of long blonde hair. The lips formed a knowing smile.

Gemma realized she was staring, and closed her mouth.

"Beautiful, yes?" asked Elaine.

Gemma nodded, then remembered and whispered; "yes."

"But more than that as well," Elaine continued, "far more." She turned her unseeing eyes back to the picture and placed a pale hand on the damp canvas. It drew slowly into a tight claw, as if she was sucking her vision back out of the image. She spun round, her hand drawn into a fist, and fixed Gemma with white gold eyes, filled to the brim with the painting.

She took a hesitant step back but Adrian stood

firmly in her way, so she couldn't retreat any further.

Elaine spoke slowly and rhythmically.

"An autumn night. The leaves cling half dead to the trees; they litter the road and make it treacherous. A car approaches. Its headlights are set to full beam against the shadows; slicing the darkness with parallel lines. A second car approaches from the opposite direction. The man inside drives recklessly, weaving between the lanes, unaware of anyone else on the road. Ahead, the woman sees him speed towards her. She knows he'll hit her car. She tenses with fear, and her baby kicks inside her. The impact will come any moment. Some might say that her death had already been decided. But it isn't just fate that holds the power to shape a life. Someone had a reason to keep her alive. A figure bursts onto the road on a white horse and halts, rearing up between the cars. The drunk driver shields his eyes from the painful light, taking both hands off the wheel. His car swerves off the road, crumpling against a tree. The woman's car rolls to a halt. She pushes open her door and stumbles out of the car. Her saviour has already gone. All she saw was a glowing outline, burnt into her mind by the lights of the oncoming car. But she knew she had seen an angel."

Gemma had turned pale. She shook her head, and then threw another angry look at Adrian.

"Does that mean anything to you?" Elaine asked curtly, her voice normal again.

Adrian watched Gemma expectantly.

She glanced from Elaine to the painting. A long time ago she had put some thought into how an angel might look, but the figure captured on the canvas was a better depiction than she had ever managed. She remembered her mum telling the story in hospital, every

15

word spoken in a whisper for fear her dad might come in and overhear. He'd sent her back there because he thought she was ill again, just as she had been after Gemma was born. The doctor told him that the visions were brought on by stress. Patients reported seeing angels after they had been through traumatic experiences, such as the car crash and consequential early birth. Everyone but her mother had thought Gemma would die.

"I don't think so," she replied.

Elaine smiled and raised her index finger towards the ceiling. "The angel still watches over you now, just as it watched over your mother and made sure that you were born."

There was a dense silence that seemed to seep from the canvas, rolling outwards like a heavy mist, and then...

"That is so cool," said Adrian.

"I'll make tea," said Elaine. The spell was broken.

Gemma watched her stride out of the room without hesitation. She must know the house like her own body. As soon as Elaine was gone she turned on Adrian. "I can't believe you told someone else that story, you knew it was a family secret."

His eyes widened with surprise. "What are you talking about?"

"I trusted you with that story, which is ridiculous anyway, and you told it to Elaine. Can't you keep a secret?"

"Of course I can," he crossed his arms over his chest, "but you've never told me that story. That's the first time I've heard it."

Gemma shook her head jerkily, her eyebrows

drawn close with confusion. "I must have told you."

"No, but you should have. What a story!"

She put her hand over her mouth and stared back at the painting. "Just forget about it. I wish no one knew, because it's all nonsense anyway."

Elaine returned with three cups of steaming tea and a bowl of brown sugar. She set them down on the small coffee table tucked away in a corner, and they each took a seat. Adrian guiltily poured five spoonfuls of sugar into his small cup.

"You haven't visited me just to introduce your friend," Elaine told him.

He glanced nervously at Gemma and then back to Elaine. "No, it wasn't quite the whole reason," he paused for a moment and looked down at his hands, "I also think I've had a visionary dream."

"What makes you think so?" Elaine asked.

Dear Lord no thought Gemma.

Adrian looked up and spread his fingers in front of his chest. "The feeling I got with it. It stayed with me when I woke up. It was a call for help."

Elaine took a long sip of her tea and settled back in her chair. "Dreams are difficult Adrian. Even I find them hard to interpret. There's too much of yourself in them."

He swirled the tea slowly round his cup. This wasn't the reaction he'd been hoping for. "I'm sure about this," he said firmly.

Elaine looked at him for what seemed like a long time. "What did you see?"

"It was a dead child in an underground chamber. There were two old skeletons as well. He had died trapped in there, hugging one of them for comfort. I think his spirit is still stuck there. He wants me to free him."

She considered this carefully, sipping from her mug as she did so. "I think you need to be very careful. What you saw was probably just a normal dream. Dark, yes, but nothing to worry about."

Adrian pursed his lips, tapping the side of his cup with his nails. "What if I ignore it and I was right?"

Elaine placed both her hands, palm down, on the table. "What you do is your own choice. I can only advise you. I think your dream is not visionary, but then I am not you. Do you know where to go?"

"Dartmoor. Before I was underground I was out in the open. There was a symbol on a gatepost that I traced online."

"Then go. Go to Dartmoor. If there truly is meaning to this, then perhaps you will find a guide."

Adrian grinned broadly. He drained his cup in one go and set it down firmly on the table. He was eager to be gone.

Gemma wasn't so pleased. Of course Elaine's vision was nothing more than an elaborate party trick, although it had shaken her up all the same. The idea of a few days away was more appealing than ever, but searching for dead children underground wasn't her idea of holiday entertainment. Adrian could go looking for dead things on his own. She'd find a pub.

Elaine unlocked a tiny drawer in the table and handed Adrian something wrapped in brown paper. "Keep it safe and read it somewhere alone. Follow the instructions if you need to free a spirit."

He nodded rapidly.

"Ring me if you need to," she said.

Adrian thanked her again and stood up, almost knocking over his chair.

Gemma glanced back once as they left. Elaine was working on the painting again.

The rest of the drive passed quickly. Adrian turned the radio up and began to sing along.

Gemma was glad to avoid talking. She gazed blankly out of the window, her thoughts going back to the story Elaine had told. How had she known? As far as she knew, her mum hadn't told anyone except her and dad, and after his reaction she kept what happened to herself. She refused to do as he asked and admit it was a hallucination caused by stress; instead she just stopped mentioning it. In time it was forgotten. Until now that was.

Adrian turned the music down. "What if you saw your angel in Dartmoor?"

"I won't."

"Why? Don't you want to meet her?"

"No, I don't. I have enough paranormal activity in my life with you, thanks."

"I think you're lucky," he said wistfully, "I wish I had an angel to look after me."

"Have mine."

Adrian shook his head and turned the music back up. There was no hope for some people. They drove on without talking for a while.

Eventually Gemma began to feel guilty. Crushing Adrian's enthusiasm was like taking a stick from a child. She turned the music down. "What's the plan if you do find this spirit anyway?"

"*When* I find it," Adrian corrected her, "I will use the power within me to set it free. Of course I'll check the instructions Elaine gave me, but I imagine I will call upon the cleansing power of a white candle to summon the spirit. Then I will use a black candle to open the portal to the world of the dead..."

Gemma let him talk on, his voice soothing when she wasn't concentrating on the exact words. Winding down her window, she closed her eyes and sat back to enjoy the warm air on her face. She resolved to avoid any portals to the world of the dead. The world of the living was tricky enough.

2.
MASK

"Welcome to Dartmoor," said Adrian, taking in the patchwork of hedged fields with a wave of his arm.

Gemma turned to look and was thrown hard against the car door, her lungs emptying in a ragged gasp. He grabbed the steering wheel, spinning it wildly as the car bucked beneath them. The cattle grid had caught him by surprise. With another bump the wheels rattled clear of the grid, but hit the tarmac at the wrong angle and dragged the car off the road. Gemma screamed. The car mounted the grass, shaking like it would fall apart. "Slow down!" she yelled. There was a metallic screech as the vehicle found the road again, throwing up clumps of earth from the back wheels.

"Just checking you're awake." Adrian grinned, glancing back to check he hadn't dislodged anything important. The brown track across the grass was the only evidence, and that was soon left behind.

"Of course you were." She looked out of her window, rubbing her shoulder, and watched green fields giving way to wild grass and patchy scrub. They stopped seeing houses. The small road became narrower and in places it was uneven or crumbling into gravel. Civilisation seemed a long way behind, and the moor was a wilderness empty of life.

Gemma shivered and shut the window. It was late afternoon and already she was thinking longingly of her own flat. Back in London there were proper roads and signposts; out here there was nothing but plants and grass. It would be so easy to get lost.

"Stop!" she cried.

Adrian rolled the car to a halt. Next to the road was shaggy brown pony which stopped grazing to look up at them. A tiny foal peered up from between its legs. Gemma wound down her window and reached out. The pony sniffed her hand hopefully, but turned away when it realized there was no food. "We should tell someone they've got loose."

"They live out here," said Adrian, "people turn them out on the moor to graze."

"How do you know all this?"

"Waking up at three in the morning allows lots of time for research."

Gemma crossed her arms. "Where are we staying?"

"Well Princetown is the largest town, and it's right in the middle of the moor. I thought we'd have the best chance of finding somewhere there."

"Makes sense," Gemma replied. She was trying to lure the pony back over so she could stroke it. It ignored her, but the foal began to test whether the wing mirror was edible.

"Get off that!" yelled Adrian. He sped off and refused to stop again.

Another cattle grid marked the transition from moor to town, but this time Adrian slowed right down for it. They turned right down a wide street flanked by grey stone buildings and followed the signs for parking, which was between a small green and an old fashioned forge with a horseshoe nailed above the door. Adrian pulled into the nearest space and threw open his door so he could stretch. The air was warm and carried a hint of wood smoke.

Gemma clambered out of the car while he went to find the parking meter. She took a deep breath, flexed her arms and legs, and began to relax. Adrian could run around looking for spirits and she could stay here and explore the shops. Perhaps there was hope for the trip after all.

"It's parking by donation," called Adrian, "I want to live here."

Gemma shut her door and walked over to join him. There was a stone box with a brass image of pony and a slot for money. "What have you put in?"

"My chosen donation of nothing."

Gemma sighed and dropped in a pound coin. "Now where are we going?"

Adrian slipped his arm into hers and led her back onto what she guessed must be the main road, before stopping outside a large white building. It stood out from all the other shops on the street. A set of wide, sweeping steps led up to a double doorway, framed on each side by thick roman pillars.

"Looks posh. Is it a shop?" asked Gemma.

He strode up the steps and popped his head inside, before running back down. "It's the Visitor Centre. Shall we go in?"

Gemma shrugged, disappointed. "If you want to."

Inside, the Centre was modern and bright. A large table to the left sold key rings and light up pens for children, and to the right was a semicircular desk with a stern looking woman behind it. She looked up from whatever she was doing to stare at them.

"We shut in half an hour," she warned.

Adrian thanked her and turned to the novelty

giftware. He picked out a toy pony and lifted its tail at the woman as soon as she looked away.

"Stop that," said Gemma, "she'll throw us out."

He stuck out his tongue and walked to a display on the far side of the room.

She noticed another donation box, this time for the Visitor Centre. It was missing the cute pony; Instead it was moulded in the form of a snarling hound, the jaws stretched wide for coins and glowing with a weird green light from somewhere inside.

"The Hound of the Baskervilles," read Adrian from the display board, "was set on wild and brooding Dartmoor-"

"That explains this then," said Gemma, feeding the hound a fifty pence coin.

She wandered deeper into the centre, leaving Adrian to read on his own. The displays and diagrams created the atmosphere of a museum. On one side of the room they traced the history of mining on the moor in brightly coloured pictures that stretched to the ceiling. She eyed the timeline idly, following it through into the next room. She had moved on to a display about the different types of pony on the moor when Adrian ran in waving a sheet of paper.

"You've got to do one of these!" He danced about, fluttering the sheet in front of her face.

"Let me see that," she said, taking the paper from his hand. It was a neat brass rubbing in black crayon of some kind of animal. Adrian had written his name in the corner of the page. "What's it meant to be?"

He took her by the crook of her arm and dragged her into the next room. A massive dog was trapped halfway through clawing its way out of a wooden crate.

Splinters of wood littered the floor like spilled needles; the smashed edges of the crate were bloody from the brute's struggling. Gemma stepped back. The creature paused, and then turned two blood red eyes on her.

"Some display, huh?" said Adrian.

Gemma let out the breath she had been holding. The dog was cast in silver and the mouth was open to take coins. The red eyes were just lights.

Adrian was selecting a sheet of paper and a crayon.

She walked over to the display, waiting for the animatronics to start again. The dog didn't move. She hesitated and then placed her hand on the silver snout. It was cold and hard, worn smooth by countless curious fingers. There was a paragraph of text above it:

Many legends speak of a great black beast which stalks the tors and hollows of the moor. In one story a farmer tells of being followed home by a great black dog with sulphurous breath, reeking of death. Walkers have reported sightings of a big cat, while locals blame this creature for killing sheep and hens. In one case experts have confirmed paw prints found out on the moor to be those of a big cat, but in another the skull of a puma found on the moor was discovered to have come from an exotic rug. Is the Beast of Dartmoor fact or fiction? You must decide. Either way, the legend inspired Arthur Conan Doyle in his famous depiction of the Hound of the Baskervilles, which in his novel haunted the great 'Grimpen Mire'.

Gemma looked at the various depictions of the beast. One was taken from the cover of Conan Doyle's novel and showed an enormous black hound with glowing green eyes and a mouth dripping with slime. Another was a hugely magnified photograph showing the grainy outline of a puma.

Adrian pushed a red crayon into her hand. She looked down. He'd put a fresh sheet of paper over the brass plate.

"Give it a go," he said.

She leaned down and steadied the corner of the paper with her hand. A minute later her own image of the beast had appeared on the page. She eyed it critically. It wasn't as neat as Adrian's.

"We can stick them up wherever we stay," he suggested, taking one in each hand and holding them up.

"Because that wouldn't be weird."

"Come on, it'll be the closest we'll get to seeing it."

"Good. Shall we find this place to stay then?" Gemma wondered if there would be any rooms left. She hoped there were. A night in the car wasn't appealing.

"I'll ask for a recommendation." Adrian winked and strode back towards the desk.

Gemma began to follow, but the final display caught her eye. There was a rack of masks with a notice inviting visitors to try them on, and the well placed mirror made it hard to resist. She peered around the corner at Adrian; he was leaning against the desk in conversation with the snobbish woman. It was close to closing time and there was no one else in the Centre so, sure no one could see her, Gemma picked up a dog mask and put it on.

The inside of the snout smelt like old leather and sweat. Her immediate reaction was to pull it straight off, but she paused to glance in the mirror first. Her reflection was transformed. She forgot about the smell and stared. A pair of pert ears now sprouted from the top of her head and her eyes peered out from over a short snout. She wiggled her mouth experimentally and saw her snout move in the glass.

There was a paragraph of print on the wall near the mirror. She skimmed through it, learning that the masks had been used in a local play based on the legend of the Wild Hunt. There was a grainy picture of a man wearing a red coat, surrounded by young girls on their knees in the hound masks. Gemma narrowed her eyes to look more closely. Then she pulled back with a jolt as she felt the mask tighten uncomfortably on her face. The strap cut into the back of her head; a line of hot pain melting the hound face onto hers. She felt the ears take root in her skull; parasitic muscles latching hungrily onto her own. The mask had become her face. She was now a hound. Her nose twitched at the scent of blood on the air, her legs throbbed with the desire to run; from far away a horn summoned her to the hunt.

"Gemma?" said Adrian.

The voice called her back. She forced her nails under the edges of the mask, feeling as if she would tear off her own skin. Pulling, she felt her ears wrench from their roots as hot blood trickled down her cheek. The mask came off. She touched her face gently, expecting to find her fingertip red, but the moisture was only sweat. "Yes?"

"Do you mind getting your own breakfast?"
"No."

"Okay," Adrian went back to his conversation.

Gemma put the mask back on the rack with the others. It grinned at her, empty eyes creased into a mocking glare. The car journey had been long and tiring, and then she'd come here and spent however long reading stupid stories. That would make anyone see things.

"Realistic aren't they?"

Gemma spun round to see who was talking. She'd been sure that she and Adrian were the only people there.

A very slim young man with shoulder length red hair stood peering in from the previous room. His lips were pursed together like he was holding in laughter.

"I suppose so." Gemma began to edge towards the exit.

The youth stumbled into the room and pulled a mask on. Suddenly he dropped to all fours, his fingers curling into paws as he scampered in a circle around her. He sat down on his back legs, then tilted his head to the ceiling and let out a tuneless howl. Then he jumped to his feet again, ripped off the mask and threw it back on the rack.

"I'm Owain," he said breathlessly. His cheeks were flushed and clashed hugely with his hair.

"Okay," replied Gemma, backing slowly away. He watched her, but didn't say any more. Once she was far enough from him she turned round and ran to Adrian. She only dared to look back once she had reached the desk. There was no one there.

"You alright?" Adrian asked.

She nodded, pushing her hair back from her face. It was too hot inside. She needed some air.

Adrian followed her out a few minutes later, the woman from behind the desk right behind him with a set of keys. She pushed the door closed as soon as he stepped outside.

"Wait," called Gemma. The woman scowled at her through the glass, but opened the door a crack.

"Yes?"

"There's still someone inside."

The woman pursed her lips and glared. "You were the last two people in here. If there was anyone else I would have seen them come in the door. Goodbye." She slammed the door and turned the key in the lock. Then she turned the lights out.

Adrian turned to Gemma. "I didn't see anyone else," he said.

She glanced back at the darkened glass. "There was a youngish guy messing around with the masks. Maybe he works out back or something."

"Someone must clean the place at night."

Gemma nodded firmly. "Yeah that must be it."

"Matron in there said the cheapest place to stay round here is the Café just down the road, I think they have bunk beds."

"What's the other option?"

Adrian laughed. "The pub."

The pub was dark, dirty and fully booked. Gemma followed Adrian further down the road to the bright glass front of the Fox Tor Café. He pushed the door open and a little bell jingled to call a plump young woman to the counter. She dusted floury hands on her apron and brought with her the smell of fresh baking.

Adrian dodged through the tables to the counter. "Do you have any bunks left tonight?" he asked the girl.

She smiled, producing a large dimple on each cheek.

"I do indeed, just for yourselves?"

Adrian nodded.

"You're very welcome; you're our only guests for tonight so far so you can pick any ones you want. Follow me and I'll show you them." She lifted up a section of the counter and stepped out. "Come on." She strode ahead of them in a businesslike manner. The smell of fresh cakes and bread accompanied her like a perfume.

The accommodation was in a separate building, reached through the back door of the Café. It was built in what would have been the garden before the building had been converted into a business. The unpainted bricks and corrugated iron roof reminded Gemma of an air raid shelter. The girl took a key from the front pocket of her apron and unlocked the door.

"I bet this place has some history," Adrian whispered.

Gemma crumpled her nose. She hoped it had a history of thorough cleaning.

"Here we are," said the girl, opening the door.

Adrian followed her inside. The interior was clean and bright, with eight bunk beds pushed against the walls in two rows.

"How much is it per night?" he asked.

Gemma crept in behind him, straining her eyes to check for unmanageable levels of dirt or insect inhabitation.

"Twelve pounds each," the girl replied.

Gemma continued her look around doubtfully. *So this is what twelve pound worth of privacy looks like*, she thought.

The girl briefly showed them the single ladies and gents toilets, the four sinks and the cupboard with a small supply of rolled up towels. Then they followed her back into the café to settle up and collect their key, which hung on a key-ring with a small wooden fox. Gemma hoped it wouldn't be a long stay.

"Where would you recommend for dinner?" Adrian asked the girl. Gemma registered an interest as the girl clapped her hands together and leaned closer.

"Definitely the Plume of Feathers," she said, "they do the best rabbit pie."

Adrian thanked her politely and didn't let his stomach rumble until they were outside.

Owain snuck out of the back exit to the Visitor Centre, humming softly to himself. He glanced left to right and then, seeing that the road was empty, made a run for it. The cattle grid was in sight and he pressed his legs to move faster. The kerb took him momentarily by surprise, but in less than a second he was up and running again. He jumped the grid in one awkward bound, and then slowed to a jog as his feet hit grass. Once Princetown was a little way behind him he walked to catch his breath.

Then it had him. A sharp pain shot through his leg where it was gripped with crushing power. He screeched and beat at his captor, his fists coming down on something hard, but he was shaken until he stopped. Then he was dragged away. Grass and heather sped by either side of him as he tried in vain to catch hold of something, even the thorny gorse. His back burned from the friction.

Abruptly he came to a halt. The hold on his leg was released, and immediately replaced by a throbbing ache.

"What did I tell you to do?" asked a cold voice.

Owain dragged himself into a crouch, muscles tense like a feral cat. He rubbed his calf sullenly. "To watch the girl and watch her only."

"And what did you do instead?"

"It was just a little bit of fun. She made a good hound."

The very real hound which prowled near him rumbled a low growl. Its master stroked its head, heedless of how the matted black fur parted from slick skin at his touch.

"You disappoint me, Owain"

Owain cowered, his red hair tousled and flecked with bits of moss gathered on his journey. He looked very young, and the voice which addressed him was centuries of tired.

"No need to set her on me though," he grumbled. The hound nuzzled its master's hand and then padded over to snuffle Owain. He gave in and itched it behind the ear.

"The girl must not know. Not yet."

3.
REMAINS

The door to the Plume of Feathers was thick with dirt. Gemma let Adrian go in first, pulling her sleeves over her hands in case she had to touch something. He pulled the door open and held it for her, releasing a slick of yellow light onto the street. It came from a heavily shaded lamp just inside, similar to others dotted around on shelves and hung at intervals on the walls. Each one was shaded in matching stained brown satin. Gemma waited for her eyes to adjust to the gloom.

Thick white candles burnt in alcoves hollowed out of the bare brick walls, and on tables with lone drinkers huddled over them. The floor was tiled with thick red slabs and the route from door to bar was worn down with use. Adrian pointed to a table in the far corner. Gemma shrugged and followed him over. They sat down opposite each other in mismatched wooden chairs.

"Drink?" he asked.

Gemma nodded. She drummed her fingers on the table, absently rubbing at an old glass mark on the wood. The surface was sticky, and stained a dark brown from years of spilt alcohol. Adrian returned with two glasses and a menu. She chose quickly and then let her eyes wander.

At the far end of the pub a collection of copper cookware was strung over an open fire. Nearby, propped up carelessly in a corner, leant an old and rusty scythe. Hung on the walls were a mixture of paintings, old photographs and dusty stuffed animals. But among the dreary and dead eyed stags, dull pheasants and moth eaten foxes there was one item which caught her attention.

"I've got to try the rabbit pie," said Adrian. He tapped the menu decisively, asked Gemma what she would have, and then went to the bar to order.

She followed a few strides behind, but walked on towards the fire when he stopped at the bar. There was a single mounted skull among all the taxidermy animals. It was the odd one out, surrounded by glass eyes and old fur.

The pub door swung open behind her. She turned round to see a tall man in a waxed jacket stride in, his muddy boots clomping heavily. The sullen drinkers turned their heads at his arrival and a few nodded in greeting. He acknowledged them solemnly. His jacket was a similar stained brown to the tables, and the man's uneven gait made Gemma suspect it had achieved that shade the same way. The barman set down a pint for the newcomer just as he reached the bar.

Adrian sidled further along the bar as the man came to stand beside him. A grubby hand shot out from the sleeve of the jacket and lifted the pint to the man's lips. He drained the contents in three gulps and then sat the glass back down with a thump. The barman wordlessly refilled it.

Gemma turned back to the skull. Up close it was rather shabby; some of its teeth were gone and the black mounting was chipped at the corners. It was a few shades off white, stained from years of smoke before the ban. The jaw had been repaired at some point and now hung slack on two twists of dark wire. There was a bronze information plaque fixed beneath it which read;

The mortal remains of the monstrous
and unholy beast of Dartmoor

"You like monsters, do you?" called a deep voice.

Gemma glanced over her shoulder to see the man at the bar staring at her. He held the second half finished pint in his hand.

"Not really," she replied.

"Can't say I blame you." He emptied his glass and strode over, bringing with him the smell of stale beer and diesel. He took hold of the lower jaw and snapped it closed. Gemma jumped as the remaining teeth interlocked with a sharp click. "But he looks a bit sorry for himself, doesn't he?"

She looked into the empty eye sockets. Someone had pushed a small sachet of salt into one of them.

"I suppose so."

"There was a time people feared me." The man snapped the jaw open and shut, as if working some grotesque puppet. "But now I'm stuck here for tourists to gawp at and to take their picture with, and I can't even kill myself because I'm already dead." He let the jaw fall slack against the wood, where it dangled in limp surprise.

"I saw a picture in the Visitor Centre," said Gemma. She didn't want to make the man angry. She had learnt to humour drunks on late night train rides in the city.

He waved a hand dismissively, turning back towards the bar. "All rubbish," he muttered, "nothing like the Beast at all."

"What is it like then?" Adrian was leaning there with a full pint of beer in front of him. He pushed it forwards encouragingly. The man didn't hesitate.

35

"I'm Mike," he said, grabbing the glass with one hand and reaching out to Adrian with the other.

He clasped the grimy palm and shook it, introducing himself and Gemma in turn. "Have you seen it?" he pressed.

"I've seen him sure enough. A lot of people round here have, though not all of them will admit to it." Mike chuckled darkly.

"Does it come into the town?" asked Adrian.

"No, no, he won't come that near so many people. He isn't silly. I saw him from up at Hound Tor, but as soon as he caught me looking he was gone again. He was dragging a whole sheep with him and he still moved that fast, it was unbelievable. There were these American tourists up there with me, I was flying my hawk around for them you see, but they didn't see him. He was too quick."

"Surely people notice their livestock going missing," Gemma said, thinking back to the display in the Visitor Centre.

"They certainly do. Some of them blame it on foxes, some blame it on badgers, but only a very few whisper that it might be the Beast. Helicopters and men with guns have gone hunting across the moor for him enough times, but they'll never catch him; he's too clever. Most people don't even believe he exists."

"So what does he really look like?" Adrian asked.

"Big. Black. The Beast is like a dog, but one you drew out of your nightmares; a monstrous hound with shaggy black fur and glinting devilish eyes. He has this way of moving that's like no animal of God's creation on the earth. It's like he's got liquid inside him instead of bones, the movement's that fluid, and the legs and body bend in the wrong places. He pretty much bent himself in half to get a good look back at me." Mike sat back to savour the last dregs of his beer, pleased with the effect of his words. He placed the empty glass back on the table, his eyes shifting towards Adrian.

The barman leaned close as he poured the amber pint.

"Don't you worry yourself too much over his stories." He told Adrian, his head twitching towards Mike. "He'll tell them to anyone who'll listen, tourists especially, but he's seen the Beast no more than I have. That skull? It's a coyote one I bought off the internet. I'll tell you now, what he saw was a wild boar wandered down from Horrabridge and no Beast at all."

Adrian thanked him and carried the drinks back to the table. Mike's face was spread with a huge grin as he took the drink and toasted Adrian in thanks. "I'll work at this rate all night," he said.

The pub had filled up around them. Groups of men nodded to each other over pints of beer and couples held hands over the table. Dusk moved on towards night out through the window and in the alcoves the candles burnt a little lower. A babble of chatter thickened the air, loud enough to make speech at separate tables private.

"Have you heard the story of the Dark Huntsman?" Mike asked.

Adrian and Gemma shook their heads, so he settled himself in his chair to tell the story.

"The Huntsman goes by many names. Some say he's the Devil himself. Others say that he's Wodan, a god of the old religion returned in a new form for a changed world. But what I think is-" Mike was cut short by a waitress arriving with food. She set the steaming plates down on the table, but Adrian pushed his aside, impatient for the story to continue.

"You were saying," he prompted.

Mike rubbed his eyes and then shook his head. "I've forgotten what I was saying now."

"You were about to say who you thought the Huntsman was."

"He has many names. They're all the same to me." He took a long draught of his drink. "Now where was I? Was I telling a story?"

Adrian nodded.

"Of course I was. About the Dark Huntsman." He placed both his elbows on the table, one hand hovering near his glass, and beckoned the others forward. They leaned in.

"One dark night a farmer was riding home from Widecombe fair. He had made a good price from his wares, and had stopped at the inn on the way." Mike raised his glass and took a swig. "Silence engulfed the moor, not a breath of wind bent the grass, but in the sky clouds gathered thick round a pale moon. All of a sudden his pony began to snort and sniff at the air, but the man brought down his whip smartly on the animal's shoulder and it carried on. Moments later the sound of a hunting horn pierced the night air, and in the distance a hunter and his pack of hounds appeared, bearing down on the farmer at a wild gallop.

"The black dogs rushed past, moving like solid night, baying loudly at the moon. Behind them came a tall rider dressed all in black, mounted on a huge steed with eyes of red fire. The farmer watched it all through a haze of whisky.

"'Huntsman,'" he called, "'what be ee a chasin'? Give us zum of yer game.'" So the dark rider slung him a wrapped bundle.

'"Take that and think yourself lucky,"' he spat. With a pounding of hooves he sped off across the moor.

"The farmer quieted his pony and continued the journey back home. He wondered what tasty meal he had been given; the bundle was far too small to be a deer, but was bigger than a rabbit. At last the pony clattered onto the cobbles of the farmyard, and the farmer called his wife to bring a lantern.

'"I met a huntsman who gave me some game, and I wants to zee what us got,"' he explained. The woman quickly obeyed, holding up a lantern as he unwrapped the bloody package. He peered inside and shrieked loudly, dropping the bundle. A sad little form tumbled out onto the cobbles. The woman dropped her lantern, but too late. The image of her own dead child was already burnt onto her eyes." Mike took another long swig of his beer and wiped his lips on his sleeve.

"They don't tell you that at the Visitor Centre," said Adrian. He crammed a few mouthfuls of pie into his mouth.

"Death is bad for tourism," Mike winked.

Adrian paused with another mouthful of pie halfway to his lips. "Do you know anything about burial sites on the moor?" he asked.

"I certainly do, you're talking to the right person for that." He flicked up the collar of his coat and crossed his arms. "Why do you ask?"

Adrian popped the food in his mouth and chewed it slowly. "I just read a bit about them at the Visitor Centre. They sounded interesting."

"They are interesting, very interesting, and all over the moor. The place is covered with them; you can barely move for ancient burials. What type do you like the look of?"

"I'm not sure yet."

Gemma had been only half listening during the story, but Adrian's impulsive enthusiasm brought her back to the conversation. Why was he so interested in burial sites all of a sudden? And then she realized, with a sensation that her food had turned to brick in her stomach, that it must be to do with the dream. He was really going to do it, and he was going to drag the village drunk along to help him.

"How many types are there?" Adrian asked. He paid for the information with another pint and Mike began to list the types on grubby fingers.

"There are two main types, although the stone rows often lead to them so perhaps they count as well. The commonest ones are the cairns." He held up one finger, the nail stained with dirt. "They're a circular mound of stones marking a burial site beneath. The other type is called a barrow." He held up another finger. "And they have an underground chamber made of granite with a long earth mound over the top."

Adrian raised his glass and then put it back down without drinking. "Is it only the barrows that have a chamber underneath?"

"Well, there's some discussion over that. Some cairns may have been built over kistvaens, or cists, which would mean they do have an underground chamber."

"What's a cist?"

"It's a stone chest, like a coffin," Mike explained.

"So the chamber would be small, not big enough to stand inside?" said Adrian.

"No definitely not, the body would be buried with

the knees drawn up to the chest. A cist would be almost square."

Gemma watched a young couple flirting over their meals and tried to guess what each of them did for a living. The woman was a teacher, she decided, because she was prim and pretty. The man looked like a farmer. But however much she concentrated on what his farm might look like she couldn't keep out the image of a small child huddled in a tiny stone coffin, his knees pressed to his chest. She wasn't enjoying the dinner conversation. Resolving to tell Adrian to change the subject she turned to face him, but he spoke before she got a chance.

"You wouldn't mind that, would you?" he asked.

She stared at him blankly. "Mind what?" Something told her that, whatever it was, she would mind it. A lot.

"Mike has offered to take us on a guided tour of the moor. He'll show us the interesting sites."

"By that, do you mean graves?"

"Some burial sites, yes-" began Adrian.

Mike butted in. "But that needn't be all. I'll take you to Hound Tor, the place where I saw the Beast. And I could take you to Wistmans Wood, you'd like that I'm sure, all the wildflowers will be up this time of year. You can lie in the shade and listen to the rustling of the leaves and the flow of the river."

Adrian took advantage of Gemma's silence. "When are you free?" He asked Mike.

"How about tomorrow morning?"

"Brilliant, what time?"

Mike hesitated. "Could you do nine o' clock?"

Gemma raised an eyebrow. She tried to catch Adrian's attention, but he was already nodding.

41

"Nine would be great," he said.

"To tomorrow then." Mike raised his near empty glass and waited for Adrian and Gemma to clink theirs against it. Gemma did, but only after Adrian kicked her under the table.

Mike insisted on walking them the short distance back to the Café. He bowed unsteadily at the door and then wandered off into the still warm night. Shortly afterwards, Gemma heard him start singing.
She followed Adrian into the bunkroom, slamming the door behind her.

"I've told you before, I don't want to be involved in your little missions," she told him sharply.

"I know, no ghost hunting. I do remember."

"Then why am I booked in for this trip tomorrow?"

"Because I thought you'd like to get out and see the countryside. As Mike said, it's all very pretty."

"Don't give me that rubbish. I know you're looking for tombs."

"That doesn't mean you have to be. Look, forget about what I'm doing if it worries you that much. Just think of it as a nice walk."

"Oh yeah, it's just a nice walk out looking for dead people with a total stranger. How do you know he isn't planning to shut us up underground as well?"

Adrian let out a loud laugh and clapped his hand to his lips. "Gemma, have you seen him?"

She shrugged. "People aren't always what they seem."

"Come on, can't you see it? It's all exactly as Elaine said. You can't tell me that's just coincidence."

42

"A crazy drunk will lead the way? No, I don't think I remember that."

"He is our guide."

"To what? Liver failure?"

"No." Adrian began to pace the sparse room with agitation. "Elaine told us that we would find a guide. Don't you think it's more than chance that he just offered to be our guide tomorrow?"

"I bet he does it for all the tourists. And he didn't use the word guide at all."

"He's going to show us round sites on the moor. That makes him our guide." Adrian's tone grew more pleading. "Can't you just get over it for once and give him a chance."

Gemma was taken aback. "Get over what?"

"Your massive fear of anything the slightest bit strange. Don't you think you're overreacting sometimes?"

She opened her mouth and then closed it again. For almost a minute she was silent. Then she spoke very quietly.

"My mum was sectioned for believing in those kinds of things," she fixed Adrian with hollow eyes, "I don't want to end up there too."

He opened his arms and caught her in a firm hug. Her lungs emptied out a sigh. "I'll keep all the ghosts and ghouls away from you," he told her, "I promise. But that spirit called out to me. Perhaps no one else heard. How would you feel if I ignored your call for help? Wouldn't it be cruel of me to leave you alone and trapped in the darkness?" He felt Gemma nod against his shoulder. She pulled away, wiping her eyes quickly.

"Wistmans wood does sound nice," she said.

"I'll make sure Mike brings us there then," Adrian

smiled.

Gemma picked up her overnight bag and began to empty it onto her bed. "This is all presuming Mike manages to get up in the morning," she added.

"Why wouldn't he?"

"How many times have you seen the morning after that much beer?"

Adrian pulled a face at her. "He'll be there."

"Bet you a cream tea he isn't."

"You're on." Adrian held out a hand and she shook it, laughing. Then she turned back to checking her quota of knickers.

Opening her laptop, she sat down with the intention of beginning the inevitable search for a new job. She concentrated for ten minutes, but found herself reading the same line of nonsense, about being a dynamic and highly motivated washroom rejuvenator, over and over again. It was no use. She couldn't concentrate. It seemed like weeks ago that she had woken up in her own familiar flat and been tricked by Adrian into joining him on this crazy trip. She yawned. The day had definitely been a long one.

She changed for bed and curled up under the thin sheets. There was only one pillow and the mattress had a saggy patch in the middle that she kept rolling back into. Adrian seemed comfortable enough, as it wasn't long until she heard him snoring in the bunk opposite her, but she lay awake for a long time. Elaine's story haunted her. It was one she had spent a long time trying to forget. Eventually she did fall asleep. The sound of a horn woke her briefly, but she told herself it was a car outside and almost instantly fell back to sleep.

4.
Warning

Asterra surveyed the gloomy hollow. Even outside of the circle she could sense the strength of the wards placed around it, all their authority set against her entry. She wasn't wanted there. The wordless warning prickled like nettles on her skin. She ran her pale fingers over the weathered bark of one of the ancient trees and her breath caught sharply in her chest.

A young boy appeared at her side and bowed.

"Have you brought the sacrifice?" she asked.

His eyes filled with fear. "It escaped," he said, shrinking away from her. But Asterra was too fast. She grabbed him by the throat and lifted him so close that they were almost nose to nose.

"And you wonder why your mother disowned you?" she spat in his face. "Who'd wish to be dam to such a useless dog?"

"It won't happen again", he whimpered. "I'm sorry."

"It had better not, if you value your life."

She released him and he staggered back from her, bowing and nodding, his eyes full of shame.

The woman had promised to be a mother to him, rear him as her own. And all she wanted was one small thing in return; such a small thing. The miracle that he was born to do, but couldn't perform.

"You realise that I have no other choice now?" Asterra said, taking a knife from her waist. She grabbed his wrist and twisted it round. He howled with pain but she ignored it and plunged the knife deep into his arm

45

until the point scraped bone.

The boy shrieked and screamed but she held him fast. "How else will you learn?" she shouted at him and the dragged the knife downwards. Blood gushed out of the long wound and seeped through his clothes. His knees buckled and he collapsed, writhing to the floor.

She leant forward and cleaned the knife on the back of his shirt and then sheathed it again at her waist. "Well?" she looked at him, nudging his face with her foot. "Get on with it."

The boy got shakily to his feet and stepped down towards the base of the hollow.

Morning dew still clung to the short grass and the sodden earth sunk beneath his steps. He looked back once. Asterra stood with her slim arms folded across her chest, her body blocking the only way out. He would be killed if he was seen inside the circle, but Asterra's threats were far more immediate, and she would kill him herself if he failed. So he kept going, only stopping when he reached the centre of the hollow where there was a stone altar, stained and pock marked by the weather.

"Quickly," Asterra shouted down at him.

He reached for the stone block to steady himself. His wounded arm hung useless at his side and his knees were too weak to hold him. He slid down the side of the altar onto the ground and threw up.

"Get on with it, or I'll feed you to the feral!"

The boy dragged himself up to his knees and leant gasping against the stone. He retched again, spitting bile onto the damp grass. Shaking, he dragged his limp arm up onto the altar, placing it so that the blood ran into a shallow basin. His lips were stretched wide in a silent scream.

"Now get out," she said.

He crumpled up, his body curling into a ball. There was no strength left in his limbs and he was nauseous from loss of blood. No threat could make him move now.

Asterra closed her eyes, breathed in deeply and waited. There was nothing. Clenching her hands into fists she swore to have revenge on the scum that had sold her the boy. He didn't have the gift. Then a shudder ran through the earth. Her eyes flew open in triumph. The turf rippled and heaved around the battered body of the child. She howled as the swollen soil gave way, erupting with a last contraction of wet earth and blood. The hollow smelt of vomit and death. It had worked.

"No!" yelled Adrian from the other room. His arms hit the wall desperately as he fought off some unseen attacker.

Gemma quickly wrapped a towel around her and ran back into the bunk room.

He was sitting upright in bed, staring at the wall with a hand pressed to his chest. The laptop was open on the floor by the bed.

"Are you alright?" she asked.

Adrian shook his head slowly. "Yeah, I'm okay."

"You were screaming. What happened?"

"Just a bad dream."

Gemma sat down on the edge of the bed. "The same one?"

"No, it was different. I was out on the moor and it was dark. I could hear something following me. I walked quicker but it sped up too, so I started to run. But I wasn't quick enough. I could hear it getting nearer and nearer so I stopped and looked back, but it was gone, whatever it was."

Gemma picked up the laptop. "That's what you get for staying up late reading about creepy legends," she said. The screen still displayed a large picture of a ferocious black dog and the title:

'The Beast of Dartmoor: Fact or Fiction?'

"You must have fallen asleep looking at it. No wonder you had weird dreams."

Adrian rubbed his forehead. "Maybe."

"It was just a dream though, right?" She plugged the laptop in to charge.

He threw off the covers and swung his feet onto the floor. The fear that had come with the dream was gone. "Yeah," he said.

"Just try to forget it." Gemma walked back towards the shower room and shut the door.

She quickly pulled on her clothes and scraped her wet hair back into a ponytail. Then she picked up her toothbrush and began to wipe the condensation from the mirror with her towel, but something in her reflection made her stop still. She leaned closer to the glass and rubbed away the mist from her breath. There were two marks on her face, one near each temple. She touched one and winced. The skin was bruised where the mask had been.

When she got back to the bunkroom Adrian had gone to the men's shower room. She reached for her makeup bag and dabbed concealer over the marks. Then, following a sudden impulse, she went to the laptop and typed 'Mike Dartmoor' into the search engine. She was half expecting nothing to come up. But even with all the guide business being nonsense, it was still strange they should just happen to bump into someone who knew the moor and was willing to show them round. What made it worthwhile for him?

The smell of styling products began to waft under the door of the shower room; Adrian must have moved on to his hair.

Gemma focused on the screen. Most of the stuff wasn't relevant, but one website caught her eye. She clicked on it.

"There you are," she said to herself. An old newspaper magazine article flashed up and Mike looked back at her from the screen, a hawk perched on his wrist. She scanned down through the report.

'The well known falconer, Michael Whitley, has recently reported sighting the legendary Beast of Dartmoor near the popular tourist spot of Hound Tor. A local dog owner has quashed this claim by admitting that the so called 'Beast' is in fact her pet, a large black Newfoundland, which she regularly walks near the tor. Despite this, Mr. Whitley is adamant about what he saw. He told our reporter:
''I can tell you for a fact that I didn't see a Newfoundland. Its whole figure was wrong and the coat was a different texture. I know a dog when I see it. The creature I saw was black and grey and similar in size to a miniature pony. It had very thick shoulders, a long tail with a blunt end and large pointed ears."'

So he was telling the truth after all. Or at least what he believed was the truth. She wondered how many pints it took to turn a stray dog into a beast.

Adrian swept out of the bathroom in a cloud of

hairspray and steam. "Ready?"

Gemma shut the laptop with a snap. "Ready."

They waited for Mike outside the Visitor Centre. At a minute to nine there was no sign of him.

"You're going to owe me a scone," said Gemma.

"He's got time yet," said Adrian, checking his watch.

A smart man in a waxed jacket crossed the road ahead of them.

"Now *he* looks the business," whispered Gemma.

The man stepped onto the pavement in long easy strides. Underneath the jacket his shirt was forest green and unbuttoned at the top.

 "Mike!" called Adrian.

The man looked up and smiled.

Gemma stared. Mike had transformed overnight. He wore a leather hat that matched his jacket, and under it his eyes were sparkling. He had even shaved, and barely seemed drunk at all.

"You're punctual," he said.

"Well, you're doing us a big favour. We didn't want to keep you waiting," said Adrian.

Mike laughed, revealing stained but very straight teeth. "I'm glad to do it, any excuse to get out on the moor. Did you sleep well?"

"Not too badly," said Gemma.

Mike nodded, suppressing a large yawn. "Perfect morning for a walk."

In the car park a very large black four by four had appeared next to Adrian's Beetle, making the vintage car look like a child's toy. Mike laid an affectionate hand on the Land Rover's chunky bonnet. "We'll take my car," he said.

He unlocked the doors and they clambered in, feeling as if they were getting inside a tank. The vehicle smelt of old mud, beer and, very faintly, of wet dog. It was to be expected, Gemma told herself; this was the country after all, and Mike probably had a crate of alcohol stashed in here somewhere.

"No Beast is getting us in here," said Adrian.

Mike chuckled to himself as he pulled his door closed. "Have you had breakfast?"

Gemma was suddenly starving. "Not yet."

"Well then, I have a little treat for you at Hound Tor."

The engine growled into life and they pulled out of the car park. They drove out of town and crossed the cattle grid onto the moor.

"Aren't you bringing your dog?" asked Gemma.

"I don't have one," said Mike.

She opened her mouth to say that the smell told her otherwise, but managed to mumble, "I thought you did," instead. She saw him shake his head in the rear view mirror.

Twenty minutes later they pulled into a large square of gravel and parked up. Mike jumped out and opened Gemma's door for her while she was still caught up in the view out of the window. The moor stretched out in every direction from the car park, passing clouds skimming shadows over the green slopes and valleys. Ahead of the car a grassy hill swept upwards towards a jagged outcrop of grey stone.

"Best breakfasts around," Mike said proudly, gesturing towards a grimy white snack van. Adrian read the name painted above the serving window and began to laugh. "Hound of the Basket Meals, that's brilliant."

Gemma shut her car door and turned to the fading sign. A cartoon bloodhound held a wicker basket in its mouth, grinning vacantly at customers. Mike's reported sighting of the Beast must have been a real boost for them.

"Three of your best bacon rolls please Martin," said Mike.

The owner nodded, his wrinkled face creasing into a smile. "I see you have company today. I thought everyone knew better."

Mike stepped aside and leaned against the counter. "I'm taking them up to see Hound Tor."

The man in the snack van nodded sagely. "Nice day for it," he said. The smell of frying bacon began to waft up from the griddle. With practised hands the old man began to toast rolls, fry onions and turn bacon.

The three of them were soon sitting at one of the plastic tables devouring enormous bacon rolls.

Mike leaned in to speak quietly. "It used to be really busy here, back when it was all over the newspapers that the Beast had been seen at Hound Tor."

Gemma looked up towards the slope and tried to work out if she recognised it as the background in the internet photo.

"People came to see it?" said Adrian.

"Well, it's famous. Basket Meals got so busy that they even had their own letterboxing stamp," said Mike.

"What's letterboxing?" asked Adrian.

Gemma turned back to the conversation. It sounded like a game she had played down her street when she was thirteen.

"There are containers, called letterboxes, hidden all over the moor." Mike put aside the last of his roll to explain. "People go out looking for them. The letterbox has a rubber stamp in it, as well as ink, a pen and a notepad. The letterboxer collects a print from each stamp he finds, and then leaves a message and a print from his own stamp behind."

"Do a lot of people do it?" Gemma asked.

Mike caught her meaning and grinned. "Apparently."

The walk up to Hound Tor was short and gentler than it had looked from the car. Gemma looked back to the snack van and realised they had climbed to quite a height in very little time.

"A nice easy walk to warm us all up," Mike called from ahead.

Adrian nodded, hiding his breathlessness.

Gemma reached the summit of the hill just after Mike, and stopped there to wait for Adrian. He followed half a dozen strides behind. From this vantage point the moor stretched out in a patchwork quilt of browns and uneven greens, marked occasionally by a narrow strip of winding road. The breeze blew stronger at this height, but it was refreshing after the climb.

"You can see Grimspound from here," Mike told them, pointing away to his left.

Adrian held his hair out of his face and peered in the direction Mike pointed. A grey circle of stones was set in the side of the hill; a very human structure in the middle of the wild moor. The grass inside was a lighter green than outside, like a scar that had never quite faded. A track, worn through the grass by countless feet, led up to the circle from the nearest road and continued out through the other side until it was swallowed by the scrub.

"What was it?" asked Gemma.

"An ancient settlement, Bronze Age I believe, but long abandoned. Hundreds of years ago the moor began to change and everyone moved on. It happened quite suddenly and they left all of this behind. Even now relatively few people live on the moor, and they know to keep to the towns," said Mike.

"What changed?" Gemma asked.

"Now *that* the history books don't exactly recall, maybe it was something to do with the climate or the earth. But whatever it was, it pushed people out. Legend says that the earth was woken up, and refused to be a slave to the humans anymore," Mike said.

Adrian stood slightly apart and looked out over the moor, picking out patterns in the grass as swathes flattened in the wind. He vaguely heard Mike pointing out to Gemma the smaller Bronze Age hut circles inside the larger defensive wall of Grimspound, but he had already discounted it as the location from his dream and lost interest. They were supposed to be looking at burial sites. Why was Gemma drooling over hut circles when they should be looking for the boy? This history lesson was wasting time they didn't have. He was just about to turn round and remind Mike about the tombs, when a movement in the grass caught his eye.

He stared at the spot, away to the right and on lower ground, hoping to see whatever it was again. He started to doubt that he'd seen anything at all. The black shape could easily have been the shadow from a passing cloud, or just the movement of something in the wind. He looked for a patch of darker grass; a contrast in colour like at Grimspound might have been all he saw. But there was nothing. The moor was bright and green, with no trace of a shadow in sight. He pressed his eyes harder, willing them to pick up on the slightest detail. Then he saw it. At the very bottom of the small valley there was a hollow, dark like a crater and edged with weird stunted trees. Perhaps that was what he'd seen. The more he looked, the more it stood out darkly against the surrounding grass, pulling his attention towards it.

"Look over here," he called, beckoning Gemma with a wave of his hand.

She and Mike lined themselves up behind him and looked out over the moor.

"What?" asked Mike, rubbing his eyes as if it would readjust them.

"There," pressed Adrian.

At last Gemma saw. "There's a hole there. See the bushes around the edge of that dark patch?" she pointed for Mike.

"Could it be a meteor crater?" Adrian asked.

Mike looked again and finally made out the spot. "That's no meteor crater. More likely to be military, a stray bomb dropped during the war, but it looks more like a slump hole to me."

"What's that when it's at home?" Gemma asked.

"They're common all over the moor. The water table has always been high here and the rocks and earth are usually saturated, like a big sponge. But the weather's on the change and we're not getting as much rain as we used to, so the moor is drying out. In places the earth is sinking."

"Could we take a look at it?" Adrian asked.

Mike looked from the hollow to his car and back again. It didn't look too far. "I suppose so." He shook his head thoughtfully. "You know what, in all my years walking these moors I've never noticed that place before."

"Could it be new then? You said the ground has been sinking," Gemma said.

Mike continued to shake his head. "Those trees are old."

"But they're tiny," she said.

"You'll see when we get closer; they'll be all gnarled and twisted by the wind. Everything here has to stay low to the ground to stay alive."

Adrian stayed ahead with Mike this time, eager to talk about what they were going to see, and finding the downhill easier than the climb.

Gemma walked a few paces behind, allowing Adrian his enthusiasm, and treading carefully to avoid the prickly heather. The low tufty bushes were becoming more regular as they descended, some woody and dead but others bright with purple flowers. Here and there were patches of bright yellow.

"Gorse," said Mike, catching her looking, "watch out for the thorns."

She edged close to one sun coloured bush. Sure enough, enormous thorns pushed through the flowers, the tips needle sharp.

The terrain got wilder. The grass was long where hordes of tourists and walkers hadn't worn it down, and now and again patches of bracken punctuated the turf. The gorse and bracken became more frequent as they walked, with only narrow strips of grass in between the bushes. It was like walking through a maze where all the dead ends were prickly.

Adrian slowed and stopped for a rest.

Gemma caught up with him.

"It's further than I thought," he puffed, massaging his prickled calves. Walking boots were no defence against gorse bushes.

"Always like that out here," Mike said.

"How much further do you think?" Gemma asked.

"It's difficult to tell with the lie of the land. Distances can be deceptive on the moor, and this ground is rough going."

Adrian nodded grimly.

"Are we still going the right way?" Gemma asked him.

Adrian scanned the surrounding moor for the stunted trees that marked their goal. Eventually he saw them, but they were difficult to spot. Without the advantage of high ground it was easy to miss them amongst all the other scrub. "There," he said, pointing.

"We're getting nearer then" said Mike cheerfully. It was the signal to start walking again.

Adrian strode ahead, still breathless but impatient to get to the site.

Gemma fell in line with Mike a little way behind. He walked steadily, offering her a drink from a silver hip flask without breaking his stride. She thanked him, but refused. He took a long swig before storing it carefully back inside one of his many pockets. She didn't know what was in the flask, but it smelt strong.

Adrian screamed loudly ahead.

Mike broke into a run.

Gemma jogged behind him. Adrian had probably just prickled his knee for the twentieth time.

"Whoa," Mike gasped, skidding to a halt.

She was worried now; it must be something more serious. She sprinted to catch up, and was only saved from a crippling fall by Mike stepping in front of her.

"Help me," Adrian whispered. He was swaying right on the edge of a gaping ravine that cut like a knife wound into the earth.

"Step back slowly," said Mike, "careful now."

Adrian stepped backwards and the edge began to crumble into the ravine.

Gemma reached out for Adrian's hand and pulled him back to where she stood with Mike. The slopes down into the ravine were almost vertically steep, but still green and furred with heather and gorse. The very bottom of the rift was narrow and marshy; a line of moist brown against the green.

"Stay away from the edge," said Mike.

"It's not as steep down that way," Gemma said, pointing to her left.

Adrian risked stepping closer to peer down where she was pointing.

"There might be a way down over there," he said.

"Now listen to me," said Mike, "I'm just as curious as you are, but it mightn't be safe. You've seen the slump hole, the gorse, and now this. The moor is littered with these ravines, and they're dangerous because often you won't see them 'til the last minute. Then it's too late."

"Nearly too late," corrected Adrian.

"You were lucky," Mike said.

"I think we can handle it," said Adrian. It was spoken as a challenge.

Mike looked at him for a long moment, a grin starting at the corners of his mouth and then spreading to his whole face. "Alright."

He led this time, and Adrian was happy to stay behind.

Gemma walked with her arm linked through his. They squashed close together to avoid the encroaching bracken. "Are you ok?" she asked.

"Yeah. It was just a surprise, you know," he said.

"The bracken would probably have broken your fall."

"Knowing my luck I would have landed right in a huge gorse bush."

"No broken bones then, just a heavy prickling," Gemma said.

Adrian laughed and squeezed her arm. "I've probably had worse." They walked on in companionable silence, each trying to steer the other out of the way of the gorse.

"Do you have a feeling about this place we're trying to find?" Gemma asked.

Adrian recalled the black shape. He was struggling to believe it was a shadow; it had been quick, but solid. There was a grace about it that made him think of a predator. He walked in silence, kicking at clumps of heather with each stride. "I suppose so," he said at last.

Gemma waited for him to elaborate.

"It was just the way I saw it; I don't think I would have noticed it at all if it wasn't for the other thing..." he trailed off.

She bowed her head closer to his. "What was it?"

Adrian shook her away. "I'm not sure."

"Are you coming?" Mike called from ahead.

They hurried to catch up, and found him standing proudly by a small and very narrow path. It led in a tight serpentine down a shallower part of the ravine. There was no other way across in sight.

"I'll go first," Mike said, "Only follow when I give you the all clear." He took a careful step onto the path.

"Wait," called an unfamiliar voice. Gemma and Adrian spun round to see who'd spoken.

A stranger stood behind them, with a hand extended towards Mike. He was wearing a knee length waxed coat and tall boots. Shoulder length blonde hair had worked loose and blew about his face. "That path isn't safe," he warned.

Mike stepped back and turned to face him. "You know it?"

"Yes," the man replied.

"Well I know the moor pretty well myself, and I've never come across this track before."

"The moor can do that," said the stranger, "it keeps its own secrets. You should expect no less, if you really do know it as well as you say. "

Mike threw the stranger a filthy look but said nothing. He stepped forward and the stranger dodged around him to block their path.

"Maybe we should just go back," Gemma suggested.

"A wise decision," said the stranger.

"Do you know if there's another way to get to that ring of trees?" Adrian asked, pointing back at the goal of their walk.

The stranger shaded his eyes and looked where Adrian pointed. "What ring of trees?"

Gemma followed his gaze and found, to her confusion, that there were no trees at all, only some woody gorse bushes.

Adrian was pacing the edge of the ravine in

frustration. "They must be hidden from this angle," he said, finally.

The man nodded curtly. "I would advise you not to go any further. What you saw was undoubtedly just those gorse bushes. The ground beyond this ravine is very treacherous, and I would be concerned there may be no-one around to help you should there be an accident."

Mike finally nodded. "Thank you for warning us," He said, bowing his head slightly.

"You're welcome," said the stranger. "The moor can play tricks on your eyes. Sometimes, what appears to be a copse of trees turns out to be no more than a couple of bushes."

Gemma nodded and the stranger turned his eyes on her. It was like trying to stare down a searchlight and she felt her cheeks colour.

"Why take the risk?" he asked.

"There's no sense in hunting out danger, is there?" Mike agreed, shifting his weight from one foot to the other, as if preparing to run.

"No sense at all," replied the stranger.

5.
HOUNDAIN

"He was weird," said Adrian.

Gemma was eyeing up the plate of scones that had just been set down between them. "In what way?" she asked, once she had secured the biggest one.

Adrian started fiddling with his knife. "Mike trusted the path, and it was none of that guy's business anyway. Does he have nothing better to do than go round butting in on other people's lives?"

"I think he was just trying to help," she shrugged.

"I mean, who is he? The Path Police? I bet it wasn't dangerous at all."

"Why would he warn us if it wasn't? For all we know he could have seen that one of those sinkholes had opened up down there, and thought he'd do us a favour by telling us."

"I doubt it." Adrian dug viciously at the jam.

"Why?"

"Because then he would have said *don't go down that way because there's a sinkhole*."

Gemma finished spreading a thick layer of cream over her scone. She took a big bite which she chewed thoroughly before answering. "Maybe he thought we wouldn't know what sinkholes were. Maybe he didn't want to bore us with an explanation. He doesn't know us, so he probably has more important things to do than stand around and talk to us."

Adrian shook his head. "He was hiding something."

"Like what?"

"He didn't want us to get to that crater."

"Don't you think you might be seeing a bit much in this?"

"Listen, the crater looked dark and earthy, like in my dream. There might be some kind of burial site inside."

Gemma leant both her elbows on the table and looked levelly at Adrian. He could find the mystery in a ham sandwich. "Mike won't take us."

"He won't have to."

She shook her head, waving her half eaten scone at him for emphasis. "If you think there's any chance I'm going out there, without a guide…"

"Stay here then."

"What?"

"I'm serious; you don't have to come with me. Stay here and do some internet shopping or something, I'll be fine."

"You can't go out walking on the moor alone."

Adrian grinned. "That's settled then." He began to shovel chunks of scone down his throat.

Gemma gave up and reached for more cream.

Ten minutes later they were trundling along in Adrian's Beetle. Gemma tried to hide the scepticism in her voice.

"So do you think the boy might be there?" she asked.

"Maybe."

"Have you, you know, heard any more from him?" He shook his head.

She looked out of the car window. Green and brown moorland rolled past them on either side, the viewing spots beside the road empty of cars. The day had stayed overcast and there was no sign of the sun returning.

"Do you remember the way?" she asked.

"Of course."

There was a faint throbbing at her temples. She rubbed her eyes.

"You alright?" Adrian glanced over in concern.

"Yeah, just a bit of a headache." Suddenly too hot, she raked her hair back from her face with both hands.

"What happened to you?" he asked, leaning over to stare at her face.

"Nothing."

The car began to veer towards the verge.

"Watch the road."

Adrian looked back ahead, but his expression was still worried. "You should get that looked at, it looks like you've hit your face."

"It's nothing. I probably knocked myself in the night, those bunkbeds are pretty narrow." She opened her window and pressed her face to the breeze until they reached the car park.

Adrian pulled in smoothly between two far larger cars. The air smelt of bacon and dust. Ahead, the green slope up to Hound Tor looked longer and steeper than he remembered.

"Do we really need to do this?" Gemma asked. Her head was heavy and she didn't feel in the mood for more walking.

He nodded firmly. "It must be important. Why would our guide lead us there if it wasn't? But you can wait in the car if you want."

Gemma sighed and pushed her door open. She climbed out of the car on stiff legs and blinked hard a couple of times. The headache wasn't improving. "Look," she told Adrian as he walked round to join her, "what if Mike isn't our guide? What if he's just some local drunk who sold his story to the paper to help a friend? You heard him, those sightings made the guy with the snack van loads of money." She glanced back towards Hound of the Basket Meals.

"You think the Beast is just a made up tourist attraction?"

"I looked Mike up on the internet. No one believed him at the time."

Adrian's face flushed pink. "So that means he was lying?"

"I think he was probably drunk. There can't be a beast wandering around here, more people would have seen it. What he saw was a dog."

Adrian kicked at the gravel under his feet. "Let's just walk."

The path to the Tor ran in a straight line up from the car park, but the climb was more tiring the second time. They both reached the top breathless, with burning legs.

"Give me a minute," said Gemma. She sat down on the grass and tried to slow her breathing. Her calves throbbed from the hill. She watched some tourists retreat to the snack van. Only a few people were still out walking dogs on the slope, and they kept in pairs.

Adrian went on ahead to check the direction of the crater. From the top of Hound Tor he looked out over the moor, skimming the landscape for the ring of trees that had first caught his eye. The grass and bracken spread out below in tattered folds, less welcoming without the sun. There was no sign of the crater, or the trees.

"I remember the way we walked," he told Gemma as he strode back.

"Could you see it again?"

"I know the way," he held out a hand.

She took it and rose stiffly to her feet. The movement made the pain in her head worse. She stood still for a few seconds until it faded.

"All we need to do is find the ravine, and we know the ring of trees is on the other side," Adrian said cheerily.

"What if we can't find it?"

"We will."

Gemma walked without seeing. She had her arm linked through Adrian's and allowed him to guide her. Mike had his priorities right. He had walked them back to the Café and then slipped into the pub for a pint. She imagined him still there now, perhaps showing off his skull routine to another group of gullible tourists. Elaine had told them to forget about the dream; it had been good advice.

Adrian came to a halt. Gemma rubbed her eyes to rid herself of the strange feeling that she was looking through cling film. The ravine stretched wide ahead of them, deeper and darker in the dull light.

"Now all we need is the path," he said. A short walk brought them to the narrow track, the bracken around it bruised from their first visit.

"I'm not sure about this," said Gemma. The warning was playing on her mind; *there may be no-one around to help you if there was an accident*.

"Don't worry, the slope is shallow here," he said.

"No one knows where we are."

"We'll be careful. I just want a quick look."

She glanced back the way they'd come. The car was well out of sight, but she could still see Hound Tor rising up behind them. It didn't seem so far to walk back.

"Hold onto me; we'll go down together," said Adrian.

Gemma locked her fingers into his and allowed him to lead her to the edge of the ravine. The path disappeared immediately, swallowed by the dense bracken on the slopes. Twisted heather grew between the fleshy stems, half dead from lack of light.

"How do we know the path goes all the way?" she asked.

He indicated a faint smudge of brown emerging on the other side of the ravine. "Just there, it isn't far."

"Then let's get it over with."

Adrian stepped carefully onto the path. The earth was wet and clingy underfoot. "See, no problem," he said. He took each step slowly, parting the undergrowth with one hand and steadying Gemma with the other. The track disappeared in places, giving way to tangles of roots where rain had washed the soil away.

Gemma screamed. She jerked away from Adrian and stumbled forward, losing her balance. The bottom of the ravine swam closer. She grabbed for something to steady herself and her fingers closed over a thin branch, but her hand sprung reflexively away as sharp thorns pierced her skin.

Adrian hooked his foot under a root and held firm, steadying her as she found her footing. They stood still for a moment.

"I don't like this," she whimpered.

"We're nearly there." He linked arms with her again. He wasn't ready to give up.

They continued, even more slowly. The path had dissolved into a matted carpet of heather and wiry grass, with waist high bracken above it. Gemma didn't trust her footing from step to step.

Then Adrian slipped.

Gemma felt his arm skim through hers. She grabbed for his hand, caught the tips of his fingers, but felt them slide away. There was a rustle in the bracken and he was gone.

"Adrian!" she screamed. There was silence. No reply. She stood completely still, barely daring to move her head. She couldn't see the hole he'd fallen down, and she didn't know how safe the earth was around it. It might give way at any time.

"Can you hear me?" She called, and then waited a few seconds. It was too long. He wasn't going to answer. Very carefully, without shifting her weight, she reached for her pocket and took out her phone. She'd call Search and Rescue; they'd get him out. The phone screen lit up. No signal. She shook the phone in anger.

"What is wrong with this place," she whined. There was no one else to help. She'd have to get him out herself. She closed her eyes and took a step forward.

A hand caught her by the wrist.

She screamed, twisting away instinctively. She'd been prepared for the fall.

The grip on her wrist grew tighter. It didn't try to pull her away, but just held her where she was.

She turned back to face a tall man with wavy blonde hair. It was the stranger from earlier.

"Stay still," he said.

Gemma tried to pull away again. "Get off me!"

He shook his head, keeping a firm grip on her arm. "It's too dangerous," he said, "I told you this morning."

"My friend is down there."

She leaned back, trying to prise his fingers off with her other hand. He was too strong. Each attempt grew a little weaker. Fear was turning her anger into tears. "Let me go," she begged.

"If you follow him down there you risk harming yourself and perhaps injuring him further. You can see the ground isn't stable."

She stopped struggling and stood still. "You think he might be alright?"

"We need to take a safer way down."

The man turned sharply, dragging her back up the way she'd come. A few strides on he veered right, following a tiny track that she hadn't noticed on the way down. He moved quickly and easily over the slippery ground.

Gemma followed jerkily, watching the soil for holes. He could be taking her anywhere. She was afraid, but she was more afraid for Adrian. The stranger had warned them about the track earlier, so perhaps he did know a better way down. It didn't seem she had a choice.

"Will Adrian be alright?" she asked.

The man shrugged without turning round. "The drop is almost sheer at that point, but he might be lucky. He could have slid most of the way."

Gemma's heart heaved. He had to be alright.

The man dropped her wrist. "You'll need both hands."

They were beginning to descend. The ground grew rocky, with large boulders blocking the path at regular intervals. Gemma either climbed over them or edged around them, gripping the stone to keep steady. After a few minutes they reached a narrow gully. Gemma looked up. The edges of the ravine stretched skywards on either side, framing a wide line of grey cloud. The stranger was nearly out of sight. She hurried to catch up with him.

The path continued to narrow until it was almost blocked by two enormous boulders, tumbled down from the higher slopes at some point in the past. Only a slim gap remained where the stones had formed a narrow door. The man stepped to one side and motioned for Gemma to go through.

She shuffled through sideways, feeling the rough stone scrape past through her jumper. Ahead was a wider basin. At the far end was Adrian. For a moment she couldn't make a sound.

He was standing up, trying to find a foothold on the muddy slope. Every time he tried he just slipped back down. It was too steep.

"Adrian," she yelled.

He spun round, lost his balance and fell over.

Gemma ran to meet him. She skidded the last few feet on her knees and caught him in a tight hug. He mumbled something.

"What did you say?" she asked.

"I said the ground is really wet."

She laughed and helped him to his feet. "Are you ok?"

He nodded, still surprised. "Yeah, I think so."

She turned back to thank the stranger. She half expected him to have disappeared, but he was still there, standing by the stone door.

He spoke before she could. "You risked your life to

see a hole in the ground."

Adrian hung his head and waited for the lecture.

"I warned you once and you chose not to listen." He paused, his eyes narrowing thoughtfully. "But perhaps I was wrong. Maybe you should see it." The man turned his back on them and disappeared back between the stones.

Adrian looked at Gemma. His face was set with determination.

Gemma nodded.

Their route took them partially back the way Gemma had come, and then they turned right to follow another tiny track up the side of the ravine. The gradient was far shallower but they still had to loop back and forth to make the climb. All the way up the stranger remained silent, his gaze fixed ahead.

Adrian kept zipping and unzipping his pockets. "Do you think it's much further?" he whispered.

Gemma shrugged. "Ask him." She brushed her hair out of her eyes to glance ahead for the crater, and realized with a start that her headache was gone. A gentle prod of her temples told her that the tenderness had disappeared; the skin felt smooth and cool.

The ground under their feet began to level out. The bracken was less dense. There was grass under their feet instead of mud.

Ahead, their guide had stopped. He stood facing them as they caught up. Behind him the moor rolled away towards a few low hills and a distant tor. The only feature nearby was a clump of stunted trees. He gestured towards it. "Houndain."

Adrian looked at the trees.

"Are they what you saw?" Gemma asked him.

He shook his head slowly. "I'm not sure. Maybe."

"Inside the circle of trees is a hollow," said the stranger.

"Is it safe to go in?" asked Gemma.

The stranger hesitated, and then nodded. He let Adrian go ahead, following three or four paces behind, his eyes scanning the ground as if looking for a dropped item.

Gemma followed Adrian to an opening in the trees. It was difficult to tell if it had been designed that way, or if a tree had been uprooted at some point to make a gap. Either way, the grass had been churned to mud at the entry.

Adrian stepped inside. The crater was almost a perfect circle, as if someone had pressed a marble into damp clay. The hawthorn hedge grew the whole way around, screening the land inside from the rest of the world.

"Be careful," said Gemma. The ground in the hollow looked boggy. She wasn't sure whether to follow Adrian or wait outside with the stranger. She stood in awkward silence, glancing furtively from one to the other. Her eyes settled on the blonde man. "Thanks for helping us." She hesitated, wondering if he'd heard her.

"I would not have had to if you'd taken my warning," he said.

Gemma looked at the ground. "I'm sorry. We should have listened."

"What made your friend so desperate to find this place?"

The question locked her jaw for a moment. She had a sense that he would know if she tried lying. Sightseeing wasn't going to cover it. "He had a dream about it. Or he might have, he isn't sure if this is the place."

The man raised an eyebrow. "How interesting."

"He thinks so."

"Do you?"

Gemma hesitated again. Her instinct was to say yes, but she was very aware that it would be a lie. She wished he'd give up on the whole thing and stop putting them both in danger. It wasn't worth a trip to A and E, or worse.

The man seemed to read as much from her face. He smiled very slightly.

"Look at this!" yelled Adrian. He beckoned Gemma into the crater.

She shuffled carefully down the grassy edge. The sides weren't that steep, but they were very slippery. It was surprising how wet it was, when the ground outside was dry. Like the gully at the bottom of the ravine, the hollow must sink close to the water table.

"Look," Adrian repeated. It was a stage whisper. He pointed down at a large stone that stood in the centre of the hollow. It was cracked near the base and covered in small holes and gullies; scars from the weather, or maybe traces of an ancient pattern. One of the larger holes had caught his attention. It was in the flat surface on top of the stone, almost like a bowl. A smudge of red marked the inside.

Gemma looked at it intently for a moment. "It looks like rust."

Adrian's shoulders sagged. "It's blood."

"Blood dries brown."

"It's damp in here."

"Not on the stone. It's from iron in the rock." Gemma congratulated herself on her geographical knowledge. She sensed someone behind her.

The stranger had followed them to the edge of the hollow, and was standing just inside the ring of trees.

"Do you think it's from iron in the rock...?" Gemma called, and then paused, "sorry, what is your name?"

He strode down towards them and leaned over the stone. He narrowed his eyes at the red smear. "That blood isn't human."

She stepped away from the rock quickly.

"What would this stone be used for?" Adrian asked, turning and holding eye contact with the stranger.

"Stones would often be placed at sites of religious or ceremonial significance. There are examples all over the moor."

"How do you think the blood got here?"

"It could be from the prey of a hawk or a fox."

Adrian scuffed at the floor half heartedly before taking a last sweep of the hollow with his eyes. It wasn't really underground and there was no sign of a chamber. He lowered his gaze. "I think we've seen enough."

"I'll see you to the tor." The man's tone of voice made it clear there'd be no discussion.

Adrian lagged behind, letting their self-appointed guardian walk ahead.

Gemma slowed her own pace to walk with him. "I thought you really wanted to see that crater."

"I did."

"And? Was it the place from your dream?"

He sighed. "I don't think so."

"At least we looked. We were lucky he offered to show us it."

Adrian kicked out at a clump of heather, sprinkling the grass with tiny purple flowers. He said nothing.

Hound Tor was close now. The terrain changed again and sloped up towards the hill. The wilder moor was behind; the car and snack van ahead. Civilization made Gemma confident.

She glanced back at Adrian. He was pulling a twig of gorse out of his shoe. There was no one else to change the topic. She turned to ask their rescuer if he'd guessed they'd try to go back, and if that was the reason he'd waited nearby. But the slope was empty. He was gone.

Adrian strode past her and up the hill. She glanced back once and then followed.

A tall figure watched them until they drove out of sight. From the top of the tor they were visible for a long time, their car a small dot speeding away over the green landscape. When they were gone he turned sharply and strode back out onto the moor. A large black dog caught up and trotted beside him, head angled obediently towards its master.

"She doesn't know me," he told the hound.
It let out a low whine and rubbed its long snout against his thigh. It was the size of a wolfhound, with shaggy black fur and large eyes.

They took the path back to Houndain, moving more quickly without others to consider. He made for the centre stone without slowing, stepping lightly from one firm patch of ground to the next. His hound sniffed the red stain with interest.

"My concern exactly." He touched the dip in the stone experimentally. Without company the scent was stronger; unmistakeable. He held out his hand and the hound came to sniff the blood on his fingers. It backed away, hackles raised.

6.
Ghost Stories

Gemma and Adrian went back to the Plume of Feathers for dinner. Mike was already there, and had saved them a table. He smiled as they sat down, but was drumming his fingers together nervously.

"This meal is on me," he blurted.

Gemma raised her hand to refuse, but he continued before she could speak.

"What I did today was wrong. I shouldn't have tried to take you down a path I didn't know. Anything could have happened."

Adrian picked up the menu and began to flick through.

"But nothing did," she said, "we're fine."

"No thanks to me," said Mike. He looked towards the pub door for a moment; his eyes focusing on a point beyond it, as if for him the door wasn't there and he could see out through to the moor.

"Anyone know what they're eating yet?" Gemma opened her menu in an exaggerated motion.

"Rabbit pie," said Adrian.

"You had that yesterday."

"Hence I can recommend it highly to myself."

Gemma watched Mike out of the corner of her eye. He'd picked up the menu hesitantly and was slowly leafing through. "What are you having?" she asked him.

"Same I think." He seemed to relax a little. "You?"

"Ill have the…" she scanned through the menu quickly, "chicken."

"I'll get our order in then." He rose from the table

and headed off towards the bar.

Once he was out of earshot Gemma leaned in towards Adrian. "Look at the state of him," she hissed, "we shouldn't have dragged him into this."

"He'll be fine," Adrian said.

"He's feeling guilty as hell because he thinks he put us in danger. You're out of order if you're expecting him to carry on leading us about on your little mission without explaining what's really going on."

"Fine, I'll tell him."

"That wasn't what I meant." Gemma raised her eyebrows and turned to check that Mike wasn't on his way back. "I mean that maybe we should, you know, try to think about this a bit more. Maybe we aren't quite ready to go hunting for this place just yet. Perhaps we need to find out a bit more first."

Adrian considered what she'd said. "Maybe." He leaned back in his chair as a signal that Mike was coming.

Gemma leaned back as well, and smiled as Mike put a Diet Coke down in front of her. Adrian was delivered a white wine, and of course Mike had a pint of beer for himself. He'd remembered their drinks from last night.

"Thanks," Gemma said.

"You're welcome." Mike was smiling now. Perhaps that was down to the beer. "I hope you enjoyed yourselves this morning, despite the little hiccup."

"It was great," said Adrian, "sorry I was so pushy about seeing that crater. I'm sure it wasn't that interesting."

"Not to worry. There's no harm done, is there?"

Gemma shook her head. But her heartbeat rattled in her chest. True, there was no harm done and Adrian was fine, but as she had walked with the stranger every part of her had been convinced otherwise.

"I was actually wondering if you were free tomorrow," Adrian said.

Mike broke into a huge grin. "So you'd like to come out again, would you?"

"Definitely," Adrian cut in before Gemma could object.

She tried to catch his eye, but he didn't look in her direction. She thought they'd just agreed to leave it until they knew a bit more. Surely he'd learned just a little bit of caution from his fall?

Mike positively beamed. "Tomorrow would be great. Was there somewhere in particular you wanted to go?"

"I'm still really interested in those burial sites we talked about."

"Well that's no problem; we can visit some of those." Mike nodded quickly, the last traces of guilt dissolving as he thought ahead. "Shall we meet at the same time?"

"Same place," agreed Adrian. It was settled.

Gemma shifted in her seat. She was going to have a serious chat with Adrian when they got back to the café. He glanced at her briefly and she saw his eyes lit with a fiery resolve. Then he turned sharply to Mike.

"Do you know any good ghost stories?"

Mike took a mouthful of his beer and swilled it around his mouth as he thought. "Do you mean ones that people have told me, or-" he clacked the glass down for emphasis, " things I've actually seen?"

Adrian tapped the side of his glass impatiently. "Things you've seen."

"Well then, what comes to mind is the black

hound I suppose. It's called all manner of names in different legends: Black Shuck, Wisht Hound or the Devil's Dog. These stories make it sound monstrous, all about the huge fangs and bloody jaws and eyes as big as saucers, but whenever I've seen it there isn't much between it and a normal dog."

"How do you know it isn't a normal dog?" Gemma asked.

Adrian shot her a cold look.

"The eyes," said Mike, "They're bright red."

"How many times have you seen it?" Adrian asked.

Mike took another gulp of beer, and then suppressed a large yawn. "Most nights."

"Have you ever tried to communicate with it?"

Gemma watched a young couple in the opposite corner. They were laughing over a joke the man had just told, and holding hands across the table. Life looked so normal on the other side of the room, and here she was; stuck with two guys who saw ghosts. It had been more than enough when it was just Adrian.

"Black seems to be a popular colour around here, what with the Beast as well..." she said. No one heard her.

Mike leant his elbows on the table to answer Adrian's question. "I tried at first. In fact, I tried everything. I tried shooing it away, I tried those sonic garden alarms that dogs can hear but we can't. I even had a priest bless my garden. By that point I felt like a total crackpot, and just gave up. Now I ignore it, and it's content enough just to watch me."

"Do you ever see it on the way home from the pub?" Gemma asked.

"Well now you mention it, yes, I think I have on a

few occasions."

Gemma raised an eyebrow at Adrian, but he just scowled in return.

"Do you know what it wants?" he asked Mike.

He shook his head and fought back another yawn. "I can't think what it's after. In the legends Black Shuck is meant to follow travellers down lonely lanes at night, and to hear his padding feet foretells of a coming death. But this dog waits in my garden, it watches me from the shadows when I'm walking, and I've even woken up with it sitting at my bedroom door. I'm not dead yet though, but then maybe that's why it's still waiting."

Gemma shivered. Mike had a way of telling stories.

"Rabbit pie?" asked the waiter, and everyone leant back reluctantly. The pub was warm and the familiar candles flickered in their niches on the walls. The eyes of the taxidermy animals glinted with reflected light.

"What about you?" Mike asked Adrian, "do you have any scary stories?"

Adrian prodded his pie with his fork. "I think I have one," he said.

Gemma had just raised a mouthful of chicken to her lips, but she let her fork clatter back down on the plate as soon as Adrian spoke. He was going to tell Mike. She tried to concentrate on her food but the meat on her plate didn't appeal. She attempted to sip her drink instead. There was nothing she could do. Adrian wasn't going to give up, and reasoning with him was pointless; she had seen that much on his face. He had such a need to find this boy that he was willing to risk his life to do it. But where had this drive come from, and why did he care so much about a stranger?

She heard Adrian repeat his dream. Mike listened with rapt attention. Gemma could tell that there'd be no way he could resist the idea of a quest, not even a pathetic and dangerous one. He was going to swallow every last detail and then that would be it; she'd have two grown men chasing spirits to deal with. One was bad enough, and trying to keep both of them from death was going to leave absolutely no time for a relaxing holiday.

"Will you help us?" Adrian asked Mike.

"Of course I will."

Gemma slammed her glass down onto the table. "I think I need some air," she said, standing abruptly and making for the door.

"Don't let your food go cold," Mike called. He watched her for a few moments, but then Adrian drew him back into conversation.

It was warm outside and there was a lazy breeze that smelt of trodden grass. There were also no people talking about ghosts, which was a definite improvement. Gemma walked a little way down the road and then stopped next to a low dry stone wall. The stones had been chosen to slot together so perfectly that there was no cement between them, although over time moss had filled in the cracks. The wall was warm from a day in the sun and she sat with her back against it. On her right the moors rolled in to press against the town, and on her left the concrete began. The wall and the cattle grid marked the boundary.

She needed to talk to Adrian, but she wasn't sure how to get him to listen. He was fixated on this dream of his, despite the fact that Elaine had told him that it almost certainly wasn't a visionary one. He clearly respected her, but he'd still ignored her advice, so what chance did she have of dissuading him? It was like he needed it somehow, as if he wanted this chance to play the hero, and the fact that it mightn't be real wasn't going to stop him. She could tolerate playing along while it was just tarot cards and candles, but ravines and sinkholes on the moor were a whole different game, and getting Mike involved was only going to make it worse. The voice of reason had no hope with them encouraging each other. She would have to get Adrian alone, if she could manage to split up their little paranormal club for a moment, and make him see the danger in what he was doing. They had been lucky in the ravine, but they mightn't be again. Chasing made-up spirits was dangerous and a waste of time. She would tell that to his face.

Goosebumps prickled along her shoulders. She glanced left down the road and then looked out over the moor. There was no one to be seen, but the tiny hairs rising along her arms still warned her that she wasn't alone.

"Adrian?" she called. Perhaps he'd come to apologise. She waited a moment for a reply, but none came. Of course it didn't, Adrian would be far too busy plotting his next adventure to worry about her. The dream had taken over. She glanced down at her hands. There was a row of tiny red circles across one palm, the skin around them white and slightly swollen. The vertigo returned for a moment and she clenched her fists, making the thorn marks burn. The muscles in her shoulders pulled tight and the gooseflesh spread to her wrists. She looked up quickly.

A dog was watching her. She rubbed her arms to make the hairs settle, but she could still feel her skin prickling. The dog sat very still, its fur a deeper black than the shadow cast by the row of houses. Gemma looked around for an owner, but there was still no one in sight. There was only her and the dog watching her. Mike's story began to retell itself in her head.

"Shoo," she muttered, flicking her hands weakly at the dog. It trotted towards her. She froze. Black Shuck is a great black dog with fiery eyes. Black Shuck appears to travellers on lonely roads at night. Black Shuck foretells of your demise. She gripped the wall behind her, ready to throw herself over. *It's just a story* she repeated in her head, *just a story, just a story, just a...*

The dog stopped on the pavement nearby. Now that it had crossed into the light its fur was glossed with a sheen that split the sunlight into deep golds and greens. It showed no sign of foretelling her impending death. It didn't even have red eyes. Gemma let her breathing slow. The dog stuck out its tongue and began to pant to cool down. She looked out over the moor again, half expecting to see its owner appear. Then she felt something cold on her shoulder. She scuttled sideways and saw the dog back off quickly. She shivered. It was nothing.

"It's alright," she soothed, "I'm not scary."

The dog padded back over and snuffled her palm. She sat very still. It nudged her arm with its nose and she reached up hesitantly to touch the smooth fur. Moments later the dog had curled up comfortably next to her. She stroked it absentmindedly, her eyes following the cloud shadows as they swept slowly across the moor. Of course it was just a normal dog, some stray perhaps or a lost pet that a worried owner was looking for. There was no such thing as demon dogs, or whatever Mike had called them. She needed to stop listening to his made up stories.

She gave the dog a final pat and stretched out her tingling legs; she'd been away from the pub long enough. Mike would be starting to think she'd been eaten by the Beast or something, and the last thing she wanted was to gift wrap him another story. She rose to her feet. Her path was blocked.

"He likes you," said the figure.

Gemma tried to step back, but the wall was in her way. It was the stranger from the moor and here on the edge of town he felt too close. "Is he yours?" she asked, vaguely indicating the dog. Her heart was thudding in her chest. A quick sweep of the street told her that there was still no one else around.

The man nodded.

"He's lovely." Gemma edged along the wall very slowly.

"Fen is her name."

"That's unusual," she said, trying to glance behind her and judge the best direction in which to run.

"She can keep an eye on you."

"What do you mean?" She risked a quick look down at the dog, which was sitting obediently at her feet. Both mahogany eyes were raised towards her own. When she looked up the stranger had gone.

"Go on!" she yelled, waving her hands at the dog. It didn't move. "Go on, go away," she took a step forward, stamping her foot on the ground. The dog glanced at her shoe but stayed perfectly still. It wasn't working. "Fine," she muttered, and started to walk back to the pub. Halfway there she looked quickly over her shoulder. The dog was still following. But it kept its distance now, trailing her on the other side of the road. She resolved to ignore it, and stepped back inside the Plume of Feathers. Strange men and their strays were none of her business.

A babble of voices closed around her as the door swung shut. The pub had filled up. Mike and Adrian looked up as she walked over. Only her plate of food remained untouched on the table. The number of empty glasses, however, seemed to have considerably increased.

"Where'd you go?" Adrian asked.

"Just for a walk," she lied. She didn't want to provide fuel for their imagination, or it wouldn't be two seconds before they'd made it into some paranormal encounter.

"Meet anyone better than yourself?" Mike asked.

Gemma shook her head.

"Adrian's been telling me all about this dream of his," Mike continued, "it must be exciting having a medium as a friend."

"It's certainly something," she replied. At the edge of her vision, she saw Adrian emptying another glass of wine.

"One more?" Mike asked him.

"Naturally."

Gemma pushed her cold plate of food away. She wouldn't have thought it possible, but her evening was actually getting worse. Now she was in the company of two fully grown men who not only believed in ghosts but were also *drunk*.

"Perhaps we should pace ourselves," Mike said, noticing the sour look on Gemma's face.

"Nonsense, it's my round," announced Adrian. He stood up and sent his chair clattering to the floor.

"That's it," said Gemma, "you've had enough."

Adrian narrowed his eyes.

"Come on lad," said Mike, giving him a pat on the

shoulder. "You've got an early start in the morning and we need you fresh."

Adrian allowed Mike to steer him towards the door, while Gemma followed behind. Mike shot an apologetic look back at her and walked them back towards the Fox Tor Café in silence. The fresh air seemed to have done Adrian no favours.

"Wait," hissed Mike suddenly. The others came to a halt. "Did you hear that?" he asked.

"Hear what?" whispered Gemma.

"That padding. Listen." Mike froze with his head tilted to one side and his hand to his ear.

Gemma strained her hearing to catch the sound. Then she heard it, slow and rhythmic, the padding of large paws.

"It's the Devil's Dog!" squealed Adrian, jumping behind Mike.

Gemma tried to work out which direction the noise was coming from. She glanced around, her eyes skimming over a patch of shadow between buildings on the other side of the road. A movement made her look back; just in time to see a head dip back into the darkness. It was Fen. She failed to suppress a smile. For the look on Adrian's face, perhaps she could put up with her canine stalker.

"I wonder if that damn hound would turn up with you two here…" Mike stepped forward as if he would cross the road to investigate.

"It's probably just a stray," Gemma said.

Mike stopped. "We don't get many strays." He turned round to face Adrian again. "You'd better get inside; if it's my dog he's not after you."

Adrian needed no further persuasion. He was

through the side entrance in seconds, leaving Gemma outside with Mike, who was still watching the other side of the road. She could just pick out two eyes glinting in the darkness. She wondered if Mike saw them too.

"You'd better go look after him," Mike said, indicating the direction in which Adrian had fled.

Gemma nodded slowly. The wine wasn't going to make her conversation with him any easier. But she had promised herself she would do it tonight, so she had to try.

"Sorry he's tipsy," Mike said.

"Don't worry," she said, "he's been worse."

Mike pulled a lopsided grin and wandered off into the night. Gemma didn't wait to watch the eyes withdraw.

Adrian was lying face down on his bed and didn't stir as Gemma pulled the door shut behind her.

"Adrian?" she called.

He grunted into his pillow.

"Do you want a drink of water or something?" She waited for an answer, but none came. "I need to talk to you quickly."

"In the morning," he mumbled.

"I need you to listen now."

Reluctantly, he rolled over and propped himself up on one elbow. "S' wrong?"

"Well, I thought we'd agreed that we were going to take a step back from all this dream stuff until we knew a bit more. There's no chance of that now you've gone and told Mike."

"He's going to help us, Gemma." He said it like it was the most obvious solution.

"Why not talk to me about it first?"

"We'd already talked." Adrian yawned widely.

"Yeah, and you agreed to keep it quiet!"

Adrian sat up and opened his eyes. "What's the point of coming here to sort it out if we don't try to sort it out?"

"None."

"Exactly."

"No, none. There is no point in coming here to sort it out, because there's nothing to sort out. Elaine told you not to, now I'm telling you not to. I went along with it, and look where it got us; nearly killed out on the moor."

"We weren't nearly killed."

"Yes we were. When are you going to get it into your stupid, hairspray addled, paranormal obsessed brain that there is no trapped spirit, there was no visionary dream, because none of that crap is real?"

It was very quiet in the bunkhouse for a few moments. Then Adrian got to his feet.

"You stink of dog," he said, walking off.

"Better than wine."

He turned back sharply and the quick movement set him swaying. "You know, I can tell you exactly why you're still single," he spat, "because you're just so bloody boring!"

Gemma stared as he strode into the bathroom and slammed the door at her. Slowly, she slid down the wall and sat with her knees tucked up to her chest. At least Adrian wasn't there to see her cry. Was he right though? Did everyone who met her just decide that she was dull? She suddenly felt overwhelmingly lonely. Adrian and Mike had their spiritual investigations to work on and get excited about. All she had was a dead end job and a stray dog to talk to. Perhaps there was a case for swapping sides. Her mum had certainly thought so.

She heard the toilet flush and scuttled into her bunk, pulling the clothes over her head. Adrian walked back into the room. His footsteps stopped as he paused by Gemma's bed, but she stayed still and pretended to be asleep. She wasn't ready to talk. After a few minutes he flung himself back down onto his own bed, and soon he was snoring. She gave it another ten minutes, just to make sure, and then very quietly crept out of bed and over to the door. Still fully dressed, she grabbed her coat and stepped out into the blackness.

It was truly dark outside, a world away from the glowing half night of the city. The stars were sharp points in a clear sky. Around her the air was still and sleepy, thick with the smell of grass and damp earth.

The padding began as soon as she stepped out onto the street. For a few minutes she listened to the paws keep time with her, smiling as she walked.

"Fen," she murmured, and the dog appeared immediately beside her. They walked on, only stopping at the wall that marked the end of town. Beyond it the moor stretched from shades of green into shadow. Gemma leant against the wall and looked out over the dark land. It was silent, except for the thumping of Fen's tail.

"Am I boring?" Gemma asked the dog.

Fen looked up at her with large eyes, slightly reflective in the dark.

She crouched down to scratch the dog's ears. "Adrian thinks so. And he might be right." She stood up again. For a time she just stared, her eyes finding patterns in the dark. Somewhere out on the moor a fox barked. "Take you for example," Gemma glanced down at Fen, "most of me is sure you're just an average pet dog.

Another example of me finding the most boring explanation I suppose. But what if you weren't? What if you really were one of these Wish Hounds?"

"Wisht Hounds," a voice corrected.

Gemma screamed and trod on Fen's paw in surprise. The dog whined and retreated to a safe distance.

"What if she was?" Fen's owner materialised just beyond the wall.

"Oh, sorry," said Gemma, trying to slow her breathing, "I was just being silly."

"Why are you afraid of being boring?"

She blushed. Had he been watching her the whole time? "Just something my friend said."

"Shall I show you something?"

Gemma shuffled backwards. If a strange man followed you at night and then asked if they could show you something, the answer was always no. She should leave.

"You'll be perfectly safe and, I promise you, it won't be boring," he said.

Gemma heard Adrian's words all over again. *You're so bloody boring*. "Fine," she said.

"Good." He held out a hand.

She let him help her over the dry stone wall. "A name might make this less weird."

"My name is Gabriel."

She had to hold his arm to keep up with him. He moved quickly over the uneven ground, but as long as she let him lead she didn't stumble. Fen ran somewhere beside them, dodging in and out of the shadows. How could Adrian call her boring now?

"Here," said Gabriel. He stopped and Gemma let go of his arm.

They were standing in front of a stone circle. Outside it gorse bushes and bracken pressed against the stones, but inside the grass was short and speckled with moss. Tiny wildflowers sprinkled the turf, their white heads turned to the moon.

Fen barked and ran into the circle. She lay down and rolled on the grass like a puppy, nosing the ground and flinging her legs in the air. Gemma smiled. But something was wrong. She became very still. A low whine gurgled from her throat and a sharp crack hit the air. One back leg collapsed.

Gemma started forward, but the dog paid her no attention.

Gabriel's hand was on her shoulder, holding her back. She could only watch as Fen rapidly decomposed. Her bones cracked and folded. Her flesh hollowed and sucked skin back onto her broken frame. Her fur bubbled up and then fell away until only her white skeleton was left, which was then pulled down into the earth.

Gemma felt herself crumple, folding over her stomach which contracted with helpless horror. It was too late to help her. "What the hell just happened?"

"What do you think happened?"

Tears burnt in the corners of Gemma's eyes. She felt dizzy. The dog didn't need to die. "Is that what you wanted to show me?"

Gabriel noted the disgust on her face. "Remember, I said you'd be safe with me."

She eyed the ground where Fen had been. "Maybe you were lying."

"Nothing will harm you."

"Your dog wouldn't agree." She tried to sound confident, whilst wondering whether she'd make it back to town if she sprinted.

"Come with me." He took her arm and tried to lead her inside the circle.

She recoiled. "No."

"Trust me. Fen is still there." He pulled her towards the circle again. "You can call her back."

Gemma hesitated, and that was all he needed.

He led her into the centre of the circle where Fen had died. The ground was springy under foot, with only a few patches of upturned moss to show the dog had been there.

"Not everything is what it seems," he said.

"Really?" Fen's demise had looked quite final. He'd be too quick if she tried to run. She would never make it.

"Look at me."

She felt Gabriel's hands on both her upper arms. His expression was excited. His eyes were bright, glinting with the same night sheen as Fen's had.

"Lay your hand on the earth," he told her. She didn't move so he crouched down and pulled her with him, placing her hand on the soft ground. Gemma didn't dare resist.

"Now call her," he commanded.

"What?"

Gabriel laid his hand on top of hers. "Call her back, with your desire for her to live."

She shut her eyes and tried to concentrate on the coolness of the earth under her hand. Then she waited. Thirty seconds passed, and all she achieved was a conviction that she looked like an idiot. She was afraid of what failing this test might mean. This was Adrian's domain. She couldn't bring Fen back. All she had was her own fear, and the knot of disgust in her stomach from when she'd watched the dog die. She had looked to her when the first bone broke. The nausea turned into anger. Fen hadn't deserved that. She pictured the look on Adrian's face when he had accused her of being boring. No one deserved that. Hot tears rolled down her cheeks. The pain punched from her chest into her throat and filled her mouth with a scream.

She stopped when she felt pressure beneath her hand. She raised it slowly. There was a growing black patch on the ground beneath.

"Was that boring?" Gabriel asked as Fen clawed her way out of the earth.

7.
MISSING PEOPLE

Gemma opened her eyes. Adrian stood next to her bed with a plate of crumpets and a nervous smile.

"I was a dick," he said "and I'm sorry."

She sat up. "Don't worry about it."

"No, I was way out of order. It's your choice what you believe in, or don't believe in. You're not boring. I'm an idiot."

"I do believe you."

"I know, and that's fine…" Adrian paused, "what did you say?"

"I said I believe that sometimes, weird stuff happens that can't be explained." Gemma threw off the covers and reached for the crumpets.

Adrian narrowed his eyes. "Cold last night?"

"No," said Gemma, taking the plate. "Thanks for these."

"Is there another reason you slept in your clothes?"

Gemma looked down. She was still wearing her T-shirt from yesterday and her jeans had dark green stains on both knees. She hesitated. "I must have been really tired."

"Those are some impressive grass stains. I didn't notice them last night."

"You were probably too busy drooling over ghosts with Mike." The words came out sharply and Adrian frowned. Gemma continued in a gentler tone, "I suppose I did it when I went for some air, I did sit on the grass for a few minutes."

Adrian shrugged and she forced a smile. "Look, shall we leave the great mystery of the puzzling grass stains to someone else? Perhaps Sherlock Holmes will take on the case?" She saw Adrian laugh in response, but inside she was tense. There was no reason for her to keep what happened last night secret; he would be impressed, and perhaps jealous. But she had just had the perfect chance to tell him and she hadn't. She felt her cheeks burn and realized that she was ashamed. What kind of lunatic follows a strange man out onto the deserted moor? Adrian would call her an idiot, and he'd be right. "How are you feeling this morning anyway?" she asked him.

Adrian rubbed an eyebrow with his fist. "Fabulous."

Gemma jumped to her feet, recalling the conversation from last night. "What time is it? You said we'd meet Mike."

"Don't worry; he's waiting in the café."

"Is it late?"

Adrian looked at his phone. "Ten."

Gemma crammed the last half of crumpet into her mouth. They were meant to have met him an hour ago. She pulled her hair back in a loose ponytail and smoothed down her top. At least she was already dressed.

Mike was sat at a table in the café reading a newspaper. A mug of coffee and half a bacon sandwich sat forgotten beside him.

"We're ready," said Adrian.

Mike glanced up and smiled. "Sleep well?" he asked Gemma.

"A bit too well perhaps. Sorry we're late."

"Don't you worry. I've been catching up on the news." He waved the newspaper in their direction. The front page caught Gemma's eye.

"What does that say?" She took a step closer.

Mike laid the paper flat on the table. "You mean this?" he pressed his finger down on the front page.

Gemma read the headline.

'Search for Missing Walkers Continues'

Adrian read it over her shoulder.

"Why would it not continue?" he asked.

"It says Search and Rescue teams looked for three days and found nothing," Mike read.

"You mean they would just give up?" said Gemma.

Mike took a sip of his coffee and grimaced. It was cold. "People get lost out on the moor from time to time. You've seen it's dangerous out there. Sometimes they don't find their way back."

"Search and Rescue should keep looking."

"Oh they'll find them," he said, "eventually."

Adrian was standing very still. Gemma glanced back at him. His eyes had grown wide and were fixed on the paper.

"Are you ok?" she asked him.

"Does it give names?"

Mike scanned the article again, tracing each line with his finger. "No, no names. It just says that an Irish couple became lost out on the moor, along with their son. They'd come to Dartmoor for a holiday."

Adrian held up his hand for Mike to stop, and Gemma guessed what he was thinking.

"The boy," Mike whispered, glancing up at Adrian.

He handed over the paper.

Gemma sat down on one of the other chairs round the table. Her heart had sped up, beating hard against her ribs. There was a boy missing out on the moor. The Search and Rescue team presumed him dead. He'd disappeared three days ago. Adrian's dream had been that night.

"They were last seen…" Adrian skimmed down the page, "near Hunters Tor." He looked up at Mike.

"Lustleigh Cleave," he said.

"Pardon?" said Gemma.

"It's the nearest town. We'll park there and walk up."

Minutes later they were in the Land Rover. Mike sped along narrow country lanes at a worrying speed, branches snapping against the paintwork as he swerved for oncoming cars without slowing.

Gemma sniffed. She smelt mud, wet dog, but no alcohol.

"Do you know of any burial sites near Hunters Tor?" Adrian asked Mike.

He drove on in silence for a time. "No," he said eventually.

Adrian sighed.

"But," Mike continued, "if I remember rightly, there's the ruin of an old fort somewhere nearby. I don't think it's far."

Adrian nodded. "Let's find it."

Gemma held onto the door handle as they rocketed down tiny roads, the verge on each side so high it felt like a tunnel. She'd sworn not to get involved in any of this, and look at her now, speeding off to find some ruins. She smiled out of the window. It was kind of exciting.

"Here we are," said Mike, swinging into the car park of a thatched pub. The wooden picnic benches outside were full of smiling people enjoying a drink in the sun. "Incentive to find our way back," he winked at Adrian.

Gemma pushed her door open and climbed out. Trust Mike to find a pub. At least they wouldn't stand any chance of getting lost; his nose would lead them back to the ale.

"The tor is up that way. I think." Mike pointed vaguely to the right.

"Have you been there before?" asked Gemma.

"Of course."

"Sober?"

Mike recalled a pressing need to look for something in the boot of his car. He returned with a thick walking stick almost as tall as himself.

"Ready?" said Adrian. He was bobbing impatiently.

"Let's go," said Mike.

At first they followed the road off to the right, but quickly veered off it and turned left down a small muddy track. It weaved between huge grey boulders, furred in patches with bright green moss. The air was cool and smelt of earth. They walked in the shade cast by large trees that pushed their way up from between the stones. It was very different to the barren moor.

After a steep climb they came out of the woodland into a landscape Gemma recognised. The usual rough grass crept between scattered gorse and patches of heather. Ahead was a small rocky outcrop which she guessed was Hunter's Tor. She shaded her eyes with her hand. It was too hot in the sun after the shade of the trees.

Adrian pulled off his jumper and tied it round his waist.

Mike hesitated. His face was shiny above the collar of his usual wax jacket.

"You can't walk in that," said Gemma, "you'll roast." Her T-shirt was thin but she was still wishing that she'd changed into something strappy.

He glanced ahead and then back the way they'd come. There was no one else around. "Don't laugh," he said, "I wasn't thinking straight at the time." He pulled off the coat to reveal a short sleeved checked shirt.

Gemma's eyes widened.

Both of his arms, from wrist up to where the shirt sleeve began, were covered in tattoos. They were all depictions of the same thing, in various styles and sizes, and repeated again and again over every inch of skin.

"That is so cool," said Adrian.

"Look at this then." Mike undid the first two buttons of the shirt. The tattoos continued across his chest.

"It's definitely unusual," said Gemma.

Mike barked a laugh. "No, it's downright ridiculous. I must have been mad."

"Why keys?" she asked.

Mike shrugged. "They meant something at the time."

They walked on. Adrian went ahead with Mike, eager to ask him more about the strange tattoos. Gemma followed a few strides behind. She was wondering how someone could identify with keys. Did Mike have a secret

102

locked away? She pushed the thought to one side. Accepting the weird stuff was one thing; creating more of it was a step too far. He'd probably just been drunk.

Mike stopped.

Gemma nearly walked into him before she noticed. "Oh, sorry."

He tilted his head and smiled. "Something on your mind?"

"Not really," she lied.

"If that's Hunter's Tor," said Adrian, "where's the fort?"

"The ruins aren't much more than foundations," Mike said.

Adrian looked serious. "That's what I'm interested in."

"What if we spread out, and then yell if we find them?" suggested Gemma.

Mike started to shake his head.

"We'll barely be out of sight," she said.

Adrian was nodding. "I'll go that way." He strode off to the right of the tor.

"Well don't go too far," said Mike. He glanced back quickly at Gemma as he walked off straight ahead.

She waved. She'd go to the left then. She hadn't taken more than ten steps when a flash of black caught her eye, and a moment later Fen was beside her. She crouched down to stroke the dog between the ears. It nuzzled her palm and then ran backwards. "What? Aren't we friends now?"

Fen ran back towards her, nudged her on the knee this time, and then retreated again.

Gemma followed. As soon as she caught up the dog did the same thing all over again, nudging her and then running ahead before stopping while she caught up. "What's wrong with you?"

Fen stopped a way ahead and began to paw the ground.

Gemma glanced backwards. Adrian and Mike were out of sight, though she could still see the tor back behind her. She walked over to Fen slowly. This time the dog didn't run away as she approached. Gemma glanced down at the ground Fen had been digging at, and then bent her knees to look more closely. The thin surface of turf was turned up to reveal grey stone beneath. Gemma looked up and saw that, here and there, thrusting up through the grass were lines of stone that looked like a low wall. Slowly, a pattern became clear. "The ruins," she said.

Fen licked her palm.

She walked along a corridor between two lines of weathered rock. The foundations of various rooms spread out off to each side. The fort must have been huge. She came to the end of the stone line and found what she guessed to be an outside wall. Even in its crumbling state it was three feet thick. She stepped up and walked along it, Fen trotting beside her. Reaching a corner, she stopped. She should call the others now.

Fen froze and sniffed the air.

Gemma jumped as the dog whipped past her. Where was she going now? A frenzied barking was coming from ahead. Jumping off the wall, Gemma raced towards the sound. Fen was sniffing at something on the floor. Gemma skidded to a halt and took a quick step back. "Get away from that!" She yelled.

The dog looked up guiltily, shuffling back from the half rotted carcass. It was a dead pony.

"Come here," said Gemma.

Fen slunk to her side, casting backward glances at the feast.

Gemma gave the dog a disgusted look. It cowered at her feet, tail between it's legs.

"Oh come on, you'll make yourself sick."

Fen let out a low whimper, and Gemma noticed she was shaking. She tried to pat her on the head but she whined and cringed away. The fur had risen in a line down her back. Something was scaring her, and it wasn't the telling off. Gemma raised her eyes and looked around. They had moved away from the main ruins and now stood in the middle of three hut circles, the rings of crumbling stone similar to those she'd seen at Grimspound. The prickling at the back of her neck told her she should leave. "Fen," she whispered.

The dog had squared up in front of her and started growling. What could she see? Fen barked again, the sound sharp in the stillness of the place.

Gemma turned to dash away but a movement ahead froze her to the spot. In the nearest hut circle a section of grey stone was slowly detaching itself from the inner wall. She clamped her hand over her mouth. It was a bone thin arm. The flesh stretched over it was pale grey, mottled with brown and black where dirt caked the surface. A skeletal leg and torso followed the arm. Then she saw the creature's face. Two icy eyes fixed on her and she returned the gaze with horror. It rose slowly; its back arched over and supporting a row of vicious spikes bristling up from the spine. Gemma screamed.

Gabriel slowed from a run beside her. She grabbed his arm without thinking, pointing at the advancing monster. Fen wagged her tail at seeing her master.

"Get away from here," Gabriel told the creature.

Its pinched features drew into a scowl. Hissing, it bared two rows of sharp yellow teeth.

Gabriel matched the stare. He took a step forward and it shuffled sideways, never taking its eyes off him. Saliva dripped from spikes that hung down from its jaw. Gabriel advanced again, a low snarl tearing from his own lips.

The creature limped a few steps, grabbed the dead pony by the front hooves, and backed off with its prize.

Gemma reached out for Gabriel's arm again.

He led her back to the outer wall of the ruined fort and sat her down on it. For a moment she understood how her mum had felt when the angel appeared in the road.

Fen jumped up beside her and snuffled comfortingly at her face.

"I know where that nose has been," Gemma mumbled. She twisted backwards at the sound of footsteps.

Adrian and Mike were running towards her. They slowed as she saw them, Mike stopping for a moment to rest his hands on his knees.

"We heard screaming," said Adrian, "are you alright?"

Gemma nodded.

Adrian noticed Gabriel. "We seem to bump into you a lot."

"I was just walking my dog up near Hunter's Tor. I wandered down this way and chanced upon Gemma here.

It would seem my dog likes her."

Fen wagged her tail.

Mike caught up and stopped next to Adrian, his arms folded across his chest as he attempted to hide his raspy breathing. "You found the fort then. Why didn't you call us?"

"I was about to, but…" Gemma glanced quickly at Gabriel, "I just got chatting about the dog. It gave me fright when it ran over."

Mike eyed Fen sceptically. "I'm sure the dog holds untold scope for conversation."

"May I ask why you were looking for the fort?" Gabriel asked.

Adrian shifted uncomfortably. "It just sounded interesting."

"You think so? I find there isn't much left to see."

"But there's more underneath, I mean cellars and dungeons and that."

Gabriel eyed the ruins with doubt. "If there ever were they're well filled in by now. All you might find under those walls are earth and perhaps some bones; nothing of great interest."

Adrian kicked the floor with his heel.

"Go and look if you like." Gabriel said.

Mike untied his jacket from his waist and put it back on, even though the day was still blazing hot. He nodded at Adrian. "We might as well look now we're here."

Adrian paused, waiting for Gemma to follow them.

"I'll be with you in a second," she said.

He shrugged and walked off.

As soon as the others were far enough away

Gabriel turned back to Gemma. "What are they really here for?"

She shifted uncomfortably on the stones and began to pick at a thread on her jeans. He had probably just saved her life. "I'll tell you if you tell me what that thing was."

He nodded thoughtfully. "What you just saw is one of the feral; a degenerate and dangerous creature that lives out on the moor. Ruins provide them shelter, as they generally lack enough skill to build their own. They feed on whatever they can scavenge, or anything else they can catch. If you're slow enough they'll kill you."

Gemma shivered, despite the sun. Once again, she'd been lucky Gabriel was there. She didn't want to think about what would have happened otherwise.

"Now you," he said.

"Adrian is trying to find the place he saw in a dream. He thinks the spirit of a young boy is trapped there." The explanation sounded weak out loud, but less unbelievable after what she'd just seen.

Gabriel didn't seem surprised. "I don't find dreams all that trustworthy. How does he know what he saw was true?"

She shrugged. "I guess he doesn't."

"As a good friend, you should advise him to take care."

Gemma shook her head. "I have tried, but he won't listen. He's like that; once he gets it in his head that he's going to do something there's nothing anyone can say to stop him. Elaine couldn't even make him see sense."

"Who is Elaine?"

"A friend of his; she's psychic I think."

Gabriel considered this for a moment. "What

made him think to come to Hunter's Tor?"

"A headline in the newspaper, it said a missing family had been last seen near here. They had a son."

"The child was underground in his dream?"

Gemma nodded. "He thinks it's in some kind of burial chamber. Mike has been helping us find some."

"I can show you burial chambers if that's what you want."

She lost her chance to reply as Adrian slouched back. His face was shiny with sweat and he was frowning.

"Find anything?" she asked.

He shook his head.

Mike followed a few seconds later. "There's no disturbed earth, and no way down to lower levels that I can see." He looked just as disappointed as Adrian.

"At least we can cross this place off," said Gemma.

Adrian muttered something to himself which sounded rude, and did include the word 'off'.

"I need a pub," said Mike.

"The Cleave is nearby," Gabriel suggested.

"That's where we're parked," said Gemma.

"Sounds like you have everything arranged then." Gabriel called Fen to his side. "We might happen on each other again."

Gemma noticed a faint smile hovering at the corner of his mouth. "Why don't you come to the pub?" she asked him. She caught Adrian rolling his eyes at her on the edge of her vision.

Gabriel saw it too. "I believe dogs are not allowed."

"Then tonight?" asked Gemma, "come for dinner at the Plume of Feathers. I'm sure Fen can look after herself for a few hours."

The smile spread from the corners of his mouth and Gabriel laughed. "That is a very kind offer."

Adrian butted in. "You don't have to come. It's pretty boring really."

Mike was edging backwards.

"I would love to come," said Gabriel, "what time?"

Adrian ignored Gemma all the way back to the car park. When they got there he went straight to the Land Rover.

"Will you have a quick pint?" asked Mike, looking desperate. The sun was still shining on the tables outside and one was empty.

"I'll have a shandy please," said Gemma, making for the free table.

"Same," muttered Adrian. He sat down stiffly opposite her. A few minutes passed in silence. Mike was still inside the pub.

"Cheer up," said Gemma.

"I am cheerful. I can't wait to have dinner with your rude crush this evening, and I honestly do find being in his company far better than getting on with what we came here to do."

"What *you* came here to do."

Adrian covered his face with both hands, and then pulled them down until only his lips were covered.

"Look," said Gemma, "I don't want to argue. Gabriel got us out of that ravine and showed us Houndain, and just now he saved my life."

"Is that what you call it?"

Gemma slammed her fist down on the table.

Adrian backed off. "I take that back. I'm sorry."

"I nearly got eaten by something that looked like a

corpse and had huge spikes sticking out of it. Gabriel arrived just in time to scare it off. It wasn't an erotic experience."

He was shocked into silence for nearly half a minute. "Why didn't you tell me?"

"I didn't want to scare Mike."

"Who's scaring me?" Mike placed a cluster of three drinks on the table.

Gemma gaped at Adrian.

"I thought there was a dent in your car," he invented, "but it was just the light."

Mike laughed. "It'd take a lot to dent *her*." He took a long swig of his beer and sighed with satisfaction.

Adrian caught Gemma's eye.

Later she mouthed.

Mike parked on the verge as his usual spot was full, then walked Gemma and Adrian back to the café.

"See you this evening," Gemma called to Mike as he left.

He halted, and she saw his shoulders move as he took a deep breath. "I don't know if I'll be able to make it," he said.

"Why not?" demanded Adrian.

"I don't want to intrude on your time too much. You didn't come here to put up with a crazy old man following you around. I've enjoyed our trips out on the moor, and it felt good to have something to work towards again, but I understand that you need your own space. Gabriel will be a good guide."

"Wait!" said Gemma.

Mike turned around.

"We want you to help us. You're part of it all now.

I didn't invite Gabriel for dinner this evening to ask him to be our new guide; we're not swapping him for you."

Mike's face brightened a little, but he still shook his head. "Gabriel doesn't share."

"What did you say?" asked Adrian.

"I said Gabriel will be a good guide."

"After that."

Mike's eyebrows creased together in confusion. "I didn't say anything."

Adrian narrowed his eyes.

"Please come tonight," said Gemma, "it'll feel all wrong if you aren't there."

"Plus I might drown myself in some soup," said Adrian.

"Alright," said Mike, holding his hands up in defeat. He smiled, but Gemma could tell he was still worried.

She watched him walk off with his head down. Intruding on their time wasn't really what had him worried. But if he could laugh off being stalked by ghostly hound and talk casually about seeing the Beast, then she wasn't sure she wanted to know what had.

8.
ROGUE

Gabriel met Owain on the edge of the wood. He sunk down onto a boulder, breathless from running.

"What is it?" Gabriel asked.

Owain pointed back the way he had come, his other hand pressed to his chest. It was still rising and falling too quickly for him to speak. Gabriel crouched down and gently touched the shoulder of his apprentice. After a few minutes he was calm enough to talk.

"Houndain," he said.

Gabriel nodded encouragingly.

"I was practising the ceremony." Owain took a few more steadying breaths and hung his head. "I know you said I shouldn't."

"I did say that, and you know why."

Owain seemed to be overtaken by another attack of breathlessness and began to suck in air in short rasps. "I know, I know, I know," he gasped, gripping the boulder for support. "But I did it and I think it worked!" The last word came out as a howl.

Gabriel sprung to his feet. "What do you mean it worked?"

Owain wrung his hands and began to rock. "There was a hound."

"Are you sure of what you saw?"

He hesitated.

"Think very carefully," said Gabriel.

Owain shut his eyes and slowly became still. He thought himself back to Houndain; back to the earthy smell of the hollow and the rustling of the hawthorn. His steps were light as he descended to the stone altar, unfurling a rolled bundle from under his arm as walked. The material was torn and stained and two of the gold buttons were missing, but as he held up the coat he felt a sense of power. He put it on. It hung long on him and was too wide at the shoulders, but breathing the musk of sweat and blood that rose from the fabric he felt his own blood rise. He performed the rites efficiently, laying his sacrifice on the stone table and tracing a circle around it with his own blood, so that the hounds must accept a blood debt to him if they wished to feed. This is what would give him the power to control them.

His eyes snapped open. "There was no sacrifice," he said, "I only pretended to place one on the altar."

"Do you have a wound that could have bled? Tell me, are you certain that you didn't spill so much as one drop of blood on that ground?"

"Yes, I'm sure."

Gabriel paced with his hands behind his back. "The hounds will not answer to the raising ceremony without meat. Neither will they respond to the sacrifice of someone not born with the potential to be Huntmaster." He stopped and eyed Owain seriously. "There should only be you and I alive with that talent."

Owain steepled his hands. "You know that I'm impatient to lead the hounds myself, but you've warned me enough of the dangers to make me wary. I know I'm not ready."

Gabriel clasped his shoulder and held his gaze for a moment, before turning sharply away. "I know you wouldn't disobey me Owain. You know I hold you back only because of the law, and because I don't want to see you made meat by the pack."

He nodded. "I know. But what of the hound?"

"It was a dog you saw. There is no rogue hound."

"I'm calling Elaine," said Adrian.

Gemma pulled the door of the bunk room shut behind them. "Why?"

"Because she might know more about that thing you saw."

Gemma sat down on her bunk and tried to get the image of the feral out of her head. It must have been lying in wait the whole time, blending in with the stones in the hope that something tasty might come near enough to catch. She grimaced, imagining the feeling of those skeletal hands taking hold of her legs and dragging her off like the pony.

"So what happened exactly?" Adrian asked.

Gemma spread her fingers. "Fen saw it first." She noted his blank expression and explained. "That's the name of Gabriel's dog, the black one you saw there. Well the dog just started growling at something and when I looked up I saw that... thing... climbing out from the ruins."

"What did it do then?"

"Well that was about the time Gabriel arrived and scared it off. But it took a dead pony with it when it left. That was the reason Fen was near there in the first place, I think she smelt the meat."

Adrian sat down cross legged on the floor, his back leaning against the bottom bunk. He threw his phone from hand to hand thoughtfully.

"I get the reason why the dog was there," he said, "but why were you with the dog?"

Gemma felt her cheeks redden slightly and she

looked down. "I followed her; she seemed to want me to."

He nodded slowly, as if this piece of information was very important. "And you say it dragged off the whole carcass?"

She nodded, remembering the terrible strength of the bone thin arms. "Like it weighed nothing."

Adrian sucked in his cheeks like something in his mouth tasted sour. "How did... *he*... scare it off then?"

"He told it to leave."

"What? It just did as he asked?"

She shrugged. "It seemed wary of him somehow, like it didn't want him too close."

"But it was coming towards you?"

"Yes," Gemma stopped and bit her lip in thought, "well yeah, I suppose it would have been if he hadn't stopped it."

"Did he not say what it was?"

She looked down at the back of her hands. Her nail polish was chipped and her nails were dirty underneath. Gabriel hadn't said that she should keep what he'd told her secret, and Adrian probably needed to know as much as possible about the creatures if there was a chance he might meet another one on the moor. If she didn't tell him and he got hurt it would be her fault. But if she told Adrian without permission Gabriel might be angry, and decide that next time she met something unfriendly he'd let her take her chances alone. She rubbed her palms together, suddenly feeling a desire to wash her hands. The dripping saliva and vicious spikes came to mind and turned her stomach. "Gabriel called it feral."

"What does that mean?"

"He said that the feral live on the moor and scavenge food, or kill anything slow enough to catch."

"Including humans?"

"I think so."

Adrian jumped to his feet and began to pace the room. He took the news that there was a species of monster on the moor that might kill and eat him with the calculated interest of someone considering a chess move. "You say they're very strong, and they use pre existing ruins for shelter…"

Gemma cut him off. "But anything they caught they would eat."

He shook his head. "Even something supernatural probably couldn't finish a whole pony in one sitting. What if it hid a meal for later and forgot where it was?"

She pursed her lips thoughtfully. "I think it would have eaten some at least. Were there any marks on the boy's body?"

He stopped pacing and closed his eyes in concentration. "I don't think so, but everything's getting blurred in my memory. The main thing I have left is a feeling of purpose, as if there was a specific motive behind what happened. The boy was killed for a reason."

"Then I doubt it was the feral. I don't think they're big on reason."

Adrian sat down heavily on his bunk, letting his phone fall on the duvet beside him. He picked it up and stared at the screen. The reception icon only had one bar lit up out of a possible four. "I'm going to try calling."

Gemma took her laptop from its case and sat down on the floor next to the bunk bed. She typed the word *feral* into the search engine as Adrian dialled Elaine's phone number. The screen filled up with lots of pictures of scruffy cats and caged dogs, but there was nothing close to what she had seen. Perhaps people never usually met one and survived. She thought back to the missing family in the newspaper. Part of her felt bad for telling Gabriel about Adrian's dream; it wasn't her secret to tell, and she'd been so angry with him for telling Mike, but if Gabriel hadn't been there then what would have happened? He was probably right to question her motive for hunting out danger at every opportunity.

"She isn't picking up." Adrian snapped his phone closed.

"She's probably busy with her painting. And I don't know if you should worry her by asking about the feral anyway, there's no mention of them on here so I don't see why she'd know any more. She'll just tell you to come home. And she might have a point."

Adrian cut her short with a shake of his head, and this time she didn't argue. He stared for a few moments at the screen of his phone, watching the reception drop from one bar to none. "She'll probably ring back."

Gemma nodded. "In the meantime, I could ask Gabriel."

"Let's wait for Elaine." Adrian's tone was firm and he seemed to be concentrating very hard on pressing buttons on his phone. There was a minute's silence.

"Why do you hate him so much?" Gemma asked eventually.

"I don't know what you're talking about."

She tilted her head to one side and narrowed her eyes. "After we left the fort I put it down to you being angry because it hadn't been the place you hoped it was. When we were warned away from Houndain I guessed it was a similar thing; you were frustrated because it wasn't the right place and he happened to be the bearer of bad news. But what the hell is it now? All he's done is help us."

Adrian shut his phone again and threw it down on the bed. "What if I don't want him to help us? For some reason he's always somewhere nearby and now you've encouraged his stalking by inviting him out for dinner!"

"You believed Elaine when she said we'd find a guide."

"Yes, and we did find one; Mike."

Gemma sprung to her feet. "But what if he isn't our guide? What if we can't find the right place because we aren't looking with the right person?"

"Gabriel is not our guide." Adrian spat each word as if it tasted bitter.

"How do you know?" she felt both fists clench at her sides.

Adrian opened and closed his mouth as if he would say something, but no sound came out. Eventually he managed to say; "If you hate helping me that much you might as well just go home."

"Are you driving?"

"No."

"Then I'll have to stay, and you'll have to start appreciating the fact that I *am* helping you, even though you brought me here under false pretences. You knew I'd be uncomfortable with what you were planning to do and you lied so I'd come anyway."

"I didn't lie."

"Omitting the truth is the same thing. But I'm not angry about that. I'm here now, I'm increasingly open-minded and I don't mind helping as much as I can. I just don't need abuse for doing it." She paused and took a calming breath. "Now tell me why on earth Gabriel worries you so much."

Adrian chewed his lip and shrugged, the anger

fading. "I don't trust him." He began fiddling with his earring and then continued. "And I don't think you should rush into getting another boyfriend."

Gemma clapped her hand over her mouth, then threw herself down beside him and laughed aloud. She hugged his unresponsive shoulders.

"I don't see why it's funny."

"So you're only angry because I want to date Gabriel?"

He crossed his arms and turned away in a huff.

"Listen Adrian, I don't want to date Gabriel. I don't want to date anyone. I invited him to the pub tonight because, as I told you, he saved my life today. The feral could have killed me. I think that deserves a thank you." She smiled hopefully at Adrian's back, willing him to turn around. After a few seconds he did.

"But the way he looks at you..."

"He can look at me however he wants. It doesn't make any difference. Plus, I think you're imagining it; unless he fancies you as well of course. In fact, I'm positive I've seen him looking at you as well."

Adrian tried to hold back a smile but it spilled out onto his lips all the same. He relaxed and hugged Gemma back. "Sorry for being an idiot. Again."

"Don't worry about it. I know you're stressed out." She squeezed his shoulders lightly.

For a few seconds he stayed still. Gemma sensed him relax, but her thoughts were picking through what he'd just said. Did Gabriel look at her differently? She thought back to their meetings at Houndain and then at the fort today; there was nothing unusual about those, apart from the thematic risk of death. Then the memories of last night crept back, vivid like a nightmare and tingly like a dream. She remembered the way he had pressed his palm to her hand and knelt with her on the dew damp grass. Shaking, she felt the jolt of electricity again and realized that she'd lied.

"You ok?" Adrian asked.

"I'm fine." She smiled, but felt her cheeks betray her.

"What are you wearing tonight?

She shrugged. "This I guess."

"If we're having a meal to celebrate your continued life I think you, of all people, need to show a little effort."

Gemma got up, reached under her bunk for her overnight bag and tipped it out on the duvet. The contents were limited.

"Is that all you've got?"

"You said a few days."

"Yeah, but you haven't even considered eveningwear." His expression was both disappointed and concerned. Gemma felt a makeover coming on.

"Any good?" Adrian called ten minutes later.

Gemma emerged from the bathroom in her black jeans and the fourth top of his that he'd made her to try on. This one was grey with small silver studs round the neckline.

Adrian nodded critically. "I think that's the one."

She looked at herself in the shower room mirror. The top suited her surprisingly well and it made her jeans look smart. She leaned in, wondering if she should put on some makeup, and then remembered the bruises on her face. They had faded to the lightest grey, barely noticeable now against the rest of her skin. With foundation they were hidden completely.

"Ready," she said.

Adrian opened the door for her and they walked the short way to the pub. Mike was already waiting for them inside and he smiled awkwardly when he saw them. It looked like he'd had a makeover of his own. His hair was freshly washed and had dried in tight curls; he'd also shaved again and was wearing a clean white shirt.

"Is that new?" Gemma asked, nodding to it.

He looked flustered. "No, no it's old. I just don't wear it that often." He flattened the cord that laced up beneath the collar. Part of one of his key tattoos was just visible.

"Usual?" asked Adrian.

Mike nodded gratefully. He looked down and began to push a beer mat along the table with his forefinger. "So we're still waiting for another guest?" he asked Gemma, his eyes still on the mat.

"Yeah Gabriel should be here soon." She checked her watch. "I guess he's on his way."

"I guess so." Mike halted the place mat directly in front of him and continued to stare at it.

"Are you alright?"

He looked up. His mouth was pursed tight in thought and his eyebrows were furrowed. "This Gabriel," he said, "how much do you know about him?"

Gemma shrugged. "Well he walks a lot so I guess he likes the moor. He seems to know quite a bit about the wildlife," she stalled for a moment, struggling to place the feral in the same category as rabbits and ponies, "so I suppose he's into that as well."

Mike folded his hands on the table. "Quite the naturalist then."

"He probably knows loads of good stories about the moor. I think you'll like him when you speak to him."

He moved his head in answer but Gemma suspected that he'd stopped hearing her. His thoughts were far away and the expression on his face was worried. She looked over to check Adrian's progress at the bar; he was nearly done. It was weird that they could both talk for hours about dead children, and yet find the idea of having someone else join them for dinner so disturbing.

Adrian put down the drinks and Mike reached for his beer straight away. He drained it in one go and then stood up with the empty glass. "Another?"

Gemma watched him stride to the bar. "He isn't acting right today," she told Adrian.

"You know he drinks."

"Yeah, but he isn't happy."

"Let him get a few more beers in and he will be." Adrian was studying the familiar menu as if concentration might reveal something new.

"You know what's going on," Gemma pulled the paper from beneath his hand, "tell me."

"It's nothing."

"Look, I'm actually quite worried about him. He had convinced himself that were dumping him to take Gabriel as our guide, and he was devastated, but he just took it like it was what he expected from life. What's happened?"

Adrian looked back over to the bar. Mike was drinking one pint while he waited for another one. "While you were off having your little walk last night he told me that Gabriel gave him a bad feeling, that's all."

Gemma caught hold of Adrian's hand to stop him tapping the table. "There's more to it than that."

"He said it was a feeling that brought him back to a part of his life that he was ashamed of, and he didn't want to be reminded."

"Is it to do with the keys?"

He nodded. "I think so."

"Carry on."

He sighed and glanced once more back at Mike, whose glass was nearly empty. "I'm not sure if I'm meant to be telling you this, so don't mention it to him unless he tells you about it himself, ok?"

Gemma nodded, feeling another prickle of guilt for telling Gabriel about Adrian's dream.

"While you were away he told me that there was a time when he wasn't sure who he was."

"Had he been drinking?"

Adrian scowled. "It was before all that, and if you're going to mock him I'm not going to tell you."

She held up a hand in surrender. "I'll shut up, carry on."

"He said that he woke up on the moor with no idea where he was or how he'd got there. He found his way into a village and someone had the heart to look after him, and after a little while almost all of his memories came back and he thought that was that. So he thanked the woman and went on his way. But a year or so later he started to get more memories back, although this time they were strange. He began to wonder if they were his memories at all."

"What do you mean by strange?"

"These memories seemed older, as if they belonged in a world that existed long ago. He remembers riding in the forest and hunting deer with a bow, but on the other hand he remembers growing up in Bristol and taking trips to the cinema. Understandably, he began to get confused over what was real and what wasn't, because as time went past he pieced together two completely separate accounts of his past. The old world he remembers less of, but what he can see is more vivid. The newer world is a complete picture but the colours are dull, I think that's how he described it."

"And they keys?"

"He said that he went on a quest to find the key to his true past, and they are something to do with that. But I think he hates them now."

"Did he ever find the answer?"

There was a crash followed by an icy tinkling and Gemma and Adrian spun round in their seats. Mike stood behind them with three broken glasses at his feet. His face had turned white and his hands were still shaking. Gemma heard the scrape of a chair being pushed back.

"Let me help you," said Gabriel.

9.
BREAKAGE

Mike had gathered the glasses before Gabriel reached him.

"I'd better tell someone," he mumbled, backing away.

Gemma could see his hands turning red beneath the broken glass. "Let me take that," she said, stepping forward.

He shook his head and turned sharply towards the bar, where a young woman was waiting with a dustpan and brush. The buzz of conversation dropped and it seemed that every drinker had abandoned their glass to watch in silence. In their alcoves the candles flared up and lit the eyes of the spectators.

"Only glass," said Gabriel. The flames shrunk and the light turned soft. "Nothing to worry about."

Slowly the hum of chatter resumed and Mike carried the larger pieces of glass to the bar while the young woman was sent to sweep up the shards on the floor. No one took any further interest.

"How long have you been here?" Gemma asked Gabriel.

"A short while. You were deep in conversation when I arrived and I didn't want to disturb you."

Adrian fiddled with his sleeves uncomfortably. Gemma glanced at him. Gabriel must have overheard most of the story about Mike, if not all of it.

"Would you like a drink?" she asked him. It felt awkward that they were both standing while Adrian was sitting down.

"I'll get one now." Gabriel strode off towards the bar. He seemed just as much at ease in the pub as he had on the moor.

Gemma looked around for Mike but he had somehow managed to vanish. "Do you think Mike heard us talking about what he told you?"

Adrian leaned close and shook his head. "He wasn't near enough, or at least I don't think he was."

"If he didn't then why did he react like that? He looked like he'd seen a ghost. Something's up with him, he hasn't been right since this morning."

"Can't you see why? Isn't it obvious?"

She shook her head, but then followed Adrian's gaze towards the bar. Gabriel was smiling at the girl behind the counter, who was tripping over trying to serve him and display herself at the best angle at the same time. She spilt half a glass of wine and giggled hysterically when he touched her hand to steady it. Gemma felt a sharp tug in her chest.

"I'll tell you what is obvious," she muttered, noticing the girl pretend to lean down for a glass and undo another button on her shirt.

"There's something about him," pressed Adrian, "he has this way of making people do what he wants. Look at him now, remember the way he told the feral to leave, and remember how we all just turned back when he told us to. Mike senses it as well, and he doesn't like it."

Gemma wiggled her fingers in front of her face. "It could be mind control," she let her hands drop to the table, "or alternatively, he could just be speaking to the town bicycle." Her mouth twisted at the edges as she looked back over at Gabriel. He had paid the girl and she was counting it out for the third time, her eyes wandering back to his face every few seconds. What a loser. It was true, his hair was shimmering like treasure in the artificial light from the bar, and a few curls had worked loose from the leather band and were hanging over his eyes making them look like the sea trapped in a gilt frame...

"Gemma?"

She snapped back to look at Adrian. There was a smirk on his lips but his eyes were serious.

"We need to be careful," he said.

Mike took his seat again silently. He was still pale and Gemma noticed blue plasters on a couple of his fingers.

"A bit early in the night to be trashing the place, isn't it?" she said.

He smiled weakly. "Sorry about that. I had a bit of a funny turn but I'm alright now."

"You'll be alright after getting some food in," said Adrian, "if you tell me what you want I'll go up and order."

"Don't forget to ask Gabriel," said Gemma.

He looked back briefly. "Oh I won't." He patted Mike gently on the shoulder and walked away.

Gemma watched him reach the bar, his head held high, and lean his elbows on it as he waited for service. It looked like he might be waiting a long time, as both barmaids were now talking animatedly to Gabriel, and the lone barman had skulked off out back to avoid the show. She thought she could just catch sight of him in the kitchen, complaining to the chef and pointing down his throat with two fingers. Adrian cleared his throat politely and Gabriel appeared to notice him for the first time. He welcomed him into the conversation with a sweep of his arm, but Adrian stayed where he was and stiffly pushed forward a spare menu. Gabriel glanced back at the table and Gemma dropped her gaze.

Mike was idly rubbing at a water mark with his finger. His eyes had taken on a glazed quality, as if she was looking at a house with the blinds drawn.

"Shall I ask Adrian to get you another beer?" she asked.

Mike didn't seem to hear, he just kept rubbing at the stain on the table. The ponderous rhythm seemed to soothe him, but Gemma felt his inwardness pushing her away like a physical barrier.

"What are you afraid of?" she asked him. The question came as a surprise to her almost as much as it did to him. She had been thinking it but wasn't aware of planning to say it out loud. Mike looked up at her.

"Midsummer eve in the forest. The last sunlight trickles golden through the green leaves and a young couple stroll by laughing. The woman has long black hair and she has taken off her shoes, which she carries in her hand. Ahead of her, the man stops and reaches out a hand. He smiles and she throws away the shoes.

"In the deepest glade they halt and he embraces her. The clearing has been used in the past and the crumbling relics of a stone altar remain, although the years have draped it in honeysuckle and ivy. She clings to him but he pushes her away. The stone feels rough as she lies down.

"The woman beside her is her likeness. The woman beside her is dead. She looks back into those drowning eyes and finds she can't make a sound. He places her hand in the other woman's hand. The last thing she feels is fire in her palm."

Mike's head hit the table with a dull thump.

Gemma watched in horror and scrambled to see if he was still breathing. To her relief she noted the gentle rise and fall of his shoulders. He stirred groggily and reached for his empty pint glass.

"There's a drink coming," she said, glancing quickly towards Adrian at the bar. She saw him and Gabriel start to walk over with the drinks carried between them. "Mike are you alright?"

He looked up and she saw that there were tears taking a shiny path down from the corners of his eyes. But his expression was confused. "Are you alright?" he asked her.

"I'm fine. I was more worried about you."

"I had another dizzy moment but it's gone now. Did you say there's drinks coming?"

She smiled with relief. There didn't seem to be any serious harm done.

"All ordered," said Adrian, taking his seat at the table.

Gabriel sat down next to Gemma. She felt his presence like the heat of a fire that has died to embers, and what Adrian had said earlier made her skin prickle. *The way he looks at you...*

He was looking at her now and she could feel it. The air smelt sweet with honeysuckle and pooled thick in her lungs.

"Thank you for inviting me here tonight. It has been a long time since I stepped through these doors."

"Have you seen the skull on the wall?" she asked.

He eyed the mounted remains of the Beast with distaste. "That would be a new addition. Fortunately it isn't real."

"How can you tell?"

"It's dead."

Adrian unfolded a newspaper on the table. Gemma recognised the headline from the morning, which felt like at least a week ago now. He flattened the pages very deliberately and she guessed what was coming.

"Look at this," he said to Gabriel.

He leaned in and scanned the paper with apparent interest. "People get lost out on the moor from time to time. It's unfortunate, but you've seen it can be dangerous out there."

The words hung for a moment in Gemma's head. They were almost identical to what Mike had told them in the café. Gabriel began to list the numerous dangers of the moor: old mine shafts, slump holes, ravines, and Gemma recognised the same rhythm as in Mike's stories. Even some of the hand movements were the same. Realization washed over her like a tide. Was Adrian right? Did Gabriel have some way of controlling Mike's actions? Some kind of link would explain why he was always able to find them. But the tide drew back just as quickly, and as Gabriel glanced in her direction all she thought about was how the candlelight glowed on his skin.

"What do you think happened to them?" Adrian asked. He sat very straight in his chair and kept adjusting the position of his glass.

"What would you like to have happened to them?"

The question took Adrian by surprise and he chose to ignore it. "Could the Beast have taken them, or are there worse things out there?"

Gemma saw a shadow of concern on Gabriel's face. It sharpened the lines of his cheeks and jaw, but it was gone in a heartbeat.

"I'm not sure that legends feed on walkers."

Mike laughed gruffly. "Oh they're gone they are, that's for sure."

"They may yet be found," said Gabriel.

Adrian shook his head. "I'm inclined to side with Mike here. Besides, the Beast isn't just a legend. You know that."

Whatever Gabriel's opinion was, he didn't voice it. Instead, he turned to Gemma and smiled. "What do you think of this Beast?" he asked her.

She looked at him and suddenly felt like she'd had too much to drink. Imagine him caring about her opinion. She scrabbled for something impressive to say. "Experts seem to agree that it is all some kind of hoax." She congratulated herself inside; that definitely sounded knowledgeable. "I think that sometimes people see what they want to see, and perhaps they think seeing the Beast will get them attention." She thought back to the soaring trade at Hound of the Basket Meals after Mike's supposed sighting of the Beast.

"I would agree with that," said Gabriel. Gemma beamed and he continued. "Sometimes people want to see something special so much that eventually they do see it. Then they believe in what they saw with all of their will, even if in truth they saw something entirely mundane" He looked pointedly at Adrian.

Adrian opened his mouth to assure Gabriel that he was perfectly capable of telling the difference between reality and his imagination, but the expression on Gabriel's face stopped him. He looked serious, and if Adrian understood the expression correctly, desperately sad. Then the moment passed and he looked away.

"Sometimes, when people set their minds on something they're going to do it whatever people say. Even if their friends tell them not to. Even if what they're looking for isn't there." Gemma added, sipping her drink and looking at Adrian.

He looked back and narrowed his eyes. Gemma was acting as if she was drunk, but she'd only been drinking Diet Coke. "Do you need some air?" he asked her.

She shook her head. The marks at her temples were beginning to hurt again and the skull on the wall had begun to float through the air. She felt a warm pressure on her arm and the smell of wild honeysuckle filled her head.

"Gemma are you ok?" Adrian's voice sounded far away and different. There was pressure on both her arms now and she felt herself being lifted from the chair.

"You need to give up," she mumbled, "Elaine told you that the dream wasn't important. You're looking for something that isn't there." She heard Adrian hissing for her to be quiet, and for some reason it seemed absurdly funny. "Everyone knows you're imagining it. You just want it to be there so much because you want to play the hero. You want to be the one who rescues us all from the monsters. But you can't Adrian, you aren't any different and chasing lies won't make you special!" She felt the pressure lift from one of her arms. Then she leaned forward and folded up.

Asterra struck the rough bark of the oak tree with her fist. Her pale gown was stained with mud and thorns had snagged threads which were rapidly unravelling into holes.

"It isn't good enough," she growled.

Fian picked his way through the woodland after her, every step burning as dirt pushed deeper into the cuts on his soles. He tried to keep to the patches of moss, which felt cool and soft on his bare feet. It was good to be in the shade of the trees after the scorching heat of the open moor, and entering Wistmans Wood meant that the Keep wasn't far ahead. At least there he might have a patch of dirt to sleep on and a drink from the bowls for the animals.

"Sorry mistress," he said.

She turned on him like a viper. "One hound? One miserable stinking hound which you can't even keep under control, do you think that's what I bought you for?"

Fian watched a fly settle on his bloody foot and didn't answer. A few days ago she wouldn't have said bought. She was still telling him that she had rescued him from the feral back then, out of the pity of her heart and regard for his special gift.

"Speak to me dog!"

He kicked the fly away. "No mistress."

Asterra stabbed a slim finger towards him. "I need the whole pack for this to succeed. One hound that is more interested in sniffing for rabbits is absolutely useless!"

"I will try harder tomorrow." Fian was exhausted and he knew his voice showed it. Weeks of sleeping curled up on the ground after spending most of the night practising the raising ceremony had taken their toll. The pre-dawn trips to the Hound Grave and the energy spent on trying and trying to call a hound from the earth were sapping the last of his strength. She had told him that if he raised the pack without completing the correct procedures to gain control of it then the hounds would

135

turn on him and devour him. This morning he had found strength by hoping it was true.

"Yes, you will," she said coldly. "You will try until you either raise the whole pack or die in the attempt. The Master does it as easy as breathing."

Fian grimaced at the mention of that name. Of course the Huntmaster could raise the hounds; it was what he was born to do. He and his apprentice were guardians of the pack and the greatest weapon that any Clan had. It was the duty of the Huntmaster to uphold the law of the Clan and punish any who disobeyed it. It would have been he who dragged Fian from the arms of his mother to the sleeping place of his pack in readiness to feed him to the hounds. There was only master and apprentice. No other with the gift was permitted to live.

"Perhaps with more food I would be stronger." He knew the suggestion would infuriate her but he was too tired to care.

"Catch that rabbit you lost," Asterra spat. She stepped forward and stalked ahead through the woods.

Fian limped after her. She already seemed keen on killing him, and that was if the hounds didn't get him first, so there was no point in sharing his suspicion that someone else had been with them at Houndain. If she heard that she might murder him even sooner.

10.
HELLHOUND

Gemma let her forehead rest on the ground while she waited for everything to stop spinning. It was a surprise to feel grass beneath her fingers.

"I should never have tried," she heard a voice saying. "She was fighting it too hard."

Slowly, she opened her eyes and let the world slide back into focus. There was a sound of fast movement and then Gabriel was beside her, helping her to her feet.

"What just happened?"

"You had a strange turn for a few minutes."

"Like what happened to Mike?"

"Similar, I suspect."

She leaned on his arm and looked out over the moor. They were standing near the old dry stone wall, in almost exactly the same place that she had met him yesterday. "We need to stop meeting here," she said. The attempt at humour sounded weak even to her. The last few minutes were a blur and she didn't remember how she had got from the pub to the edge of town. "Where's Adrian?"

"They must have served our food by now," said Gabriel. He steered Gemma back along the road towards the Plume of Feathers.

For a few strides she let him lead; her legs were feeling unpredictable. "Is he still in the pub?" she asked. There was a thought rattling at the back of her head, and even though she couldn't quite catch hold of what it was, it worried her.

Gabriel held the door open. Mike was still sitting

at their table, along with four plates of food and three empty chairs. He nodded when he saw Gabriel and Gemma sensed that something had passed between them. Gabriel pulled out a chair and she sat down.

"Feeling better?" Mike asked her.

She stared down at her food, and then glanced over at Adrian's empty seat. "Do you know where he's gone?"

Mike shifted uncomfortably and pushed his food to one side of the plate. "Just to get some air I think," his eyes flicked quickly towards Gabriel and back. "Like you did yesterday," he added.

Gemma pushed back her chair and stood up. "I need to get something from the bunkroom."

"But your food will get cold," protested Gabriel.

She looked down at him and felt the air thicken in her lungs. There was the smell of honeysuckle again; it was so sweet that it made her dizzy. She stepped back. Gabriel stood up. The air burst into flame. But nothing was burning, and there was no heat. A moment stretched between them, and Gemma realized that instead of fire it was light. But it was light so bright that it scorched her vision into monochrome and pinned her to the spot like the blazing beams of an oncoming car. Gabriel glowed. His hair drifted about his shoulders as if caught in a slight breeze, every strand shining like spun gold. The light spilled from his pale skin and it glinted pearl silver, while his eyes remained bright blue, two lakes in a luminous abyss.

Gemma ran.

Mike's screams followed her.

She didn't stop until she had thrown herself

against the bunkroom door from the inside. She sat still for a minute, waiting for her breathing to slow. Elaine had told her and she hadn't believed it, but there was no doubt about what she had just seen. There was the white light and everything. Gabriel had been there to ensure that her mother survived to bring her into the world. He had ridden out in front of that car and sent it swerving off the road. He had killed to save her, and he was here now, probably still waiting for her in the pub. A real live angel.

A phone began to ring somewhere in the room. Gemma got up and followed the sound to Adrian's bunk, where his phone lay on top of the duvet. She picked it up, but the tone chirruped to a close in her hand. Whoever was calling, she'd missed it. A message flashed up on the screen and told her it was Elaine. She wondered whether she should try and call back; if Elaine was ringing it might be important. But then she remembered that Adrian had been trying to call her earlier. She was probably just returning the call. It might be best if she left it. It was Adrian's place to talk to Elaine and besides, she didn't want to find herself being questioned; especially as she didn't know where Adrian was right now. She was about the put the phone down when the screen flashed again. Elaine had left a voice message. For a moment Gemma hesitated, and then she pressed the phone to her ear.

The message was garbled by the lack of signal, and Elaine was speaking so quickly that it was hard to understand her. Gemma listened while a knot of nausea grew in her stomach. She hadn't understood everything but one part was dreadfully clear.

…I was wrong, I'm so sorry, I was wrong that… thing isn't an angel at all. Tell Gemma it isn't her angel.

Tell her to stay away, tell her to run if she sees it. I've never been wrong but it isn't an angel. Tell her...

Gemma sank down to the floor. She needed to talk to Adrian but there was no way of contacting him with his phone here. Mike had implied that he might come back to the pub, but even he was acting strangely. Adrian had warned her to be careful around Gabriel, and now Elaine had said the same thing in stronger terms. But if he really was dangerous, wouldn't he have done whatever awful thing he was plotting when they were alone out on the moor the other night? It had been the perfect opportunity. Why would he save her from the feral if he really intended to harm her? Why had he saved her mothers life?

She was getting a headache and none of this was helping. If Adrian thought she was still at the pub that would probably be where he'd go back to. She struggled to recall what had happened just before she rushed outside. It was difficult; everything had seemed like a dreamy blur. Maybe that was how Mike felt all the time, with the edges of the world softened by drink. But she felt fine now, whatever it was had passed. Then memory began to surface. She let the phone drop from her hand. Adrian had left because of her.

Gabriel had been all she could think about since the moment he stepped into the pub; she had been fluttering around him like some overgrown moth. It was only just before they went out that she'd promised Adrian that she wasn't interested in Gabriel, however he looked at her, and now he'd think that she had lied to him. Her heart sunk even lower. She had spilt all the information on the dream as well, and told Adrian that he was making it all up because he wanted to feel important. They were the deepest darkest thoughts that she would never, ever have voiced, and she'd blurted them out in the pub with everyone watching. What had come over her? Suddenly the mind control idea didn't seem quite so ridiculous.

She forced herself to her feet. It was no good coming up with supernatural excuses for her own idiotic behaviour. She would go back to the pub and wait for Adrian to come back, and then she would apologise.

The door to the bunkroom clicked shut behind her and she headed back onto the street. She looked around hopefully, half expecting to see Adrian sitting on the stone wall on the edge of town like she had done, but he was nowhere to be seen. There was a clicking of claws on concrete and then Fen was beside her, her head tilted upwards in supplication for a stroke. Gemma stopped to scratch the dog's ear. Elaine must be wrong. Fen and Gabriel couldn't be bad. Could they?

She pushed the thought from her mind and slid into the pub. Gabriel and Mike were talking quietly, their heads bowed over the table, but they stopped as soon as they saw her.

"All sorted?" asked Mike, in his best cheerful voice.

"Fine," said Gemma.

"Did you find what you were looking for?" Gabriel's tone was light but he was watching her intently. For a second she panicked, feeling her pockets for something to pass of as the item she had needed so desperately. Her hand stopped on Adrian's phone.

"Yeah I'd forgotten my phone, but I have it now." She flashed the phone quickly to prove her story.

"Not much point in having a phone round here,"

said Mike, "the signal's so bad. They've put in all the masts but something messes with it." He waved his hand in the vague direction of outside. Gabriel must have been buying him drinks.

She looked down at her plate and frowned. Eating was the last thing on her mind, but Gabriel was pushing a knife and fork towards her.

"You should eat," he said.

"I don't think I'm hungry."

"You'll be weak after being unwell, you need to try and eat something."

"Shouldn't we wait for Adrian?" She noticed that Gabriel's plate was untouched as well, although Mike had nearly finished his.

"I'm sure he won't mind." Gabriel cut a piece of steak and put it in his mouth. "No doubt he will be back soon anyway."

Gemma sighed and loaded her fork with some cooling pie. If she was going to have to beg for Adrian's forgiveness she didn't want to black out again in the middle of it.

For some time they ate in silence. Then Mike began to snore. He was asleep at the table, with his head resting on his folded arms. An army of empty pint glasses surrounded him. Gemma suddenly felt very alone. She turned back to Gabriel and caught him watching Mike with a pleased smile.

"Did you do that to him?" Gemma asked. Adrian was missing and Mike was out cold. She was beginning to get frightened. Elaine's warning crept back into her thoughts. *Tell her to run...*

"If you mean did I buy him the drinks, then yes I did. I know that he likes to forget certain things for a little while and the ale helps him with that. But if you're asking if I've done anything else to him, then no I haven't."

His honesty was somehow reassuring, even though she had been warned not to trust him.

"What about all that bright light? Why isn't the pub empty?"

"Only you saw that."

"But Mike was screaming."

"He saw you run and he was afraid. He doesn't want you out alone after those walkers disappeared, and I can't say I blame him. But also…" Gabriel paused as if trying to think of the right words, "he sensed what I did somehow."

"He sensed that light trick?"

A small smile curled at the corners of his mouth. "Yes, he sensed that light trick."

"Why did you do it?"

"To help you trust me."

Gemma rubbed one eye with the back of her hand. "I don't know what to think."

Gabriel templed his fingertips patiently.

"I didn't believe in any of this stuff before I came here. I knew Adrian was into his spiritual things and to be honest I just stayed out of it as much as I could; there was nothing to see in the old houses that he dragged me to at weekends, except dust and some bright sparks business idea. It was all a fraud. But last night I saw a dog decompose and then come back to life, and today I've met an angel in the pub. I'm all over the place. I don't trust myself." Gemma sighed.

Gabriel reached out a hand and laid it on top of hers. His skin was smooth and cool, and on the very edge of sensation she could feel the slow pulse of that same electricity that she'd felt the night before.

"I wish Adrian would come back," she said.

Outside the pub the sunlight was beginning to thin. Soon it would give way to that long stretch of summer twilight that came before full night.

"He probably just wants a little time alone," Gabriel suggested. There was nothing to do but wait.

"Were you really there that night my mum crashed?" Gemma asked.

He pushed his plate to one side and leaned both elbows on the polished wood of the table. Mike was still snoring contentedly and the conversations of everyone on the other tables had dropped to a pleasant drone.

"What did she tell you?"

"She said she was driving home and she was nearly hit by a man that was too drunk to control his car. But just when he was about to hit her car he swerved to avoid something in the road and crashed his car into a tree. She said she saw a glowing white figure and that it was an angel."

Gabriel looked down at the table as he spoke.

"I was there. I had been watching your mother to make sure that she was safe, but that one night my concentration was elsewhere and I was almost too late to save her."

"Why were you guarding her?"

"I've been watching your family for four generations."

"Why?"

"I've been waiting for you."

Gemma almost knocked over her drink. She caught it in time and moved the glass carefully out of her way. It made her skin prickle to think that someone had been watching her all these years and she had never known. She needed Adrian for all this; she was out of her depth.

A howl ripped through the air outside. Drinkers turned their heads in surprise and the barmaids squeaked and scuttled into the kitchen. The barman who had bought the fake beast skull from the internet looked to have his hands clasped on something hidden behind the bar. Mike sat bolt upright.

"The Devil's Dog," he slurred.

There was another howl, followed by a scratching at the pub door. Claws raked against wood and Gemma heard it splinter away under each renewed attack. Gabriel was on his feet and his knuckles had turned white where he grasped his chair.

"Get back," he told Gemma.

She could hear snatches of conversation from around the room. Some people were afraid but others were excited.

"I've heard about this one before, but it was a church not a pub," sniggered one man. He was clearly drunk.

"What happens in the story?" Gemma asked, turning to Mike. His eyes had rolled back in his head and he looked like he was going to collapse again. His shirt had pulled further open and the keys were tar black on his milky skin.

"What happens, Mike?" she demanded, her voice turning shrill with fear.

He held the back of his palm over his mouth as if he was about to be sick, and beneath his eyelids his eyes were flickering like he was having a terrible dream. His lips moved sluggishly as he struggled to form the words.

"Everybody dies."

"I thought there was meant to be fire," said an older woman with flushed cheeks, "how else will he leave scorch marks on the door?" there was the sound of drunken laughter.

Gemma glanced around. A group of sensible people had backed away towards the bar, and the barman was slowly filtering them through into the kitchen. She guessed that they were the locals. The tourists in the pub were treating it like some form of free entertainment.

"These people need to leave," said Gabriel.

The animal howled again, the note dipping and fading out into a gurgling snarl. The attack on the door came again with redoubled force, and the heavy wood began to buckle beneath the blows.

"Why is it smashing the door, couldn't it just pull it?" Gemma whispered.

"Blind hunger doesn't think."

Gemma turned back to see Mike slumped over the table again. Gabriel followed her gaze and his eyes clouded with concern.

"Help him," Gabriel told Gemma. His tone was gentle but commanding.

She did as he asked.

Mike was heavy but not quite a dead weight. He complied with her unsteadily as she pulled his arm up over her shoulder and stumbled beside her like a sleepwalker. Their progress to the bar was painfully slow.

"Hurry!" Yelled Gabriel. The words came out in the same hiss that she'd heard when he was dealing with the feral. Whatever was outside was deadly.

"Come on," she told Mike encouragingly, and at last handed him over to the stronger arms of the barman.

The exchange was wordless but the man knew what to do, there was wariness in his eyes that suggested he was ready for whatever came through that door. The weapon he had been clutching was a thick wooden staff topped with a spur of antler.

Gemma turned to the drunken tourists. "You need to get out back right now," she told them. Public speaking had never been her strong point, but a few people did turn to listen.

"What? And miss all the fun?" the red cheeked woman snorted.

"It's not open air theatre, that thing outside will kill you!" Gemma told her.

"There's no fun in trying to breathe when your throat's on the other side of the room," Gabriel added grimly.

A few of the tourists stopped smiling and shuffled over towards the bar. The barman let them out through the kitchen as he'd done with the others, and then wedged the door shut.

The front door groaned and then finally splintered, flying open in a shower of wood and flaking paint. A low growl ripped through the wreckage, darkness spilling in through the gaping hole where the door had been. Everyone held their breath.

"Have you come for me hellhound?" taunted the obnoxious woman, her accent thick with drink.

A final howl pierced the air, twice as loud now without the barrier between them, and the creature opened two blood red eyes. They glowed with an eerie luminosity of their own that was more than just a reflection of light; both crimson irises looked like rings of fire.

Gemma wondered if the woman with the big mouth deserved to be eaten first for being such an idiot.

The hellhound placed a large black paw over the threshold and four razor sharp claws clicked down on the slate floor.

"Get behind me," said Gabriel, "all of you!"

The tourists moved immediately on his command. Even the loud mouthed woman dragged her feet over, although her bloodshot eyes were fixed on the hound. There was no laughing now. Gemma glanced back and saw the barman raising his staff.

With slow steps the monster shed the darkness of outside and emerged into the yellow glow of the pub. It was terribly lean, with every rib showing beneath its matted fur, and the fiery spittle that dripped from its jaws was undoubtedly expectant. It was starving.

Gemma waited for Gabriel to send it away like he had done with the feral. He had it locked in eye contact just as he had done then, only this time the creature wasn't retreating. It was getting nearer.

"Gabriel," Gemma whispered, "why isn't it afraid?"

He sighed and she saw his body tense as if he was trying to lift a huge weight. "It doesn't know fear" he said through gritted teeth.

"Then how do we stop it?"

Gabriel let the question hang in the air unanswered. There was sweat seeping through the back of his shirt and his shoulders were shaking. The hound stalked closer.

"You won't touch me, devil!" screeched a voice from the back of the pub.

Gemma looked round in time to see the drunken

woman, her hair loose and her cheeks crimson, running toward the creature with a gold crucifix held out in front of her.

Gabriel fell to his knees.

The hound fixed both fiery orbs on the woman and licked its dripping lips.

"No!" Gemma screamed.

Then the one hound became two. Gemma clasped her hand over her mouth as the first hound lunged for the woman's throat, only to be knocked back by another black dog. The hellhound turned on its attacker and braced to defend its prize. For a moment the woman spun between the two hounds, trying to ward off both with her crucifix, and then she fell abruptly to the ground. The hellhound snarled at its competitor and leapt. The second hound was much smaller, and as Gemma watched it crouch ready for the attack she saw that there was no fire in its large eyes.

"Fen!" she cried.

The dog looked at her once before disappearing under the bulk of the hellhound.

Gemma turned to Gabriel. He was still on his knees, holding his head in his hands and not doing anything to help at all. She put a hand on his shoulder and shook him.

He lunged at her, snarling, and she stepped back enough to not be caught but still felt his sharp nails tear through her jeans. The face that looked up at her was unrecognisable. Gabriel's skin had drawn tight over his bones and his blue eyes were gone; sunk back into their sockets and turned a tarry black. The darkness was hypnotic, but she forced herself to look away.

Fen was fighting with the hellhound on the pub

floor. Again and again it caught her by the neck but she managed to wiggle free and dart sideways to lunge at its stomach. The slate beneath them was getting slippery with the black blood that oozed from the monster's wounds. Gemma saw smears of red on the floor as well. The other hound was going to eat Fen alive.

In the midst of the carnage Gemma paused for half a second. Had Elaine been right after all? Perhaps Gabriel was a devil instead of an angel, and that creature was his dog.

Fen squealed in pain and Gemma saw that the hellhound had hold of her leg.

"Go for the eyes Fen!" she yelled.

The dog glanced at her, and then threw itself at the hellhounds face. The creature howled and Fen pulled her leg free. It was bleeding badly. Then, while the monster was still batting at its eyes in pain, the smaller dog grabbed it by the scuff of the neck and dragged its bulk out into the night. For a few minutes there was a chorus of wails and howling, but soon there was silence.

Gemma glanced at the woman on the floor and then down at Gabriel. Other people were already rushing over to check on her, so she went back to him. He lay flat on the ground with his face on the slate. She leaned closer carefully. His face had gone back to normal and it was shiny with sweat.

As she watched he slowly opened his eyes and reached out to her. Her instinct was to jump backwards, but the look in his eyes kept her still. He let his outstretched hand fall to the ground and she hesitantly laid her hand on top of it.

"What are you?" she asked.

11.
CONFESSION

Gemma helped Gabriel to his feet while the barman moved to attend the woman on the floor. Behind him, one of the barmaids had emerged from the kitchen and was dialling for an ambulance on the land line.

"She had too much to drink and hit her head," the barman told the girl on the phone firmly.

She nodded once to show she understood.

Then he turned to the rest of the drinkers, some now slumped on chairs and others shaking where they stood. "The pub is closed," he told them firmly, "I would like to give each of you a drink for the road, and then I suggest that you all go and sleep it off. Don't let anyone walk alone, one tipsy accident is enough for the night."

The barmaid finished her call and came to stand by the ruins of the door with a silver flask. She made sure that each person took a sip of it as they left, wiping the top with her sleeve between drinkers. Gemma and Gabriel came last and she stood blocking their path, the flask in her outstretched hands. Gabriel shook his head.

"Take it with our compliments," pressed the girl, holding the flask in front of his face.

"He said no. Can't you see he's in no state to be drinking?" said Gemma.

The girl turned her attention to her. "Then you'll have a sip for the road?"

Gemma raised her hand hesitantly, the other gripping Gabriel's waist to help him stand. She reached out for the flask but he caught her hand and held it, pushing it down and away from the drink.

"I think I'll pass," she said.

The girl's eyes narrowed. "It's rude not to take a drink offered in goodwill."

"And it's weird that you're trying to make me drink something when I don't know what it is, whilst also blocking my way out." Gemma stood as tall as she could with the weight of Gabriel on her shoulders and looked the girl in the eye.

She didn't move.

"Let them go, Fiona," said the barman.

The girl looked back at him in surprise.

"Go and make sure our other guests have a sip before they leave out back," he told her.

She blinked once and then strode away.

"Thank you," said Gemma, once the girl had left.

The barman dipped his head. "I have no quarrel with you, Huntsman."

Gemma noticed he was keeping both his hands out of sight. Something told her they were grasping the staff behind the bar.

They stepped through the remains of the splintered door and into the night. The air was thick and warm, smelling faintly of dust and dry grass. Everyone else had gone back to wherever they were staying and the road was empty and silent, except for a low whine.

"Fen," said Gemma. She felt Gabriel pull away from her. "Wait, let me help you!"

But the dog had already disappeared into a patch of shadow between two houses. It was the same place that she had watched Gemma from on the first night she met her, but this time there was no glint of curious eyes.

Gabriel emerged from the gloom with a limp black bundle in his arms.

Gemma felt her eyes begin to sting.

"You can save her right? You can bring her back like last time?"

He kept his eyes on the still form he was holding. Each step looked like an effort, as if the lean dog was too great a weight to carry. It was a world away from the lithe and effortless way she had seen Gabriel move on the moor.

"Let me carry her for you." She held her arms out to take Fen but Gabriel shook his head, so instead she followed behind, ready to help if she could.

They formed a strange procession to the edge of the moor. They had just reached the dry stone wall when Gabriel suddenly fell to his knees. Gemma rushed forward and caught him. His arms were still cradling the dog and he hadn't put out a hand to save himself.

"Take her," he said quietly, offering Fen to Gemma.

She took the dog gently. Fen was cold and she couldn't feel a heartbeat. Hot tears began to roll down her cheeks.

"Take her over the wall to a place that feels right," said Gabriel.

She hesitated. How would she know what was right? If Gabriel wasn't coming then how could he make the dog come back to life? Then an awful thought hit her; she wasn't taking Fen to be healed.

"Go," Gabriel told her. He was kneeling with both palms pressed to the floor, almost as if he was praying.

Gemma stepped over the wall. Fen felt light in her arms, far too light for a dog of her size. She also felt bony beneath the fur, as if she hadn't eaten in a long time. Maybe she had been sick even before today. Perhaps she was old. Gemma could feel her sleeve turning sticky; the dog was still losing blood from the wound on her leg.

She walked for what seemed like a long time. The bracken and the stunted trees of the moor stood still around her, and the only noise was the occasional call of an owl. When the tears got too thick for her to see properly she stopped and closed her eyes for a few moments. When she opened them she found herself on a piece of flat ground, covered in the short springy grass that was all over the moor, and surrounded by three young trees. It seemed like a good spot for Fen. She could almost imagine the dog sleeping there in the sun.

"There we go," she whispered as she gently laid the dog on the ground. Fens eyes were closed and she lay on her side, with her legs stretched out like she was dreaming of running. The trees rustled quietly and Gemma stepped back. Fen sunk slowly, and then the earth closed over her. Only this time she wouldn't be coming back. It didn't seem right. Wasn't all this supernatural stuff supposed to be about defying death? How could a child in a tomb refuse to go quietly but Fen could just die like this, without fighting back?

Gabriel put his hand on her shoulder. She knew it was him because of the smell of honeysuckle.

"Fen's gone," said Gemma.

"She is sleeping now."

Without thinking, she turned and let him hug her. He just held her and let her cry. It didn't feel like being hugged by an angel, not that she was exactly sure how that would feel anyway, but perhaps a bit more airy fairy somehow. This just felt like being hugged by a man.

"Adrian!" She pulled away sharply, remembering why they'd been waiting at the pub in the first place. "If he goes back to the pub now it'll be shut."

Gabriel folded his arms behind his back.

"He might be back at the café, I'll check there." She took a step and then hesitated. "And Mike?"

"Is not in any danger."

"But what if they made him drink that drink, whatever it was? What's in it anyway?"

"Alcohol."

"Yeah I'd guessed that."

"It's very strong. It will make sure that those tourists believe what they saw was due to drink in the morning."

"So Mike won't remember?"

Gabriel sighed. "I might wish that he wouldn't, but he will eventually. Where others find it easier to forget, he persists in trying to recall."

Gemma shook her head in an effort to make what she was hearing sink in. "So let me make sure I understand all this; the staff at the pub are prepared for attacks from terrifying hellhounds, and keep a big stick under the counter and a drink that makes punters forget just in case?" It was a big turnaround from the crappy internet skull. She thought she caught a faint gleam of humour in Gabriel's eyes.

"Where do you think legends come from?" he asked.

They walked back into town as quickly as they could. Gabriel seemed to be back to his normal self, striding easily across the uneven ground.

"What happened to you in the pub?" Gemma asked.

The question brought him to a dead halt.

"I just-" he lengthened the word to give himself

more time to think, "wasn't myself for a little while."

"I noticed that. The claws and the skull face gave it away." Gemma inwardly congratulated herself on being so to the point; she was all over this paranormal stuff. Adrian would be proud. Wherever he was.

"It won't happen again," said Gabriel. His tone sounded final.

Fian lay on a rough blanket thrown over the quilt of an ornate four poster bed. An old cloak that was ripped and stained with use had been laid on top of him, and a woman with raven black hair looked on with her arms crossed. He had lay in the same place since morning, trapped in a strange state between asleep and awake, and if his face was anything to go by he was having terrible nightmares.

"Will he live?" Asterra asked the woman.

The woman leant down and touched two long fingers to Fians neck. "His pulse is a little stronger, with care he may survive."

"But when will he wake up?"

The woman shrugged.

"When he's strong enough, that's if his mind is still intact."

Asterra hit the wooden frame of the bed with her fist.

"You know I haven't got the time to wait for his useless little brain to fix itself. I don't need his mind to work Morgana, just his talent."

Morgana stood up. She was taller than Asterra and her hair hung in waves down to her waist.

"You forget who you are speaking to Asterra. If you let you tongue run away with you like that one more time I swear I'll cut it from your mouth."

Asterra let her hand fall back to her side and inclined her head at her dominant companion, making her own blonde hair fall in front of her face. "Apologies, Lady."

Morgana's lips curled into a frown at the formal address.

"You spend too much time listening to human legends." She spat contemptuously on the floor. "The boy sleeps because his mind is damaged after trying to control two hounds when he is not strong enough. You're lucky that it is only one that got loose, and that he is still alive at all."

Asterra hung her head.

"I was assured that he would be powerful enough."

"And he might be, when he comes of age, but as he is I am shocked that he called a single hound from the earth. Gabriel's hounds are bound to him as strongly as if they'd given the vows. I have heard tales of the dark magic which has melded their spirits, an abomination that even I dare not attempt. You are unwise to pursue this any further. You will kill the boy, and a rogue hound cares only for meat." Morgana held Asterra's gaze for a long moment and then turned back to Fian. She lay the back of her hand across his clammy cheek. "I would guess that the hound sleeps again. His skin is warmer."

Asterra looked down at him with disgust.

"What use is he to me if he can't raise the pack? I can't wait until he comes of age, I need to strike now while Gabriel is distracted."

Morgana smiled to reveal a set of pearly white teeth, the canines of which ended in sharp points.

"Oh yes," she purred, "his human lover."

157

It was Asterra's turn to spit on the floor.

"And her fate will be the same as the last one. But while he disgraces himself and the Clan I will turn his own hounds against him and let him feel how I felt all those years ago."

"You think the boy will do this?" Morgana glanced at Fian and then laughed. "He will never control the pack without help."

Asterra narrowed her eyes, a greedy look spilling onto her face.

"What kind of help?"

"You will need to enhance his powers for long enough for him to raise the pack, after that he needs only make one command. Once he tells the hounds to kill their old master, then what will it matter if he is burnt out himself?"

"And you know how to do this?"

Morgana smiled again.

Fian moaned softly in his sleep. Cold sweat laced his forehead and neck, and the two skinny arms that lay on top of the covering were patterned with a network of cuts. The newer wounds were still an angry pink, but beneath them was a spider's web of older scars that had faded to dull silver.

"And the price?" Asterra asked.

Morgana sat back down in the high backed chair, taking a moment to rearrange the embroidered cushions to her liking. She then took a phial of red liquid from a pouch at her waist and began to reapply the dye to her already crimson lips.

"Your brother's body when it's done."

Gemma and Gabriel reached the front of the Fox Tor Café

and stopped. Gemma fumbled for the key in her pocket and eventually found it.

"I'll see if he's there," she said.

Gabriel nodded.

She skirted the café building itself and walked through the dilapidated garden around to the bunk room. There was no light showing in the high windows and she felt her heart begin to thud in her chest. Perhaps Adrian had got back and gone to sleep, she told herself; but she struggled to believe it. The image of the terrible hound tearing its way through the pub door as if it was plywood was all she could think of, and it was pushing all other thoughts to one side. What if he had met the monster before it got to the pub? She shivered. There wouldn't be a lot to find.

The bunkroom was not as she'd left it. An unfamiliar rucksack had appeared next to one of the beds at the far side of the room, and an intermittent snoring told her that someone else had bought themselves twelve pounds worth of privacy. She checked Adrian's bunk silently, not wanting to wake the new arrival. Everything there was just as it had been when she left earlier. He hadn't been back there since.

She found her way back to the street in a daze. Gabriel was waiting exactly where she'd left him. "He hasn't been there." She covered her eyes with her hands and slid down to sit with her back against the brick shop front. Adrian had disappeared, just like that family on the moor. Then an idea came to her; Search and Rescue would help look for him. She rummaged for her phone and eventually found it, only to find it had no signal. It refused to even dial 999. She flung it on the floor in disgust and heard pieces go skittering across the path. The anger flared like wildfire.

"It seems strange," she spat, rising to her feet, "that people should start disappearing so soon after you arrive on the scene."

Gabriel held his palms up in defence.

"You just let your dog die after it saved our lives, even though I've seen you raise it from the dead. What's all that about? And why was the barman so scared of you? Why did he call you Huntsman?"

Gabriel braced himself against the torrent of Gemma's rage. "I suspect you want answers, and-"

"And nothing!" she cut him short, "what the hell is going on? Did Adrian offend you somehow because he thought you were weird? And you got rid of Mike easily enough. How do I know he isn't *sleeping* in the ground as well?"

Gabriel flew forward and hit the wall with his fist. The howl of rage that tore from his lips set off car alarms two streets away.

"I would never do anything to harm Michael. I owe him that."

Gemma shuddered at the sudden noise.

"Come," said Gabriel, taking her hand.

She planted her feet on the pavement. "Why would that ever be a good idea?"

"You trusted me before."

"That was before my friends started disappearing." It had been exciting to sneak out and scare herself on the moor, but now the freaky stuff wasn't fun any more. The people in the pub had been in real danger.

"We will find your Adrian."

She hesitated for a few seconds, and then clasped her free hand over Gabriel's. It was a stupid idea, but she had no idea who else could help.

"Swear it."

The action set him cowering away, as if the two simple words had stung somehow.

"Promise you'll help find him," she pressed.

Gabriel sighed and hung his head. Just for a second, it felt like his hand was shaking.

"I promise."

She let him lead her out onto the moor. They halted when the town was out of sight.

"You want answers," said Gabriel, "so ask." He dropped Gemma's hand and she suddenly felt very alone. Her mind was a confusion of fears and she didn't know what to ask first.

"Why Huntsman?" she managed finally.

"I thought you might have worked that out for yourself. Mike tried to warn you with his stories, even if he didn't entirely know what he was doing. The display in the visitor centre you saw with your own eyes, although Owain says it is a crude likeness."

Gemma clapped a hand to her mouth. Her mind went racing back to the visitor centre, the Dark Huntsman and the hound masks.

"That's you?"

"That's what legend says about me."

"And what do you say about yourself?"

Gabriel fiddled with the cuff of his waxed jacket, brushing off dust that wasn't there.

"I say that I didn't choose this." He took a deep breath and then threw back his shoulders and held his head high. The weariness instantly faded and he was as he had been when he turned them away on the moor. "But I have played this role for a long time. There must be a

Huntmaster to lead the pack, and every generation a child is born with the power. If the master has no apprentice, then the boy is trained. If that position is already filled then the child is fed to the hounds, so as to not dilute the power. Huntmasters don't often die, so I have been congratulated on my luck."

For a moment Gemma felt sorry for him, but then she remembered the monster in the pub.

"Was that hound yours?"

He looked at her steadily and she felt like he could still see the image of the creature that was burnt into her eyes.

"Yes."

She retched and doubled over as her stomach turned. Gabriel reached out to steady her but she hit him away. That monster belonged to him and he had just let it go rampaging through town, killing whatever it could get its paws on. Had he meant for Adrian to get angry, and had the hound waiting outside accordingly? Had Adrian really been right when he had tried to tell her that Gabriel was able to control how they acted? Had he *made* her say that stuff to Adrian?

It felt like her knees would buckle, but the anger gave her strength. She turned on Gabriel with tears in her eyes.

"Did you kill him?" The words came out in a cutting hiss.

Gabriel began to shake his head but she was already on him, hitting any part of him she could reach. She felt her fists make contact with his chest over and over again, but he made no move to stop her or to fight back.

"Did you kill Adrian?.... Did you kill him?" She

screamed until the words corroded into sobs and her arms got tired. Only then did Gabriel gently take her by the shoulders and take her weight as she sunk against him.

"I have never intended your friend any harm and I certainly intend him none now." He waited a few moments for Gemma's sobs to quieten. "That hound was mine, just as Fen is mine. You saw how Fen fought it off. The hound that attacked us in the pub has been tampered with; someone else has called it up from the earth. But they weren't strong enough to control it, because the beast is mine, and obeys my will alone. That is how even Fen would act, if there were to be no Huntmaster."

Gemma struggled to calm her breathing.

"And Adrian?"

"That hound still looked hungry to me."

Relief washed over her and folded her knees. She fell to the floor, dragging Gabriel with her.

12.
HUNT

Adrian hit the ground with a yelp. It wasn't the first time he'd fallen, and his hands and knees were already scratched and bloody. He dragged himself to his feet and kicked at the rabbit hole in frustration. At first it had been thrilling, striding off onto the moor resolved to find the trapped spirit or die trying, but now that the alcohol was wearing off so was the adrenalin. The ground was uneven and in the hollows the darkness was so thick he couldn't see his hands in front of his face. Gorse caught on his clothes and sliced his arms, while the wiry heather tangled round his shoes and made him stumble.

He reached a point of higher ground and stopped to rest. The rising moon cast a weak light that only seemed to make the shadows deeper. The air was very still. He threw his hand to his chest as he saw hunched figures gathering around him, but forced his heart to steady as he realized they were only scattered boulders. Looking up he noticed the stones covering more and more of the ground until a mass of rock burst from the top of a hill nearby. He took a moment to massage his throbbing legs and then made for the tor.

The stone felt cold against his back and evening dew was seeping into his jeans from the damp grass, but it was refreshing after the walk and it felt good to sit down. He checked his pockets for the hundredth time, but his phone still wasn't there. He must have left it in the café. All he could do was sit where he was until morning. His legs were already stiffening and soon they would begin to ache; there was no way he could walk any further. In daylight he would try to spot a road, or cross his fingers for a helicopter. Mike and Gemma might have called Search and Rescue by now. But her words in the pub still clung to him. *'You aren't any different and chasing lies won't make you special!'* Would she be glad he was gone?

He shook his head and felt dizzy for a moment. She couldn't have meant it; it was Gabriel putting those words in her mouth. It was Gabriel who'd be glad to see him gone, and the thought of him comforting Gemma made Adrian's blood run like lava. He was a complete weirdo, and whatever it was that made him so interested in her it couldn't be good.

"Arise!" A cold voice carried upwards on the night air.

Adrian dragged his knees to his chest and clasped them tight. The noise made the hairs on his arms and neck stand on end and his skin prickle. He shivered. The dew wasn't refreshing any more and his sweat had cooled icy cold. He held his breath and listened. The moor was dead silent. He breathed out quietly and tried to convince himself that it was wind blowing through rocks, or an echo, or an animal. A fragment of him acknowledged the truth in what Gemma had said. When he'd dreamt about the boy in the tomb he had wanted it to have meaning so much that he had forced it to mean something. He hadn't listened to Elaine's advice because he didn't want to lose his own sense of importance. But all alone, in the dark, on the moor, he was ready to believe that he wasn't special at all and that the dream meant nothing because there was no such thing as the supernatural. Except every sense he had told him otherwise.

"Hear me and arise!" called the voice again.

Adrian instinctively pressed himself closer to the rock. He heard snatches of muttered chant, and the few words he could make out made him want to cover his ears. The chanting grew louder and took on a rhythmic beat. From somewhere a drum began to pound. He pressed his hands over his ears but the drumming continued, as if someone was beating the instrument inside his own skull. The beat was inescapable, and it called to him. He felt the ground beneath his palms and realized he had uncovered his ears. Slowly, he began to crawl around the base of the tor.

The drumming reached a climax as the horrible voice rose to a frenzied screech, and then cut short abruptly. Adrian listened as the echoes settled. There was no more speaking, just a heavy scraping sound, and every so often a grating noise that set his teeth on edge. He felt the ground begin to slope downwards slightly beneath him and saw that the tor overlooked a steep sided valley. On the opposite side a twin tor shone silvery in the moonlight, the silent stones looking like a hunched guard keeping the night watch. The noises were coming from somewhere below.

A thin mist began to rise and he struggled to keep his teeth from chattering. He dropped to his stomach and wriggled from stone to stone, abandoning the cover of the tor to get a glimpse of the valley floor. It felt better to be moving than to wait huddled up for something unpleasant to find him.

He gagged suddenly. A rancid sweetness filled his lungs, pulling his stomach and throat tight. He buried his face in the grass in an effort to escape the overpowering smell, but it was no use. When he breathed through his nose he could smell it, but if he breathed through his mouth he could taste it on his tongue. Something must have died nearby, and not that recently. The smell surrounded him and he was afraid that he might crawl straight into the source of it in the darkness. The thought of putting his hand down on something slimy and seething with maggots made him want to crawl back to the tor and press himself between the stones, but he didn't dare turn his back on the valley. Whatever was there was worse. But he needed to see it.

The ground grew steeper and he moved slowly to stop himself sliding. He dragged himself forward with his elbows, afraid of what his fingertips might feel. The ground beneath him was springy and covered in short turf; there was no bracken to hide him and he was running out of stones to creep between. He curled up behind the biggest of the remaining stones and risked a glimpse down the slope. A scream gathered in his lungs but he clamped his teeth together and stayed quiet. His fast breathing flooded his chest with the stink of rotting flesh, but it seemed almost bearable in comparison to what his eyes were fixed on now.

"Take of my offering and serve me," commanded the voice. It came from a tall man in dark clothes, his arms spread wide in welcome. At his feet lay two bodies. "Take it!" he yelled, his arms sagging as he looked from side to side. Dark shapes began to gather around him. At first Adrian told himself they were just rocks, but there was no doubt they were moving. Each one was dragging itself, painfully slowly, towards the offered prize. The scraping sound was coming from them.

"Come," called the man, his tone turned coaxing. He swayed where he stood and his shoulders dropped with exhaustion.

Adrian felt the earth heave beneath him. The first of the creeping things had reached the dead woman. The body beside her was male; perhaps her husband. The headline in the newspaper rose through waves of nausea to the front of his mind. But if the two bodies in the valley were part of the lost family of walkers, then where was their son? The creature dipped its head low until its rank lips must have been touching the woman's skin, and then it curled up comfortably to feed like a leech. Other dark shapes joined it until there was a mass of filthy bodies crowded around the dead couple. The man in black watched in satisfaction for what seemed like a long time, and all the while Adrian couldn't tear his eyes away. Then, the man seemed to decide that the creatures had fed enough and stepped forward to shoo them away. They ignored him, and instead pressed their faces harder into their prize. For a moment the man wavered, but then pulled a small flask from his pocket and threw something from it towards the crouching forms. They drew back immediately, moving far more quickly now they had fed, and Adrian gazed in horror as they pulled themselves unsteadily to their full height. Each one of them had been human once, but now yellowed bone showed through tattered cloth and grave stained wrapping. Every empty eye socket was still fixed on the dead walkers.

"Enough," growled the man in a low rumble, "you shall have more." A ripple of sound passed through the undead and their loose teeth rattled in their jaws like hail. "You shall have more," the necromancer repeated, "when you have earned it." There was a pause and then one of the rank figures leaned forward and bowed stiffly. One by one, each one of the others followed his lead until the entire group had indicated their submission to him.

"Now find me my dagger!"

The minions backed away as their master spread his arms eagerly.

"It lies inside this wall." he gestured out towards the faint line of encircling stone which Adrian could just make out as smudges of lighter grey in the darkness. "Bring me it and be rewarded!"

The skeletal figures spread out into the darkness and the man sank to his knees next to the dead woman. He leaned low and close, his face near enough to brush her cheek. Almost lovingly he smoothed back her hair and let his hand wander down to her neck, as he angled his head to whisper in her ear. Then her hand twitched. Adrian turned and vomited on the grass. The woman wasn't dead.

Adrian sat with his back to the stone he was hidden behind, his eyes squeezed tight shut. In his fear his senses seemed magnified and he heard the scraping and clawing of the animated skeletons searching the valley as if they were right behind him. He tried to stay still. As soon as the man had spoken of the stone wall Adrian realized where he must be; the large outer circle enclosed the smaller stone circles that were the remains of Grimspound settlement. He had half listened to Mike telling Gemma about it on top of Hound Tor. At least in the morning he would have a point of reference to look for. If he survived that long.

He wiped his mouth with his sleeve and pushed back another wave of dizziness. The stink must be coming from those things that the man had summoned, and however they fed they must need their prey to still be alive, which meant the couple on the ground might know what was happening to them. It was awful, and there was no sign of their son, unless he had escaped, which seemed unlikely. Maybe he was being kept somewhere else, somewhere that kept him out of the way. Maybe the necromancer hadn't wanted to use him, or just thought he was in the way. A tomb would be easy enough for someone like that to find and get inside; there was probably one under one of the ruined circles. So maybe this, in a weird turn of fortune, was his one chance to keep the promise that had called him all the way to Dartmoor.

The moonlight was brighter now that some of the cloud had cleared, and the mist seemed to be staying low and inside the valley. Adrian manoeuvred around his own vomit to look back down. The necromancer had moved away from the prone walkers and was observing his minions as they searched the site. They disturbed the mist and sent it up in dwindling tendrils as they scurried between the hut circles, bent nearly double and rooting the ground like animals. The remaining stone foundations of the dwellings rose like ghostly wrecks from a sea of mist, glimmering eerily in the moonlight. There was a sudden commotion round one larger stone and the noise of many bony fingers dragging at it, and then a dull thump that set the mist recoiling back as the stone fell. The minions clustered around the wound in the earth like it was fresh meat. This was the time to act, while they were distracted.

Adrian darted out from behind the stone. If he could skirt the valley and come down from the other side then he wouldn't be seen. He would know when he was near the boy, he told himself; he would feel it. As for the parents, what could he do, except maybe make sure they really were dead before this dagger was found.

He tripped once, but got up quickly and kept running. It was downhill and small gulleys and streams crisscrossed the land, running down from the higher ground. He jumped without slowing when he heard the trickle of water. Only one thing made him pause for a moment; the moonlight glinted on a flat surface a short way away and Adrian realized it was a road. If he turned and ran that way he could be on it within a few minutes, and maybe have walked back into a town before dawn. He turned his back and ran the other way.

The cover of bracken and gorse made it easier to approach Grimspound from this angle and he moved quickly without fear of being seen. His nose had hardened to the smell and it was only there as an unpleasant afterthought. Mist began to pour past his feet and he knew he must be close. Ahead he could make out the outer wall of the settlement and he made towards it on his stomach, feeling thorns tear flesh from his hands. He pressed himself against the stones and peered over. The necromancer still had his back to him and was watching his minions work. A cover had been thrown over one of the couple at his feet. Adrian prayed it was the woman, but the positioning told him it was the man.

A scraping sound nearby locked his muscles. He rolled his eyes downwards in slow motion. The ground just inside the wall was moving. It bulged upwards and then split, the smell of decay doubling and burning in his throat. A huge mushroom began to push up from the ground, shedding dry earth from its cap. Then a bony hand shot up and grabbed at the turf. Adrian gaped in horror. It wasn't a mushroom; it was a human skull. The figure continued to drag itself out of the earth, pausing sometimes as if tired, until eventually it could stand. It

172

was smaller than the others and the scraps of skirt and jumper that clung to it looked like they had been bright colours once. This burial had been more recent; the skeleton wasn't Bronze Age like the others. It turned both empty eye sockets on Adrian. The matted remains of plaits hung down over each shoulder. It was a little girl.

For a second Adrian saw her as she must have once been; red rosy cheeks, blonde hair tangled by the wind and a jumper a size big for her to grow into. He reached out.

"Come here."

The girl didn't move.

"Come on, come with me," Adrian beckoned with both hands. He had to take the girl away, he couldn't let that man have control of her.

She raised her arm slightly. A pink and yellow plastic bangle hung loosely on her wrist, the colours untouched by their time in the earth.

Adrian nodded. "That's it!"

But her head jerked backwards suddenly and she snatched her arm away. She glanced at Adrian once, then fell to all fours and galloped off like an animal.

He slumped with his forehead against the wall. Mike had said that people got lost on the moor and were sometimes never found, but that girl had a family somewhere that didn't know where to leave flowers. All the disgust and horror of the skeleton workers melted away; they weren't monstrous or disgusting, it was just sad, and no one deserved to be dragged out of the earth like that. Death was supposed to be a dreamless sleep. He needed to find the boy. With stinging hands he gripped the stones of the wall and dragged himself back to his feet. After that, then he would try and help the girl as well. He looked up and froze. All the undead had given up their search and were gathered in a semi circle on the other side of the wall. In front of them stood the necromancer, his black robes thrown over a smart tweed suit. One of his hands was on a very real hunting rifle and his other rested on the head of the little girl.

"You look fresh," said the man, "and I must admit your arrival is most timely."

Adrian set his jaw.

The man pointed back towards the two bodies. "Because that bitch has just gone and killed her husband, I mean, how inconsiderate! My kind of woman though, it's almost a shame she'll soon be dead." He looked at Adrian appraisingly.

The woman had been brave enough to do what he had just failed to. Her husband wouldn't suffer any more. Adrian vowed to do her the same honour.

"Now," said the necromancer, "get him."

The girl dropped to her knees ready to spring.

Adrian shut his eyes.

It was cold and dark. Time had passed but it was still night. Adrian eased his eyes open a crack. His skull throbbed and his t shirt was stuck to his back where had been lying on the damp grass and his jumper had been taken off to uncover his arms. He rolled his eyes slowly from side to side. The woman lay on his right, her red hair spread messily around her like a halo. Her husband had been rolled roughly onto his side and laid a few feet away, the lingering expression on his face almost serene.

"Why are you stopping?" snarled a voice nearby.

Adrian closed his eyes and pretended to still be unconscious.

Footsteps came nearer and he sensed someone standing over him. Their clothes smelt of stale earth and blood.

"Quickly, if you must," the necromancer snapped, "and take from the boy; she's nearly finished."

There was a rattling of jawbones as multiple skeletal figures nodded hungrily.

Adrian tensed. There was no way of escaping; if he tried to run they would hit him again. All he could do was lie still and leave them unaware he was awake; it was his only chance. The red haired woman had managed it, so why couldn't he? He felt something brush against his finger and almost drew his hand back, but remembered he must stay still. A hand took his. It was weak, but living. The woman gave his hand the very slightest of squeezes, and he braced himself for the attack.

At first they leeched on one by one. Cold teeth pressed against his skin and latched on, tight enough to bruise but not to cut the skin. It wasn't so much painful as uncomfortable, but they must have felt his heart throwing itself at the bars of his chest, and it excited them. They began to feed. It felt like ice crystals being sucked out through his skin; tiny stabs of pain that cut for a second and then left behind a feeling of cold. He began to feel weak and dizzy. It was like losing too much blood. Blackness swum up to claim him and he let it, the woman's hand still grasped in his.

13.
PREY

Dawn comes early in summer, seeping into the sky from three or four in the morning. It touches the highest tors first, then it grows and pours into the valleys and trickles into the ravines and licks the singing water of the Dart. But there is one place that the dawn does not go. This place is always dark and so dense with oak and bramble and nettle that no one ever walks there; even the rugged mapmakers for the Ordnance Survey couldn't cut their way in. So they fenced it off from the surrounding forest. They labelled that area 'conservation', and the rest is signposted 'Wistmans Wood'.

It was here that Gemma finally opened her eyes.

She reached thoughtlessly for her phone to check the time and shuddered as her fingers closed on something dense and furry. Her hand sprung back as her eyes tried to take in her strange surroundings. The walls were stone, dark from past moisture and bristling with dried moss. She was curled up on a low stone bench draped over with layers of what she could now see to be soft white sheepskins. Slowly she began to sort her memories into two sections; dream and not dream. Real was too strong a word.

She was making good progress when a knock startled her. Gabriel had appeared from nowhere. No, not nowhere. When she looked carefully she could see that the stone blocks overlapped behind him, shielding a narrow passageway that must lead in and out. He had two hares slung over his shoulder and his hand was still raised from knocking on the cave wall. It could have been the tiredness or her brain simply refusing to deal with another single weird situation, but suddenly the scene was hilarious.

"I suppose," Gemma spluttered between chest wracking waves of laughter, "that you caught those with your pack of monstrous hellhounds."

Gabriel remained still for a moment, then in a careless motion threw the hares to the floor.

"You should eat," he said. With nimble fingers he began to build a fire, using wood that was clearly stored there for such a purpose. All the while he kept his eyes on his task so that Gemma could only see the blonde hair that was falling around his face in loose waves. His shirt had been unlaced at the front and hung wide at the neck. It must be well into the day outside of the cave for it to be that warm. The laughter vanished.

She pushed herself up and sat with her arms hugging her knees. From outside the cave she could hear a faint chorus of birdsong, and further away the rushing of water.

"I'm sorry." Her words disrupted the stillness and turned the air foul.

Gabriel broke the spit he was building.

"I should be sorry," he said finally. His words were not the flowing silk of suggestion they had once been. They were the words of a man who was tired.

Gemma rose to her feet to help, but realised she had no idea how to.

"But you have my word now. My vow." He looked up and the world was eclipsed in the blue of his eyes; otherworldly as ever, even if the rest of him had faded to almost human.

"You've changed your shirt," Gemma managed to

stammer.

Gabriel laughed once.

"Just as I endeavour to blend in when in your towns and on your well trodden paths, here I must make the effort to conform. The hares I caught in a snare."

The fire crackled greedily, consuming the dried twigs. Gabriel built it up with thicker branches, until it burnt low and red enough for him to begin turning the skinned hares over it. Slowly the cave began to fill with the rich smell of roasting meat. Gemma blushed as her stomach rumbled. Gabriel was too preoccupied to notice, his hands constantly moving as he drew shapes in the trodden earth of the floor with a twig and then scratched them out in agitation. Finally he seemed to come to some sort of a conclusion.

"This is a safe house, a shelter that can be used for one or two nights when needed, but your presence will not escape notice for much longer. I will need help if we are to find your Adrian, and my apprentice will meet us here. Then we must leave before you are seen." He laid these ideas out as immutable facts.

"And if I am seen?"

"It would become difficult." He offered Gemma a piece of the hare and she took the thigh, holding it carefully by a blackened leg bone, and sat cross legged by the fire.

"Difficult how?" she pressed.

Gabriel paused from peeling strips of meat from half a ribcage and looked into the fire until his gaze pierced beyond it, through the earth and back in time.

"We have always been; and your kind are ancient enough now also. But we were here before you, here at the birth of the earth, through the wracking labour of ice and fire. We watched you grow and become strong and we saw some of ourselves in you. For a time we knew each other and we respectively learnt things that we had not previously understood. In time you learnt to manipulate the earth as we do, not with will but with smoke and metal and machines. You learnt the ways of the earth from us, how much it could yield, and then you pushed it to that point and beyond. But we are not blameless; we learnt jealousy and hatred and we learnt to be afraid. Then the earth failed and we watched you leave the moor and now only the hut circles and the hatred remain."

Gemma narrowed her eyes. She was tired of grand words and pretty stories.

"And that means?"

"My Clan would see you dead."

An uneaten chunk of hare hit the floor as Gemma scrambled backwards from the sound of footsteps at the entrance. A figure visibly adjusted his posture as he stepped inside.

"Owain," Gabriel nodded.

Gemma flung her gaze between them. The new arrival stood stiffly, like a boy who is tall but not used to being tall yet. His hair was a shocking red and swept back from his pale forehead. Gabriel showed no sign of moving to defend her from murderous hordes.

"My apprentice," he added helpfully.

Then it began to come together, like the fiddly pieces of a jigsaw where too many of the colours are the same.

"You were at the Visitor Centre," Gemma said to Owain.

His cheeks blushed a faint crimson that created an

unfortunate clash with his hair. There was a softness to him that she struggled to reconcile with the predator that prowled beneath Gabriel's controlled exterior. Her eyes returned to Gabriel.

"He's lucky." She regretted the words as soon as she'd spoken them and spluttered over an apology, wishing she could grab the syllables back from the air and swallow them bad taste and all.

"I wasn't fed alive to the hounds, if that's what you're implying." Owain's voice was deeper then she had imagined, and held more of the calm control she had thought he was missing. But there was an unmistakeable twinkle in his eye.

"They would have had to catch me first." He swung himself down into a cross legged position by the fire, quickly righting the edge of the refilled spit that he had knocked with his foot.

Gemma pulled herself nearer again, catching a resigned look aimed at Owain out of the corner of her eye. She was too hot. Sitting between a person who had escaped being torn limb from limb by enchanted monsters because there just happened to be a lucky opening for him at the time and some kind of demonic Huntsman just wasn't normal. She wanted to know how Owain felt about the fate of all the others now he had filled the position. She wanted to ask Gabriel how he felt about calling his hounds to that grisly meal. She wanted to ask how many they had killed between them. What she did ask was:

"How do we find Adrain?"

He would have dealt better with all of this. He would have found a way to rescue her.

"That is the reason I have asked Owain to join us.

181

It is something of a speciality of his," Gabriel said.

On cue, Owain produced from his pocket a stone on a string and an extremely ordinary looking Ordance Survey map. The stone had a natural hole which the string was tied through, and veins of silver stood out from the dull grey in the light of the fire.

"Natural tin, collected from the river Plym where it meets the Dart," he explained as he smoothed the map open on the floor. "Gabriel is a better tracker than me, better at being unseen and well, better at most things generally," He shared a conspiritory smile, "but I can find in minutes what he might search for over days."

Gemma gave him a warm smile in return.

His blush was barely visible as he looked back at the map.

The air stilled around him as he slowed his breath. Even the fire seemed to burn lower and the birds and river outside seemed further away. He was dragging the world towards himself as he stretched his arm out over the map and let the stone fall from his fingers. Gemma felt the tug faintly on herself as she leaned in to watch the stone swing erratically then settle into a rhythmic circular path. Either the map was overlaid on the world or the world was shrunk to be thrown across the map as he swung the stone in wider circles, taking in every corner, passing over some areas twice and returning again and again to-

"Grimspound," said Gabriel.

Owain opened his eyes and the world snapped back, leaving Gemma slightly dizzy. Outside, the birdsong returned to normal.

"I've heard of that place," she said, "Mike showed us it from the top of Hound Tor."

"Excellent bacons rolls there," confided Owain.

Gabriel trod out the fire with his foot and threw the second cooked hare at Owain, who caught it with both hands.

"Eat up. We have a fair walk ahead of us," Gabriel said.

"Well on that front, if you'll permit me, I have a little something waiting in the car park." Owain's face was a battle between sheepish and triumphant, the latter of which won when Gemma shot him an impressed grin. Gabriel gave the extinguished fire a last kick and prowled out of the cave.

Outside, the sun was blinding after the dim firelight. The heat settled on Gemma's skin, reminding her that she hadn't changed her clothes since yesterday, which now seemed like at least a week ago. But it could wait. In little more than an hour Adrian would be safely found, and perhaps a little less rash for his night out on the moor. Of course she still owed him an apology, a big one, but turning up in hypothetical shining armour had to earn her a few brownie points to start with.

Gabriel strode ahead for the entire mile or so walk to the car park, but Gemma was content to hang back a few steps and match Owain's stride.

"The masks at the Visitor Centre, they look nothing like the real hounds," she said. They were just leaving the open moor behind and stepping onto a well worn path that wound between man high gorse bushes, prickling with vicious thorns among bright yellow flowers.

"The hounds look different for each Huntmaster. They're formed from old bones, the blood of a sacrifice and the will of their Master. So perhaps they look like someone else's hounds, many years ago. I'm sorry for

183

scaring you at the Visitor Centre."

"Did you do that, make me see and feel that weird stuff?"

Owain watched his leather booted feet eat up the gravel beneath them. "I didn't mean to do that much. Gabriel is always telling me that my manipulation of humans is poor; I shouldn't have tried it."

"So that's what he calls it is it?" Gemma kicked absently at a stone, sending it skittering off onto the grass and startling a sheep nearby.

Owain either chose not to answer the question or missed the significance of it.

"Gabriel chose the way his hounds look then?" She prompted after a few moments.

"It isn't a choice. They reflect the Master's personality. But then he does choose to have Fenrir look like a normal dog when they're near people."

"Fen?"

Owain nodded.

"Fen is dead," Gemma said sadly.

Owain snorted and clamped both hands over his mouth to quell the noise. "They're all dead!"

High banks spilling over with sun withered flowers sped by, followed by precarious looking dry stone walls that gave way to the sprawling moor that wreathed the ruins of Grimspound. Owain drove faster even than Mike, with oncoming cars diving out his way with disregard for wing mirrors or paint. Gabriel sat on Gemma's left, watching the scenery with an easy indifference that suggested he was used to travelling by car, even if he thought it lacked a certain elegance. The old pick up truck might have been blue under the dust, and the three front seats were so saggy with wear that Gemma was thrown against one of her companions at every bend. Their coolness was disconcerting in the afternoon heat.

Owain slid the car neatly into a well used pull-in opposite a worn path meandering up onto the moor. Gemma scrambled out of the door he left open, glad of the air, and shaded her eyes to look upwards. Something startled a flock of crows and sent them wheeling up over one of the two matching tors flanking the dip that she knew held the clustered hut circles of the ruined village. The shadow of a cloud slipped down the slope and rushed across the hot tarmac. Gemma wondered how Adrian had failed to spot the road.

"Up we go," said Owain, extending a hand to help Gemma up the small roadside bank. They walked in silence, this time with Gabriel hanging behind. Gemma glanced back occasionally, and each time she caught his expression the fist of her stomach clenched tighter; he was thinking what she was trying not to. This was too easy. Adrian would have found the road himself if he was alright.

In her head, she thought of the reasons that could stop him. A broken leg would explain it, and that could be fixed. Even if he had hit his head and was confused, that would mend in a few days. She thought of him lying in the hot sun and quickened her pace.

They stopped only for a moment while Owain drank a few handfuls of water from a small, fresh stream that followed the path for a little while and soon the outer wall was ahead of them. A few of the crows had settled on the taller rocks of the entrance off to their right. In front of them was the more modern entrance, where the stones had been knocked aside to facilitate the footpath

185

made in Victorian times. Their approach startled a magpie, which flew off untidily with the plastic bangle it had been pecking at.

"Shall we split up?" suggested Gemma. Her voice cracked out loud. Gabriel nodded and headed off around the left side of the circle. Owain wordlessly took the right, leaving Gemma to step over the fallen stones ahead and search inside the wall.

"Adrian!" she called, her voice catching in the breeze and setting the crows screaming. The moor was empty except for the carrion eaters. There wasn't a walker or pony or sheep in sight. She walked first to the largest hut circle near the centre of the village. It offered most shelter and seemed a sensible place to start. But as she stepped inside it was clear it was empty, the only sign that anyone had been there previously was some disturbed earth around the base of the largest upright stone.

She looked up. Gabriel and Owain had finished their sweep of the outer wall and were scanning the surrounding circles at speed. A searing heat gathered behind her eyes and forced its way out as tears. It was oppressively hot, too hot to breathe. Suddenly she needed to lie down and in that moment there were hands to catch her and then the safeness of stone behind her back.

"I told you to eat." Gabriel was crouching in front of her, the calm pools of his eyes disturbed by worry. Behind him, Owain had the Ordnance Survey map out again, and was repeating his search with the stone.

"He's here," he said, "it still says he's here. Gabriel rose and kicked the map out of the way. He pulled a knife from his boot and began carving into the sun baked earth. Gemma craned her neck enough to glimpse the shape and guess it was a likeness of the village. He sat back when he was done and Owain threw his searching stone over the drawing. Gemma watched the stones progress, noting the way it swung repeatedly beyond the outer line of the image.

"He's outside, up there," she pointed to a ridge of higher ground just to the right of where the modern path exited the settlement.

Gabriel narrowed his eyes at a slight swell in the earth, inconspicuous amidst the scattered boulders and tufts of dying grass. Owain yelped and dropped his stone. His eyes were wide as he looked at Gabriel, who was there to help him up.

"I've felt it for some time. Be very careful," Gabriel whispered in his apprentice's ear.

"You should stay here," Owain told Gemma. She opened her mouth to protest, but Gabriel shook his head.

"The ground up there is too rough, plus there is a bog just inside that section of the wall. You are in no state to look out for your own safety."

The will was in his voice again, and she didn't fight it.

"Take this," Owain produced a chunk of remaining hare from a pouch at his waist.

"Eat it," said Gabriel.

Gemma had a piece of the meat in her mouth before she realized what she was doing.

The climb up to the barrow wasn't hard for feet that knew the moor. In swift strides Gabriel and Owain made their way to the front end of the oval of earth that looked over the valley. Immediately, Gabriel fell to his knees and pushed his spread fingers into the dry, springy turf. Imperceptibly, the earth stirred to his touch, nearby in Houndain the wet soil heaved to his call and then settled, and from the dark hollow core of the barrow there came the stench of death and a heart shattering scream. Which was echoed from nearby.

Gabriel sprung to his feet and was sprinting downhill in a moment. Owain followed, recognising Gemma's voice.

She knew the feral. She would never forget the sluggish rhythm with which the creature had dragged off the pony, or the strong grip of those bone bare hands. Only this time there was no dead pony, there were six of the monsters, and she was the edible thing that each had sunken eyes fixed upon. Her fingers tore apart the remaining cold hare and she threw a chunk as far as she could. Two of the feral threw themselves into a lumbering burst of speed and reached the meat at the same time. In a second it was gone and their gaze returned to a more filling target. Gemma threw her last chunk of meat and screamed.

Owain was beside her, his pale fingers around a wicked knife. Gabriel collided with one of the feral before it had registered his arrival. With a downwards sweep he sunk a dagger into the putrid flesh of it's throat and tore it down to the stomach. It recoiled, hissing wetly like rain on ashes, and Gabriel delivered a kick to the chest that catapulted the creature into the next hut circle whilst cleverly leaving the innards next to him. One of the other feral fell on the green grey intestines, pushing slimy handfuls into its gaping mouth, but the others turned on Gabriel.

Gemma saw all of it, even with Owain shielding her. She gripped his arm grimly.

Gabriel faced the four approaching feral. His shirt

was already torn from grappling with the first one and he tossed it aside. Clouds had rolled over the sun and in the grey light his milky skin was laced with the grey of ancient stone. It was the same transformation that Gemma had witnessed in the pub. But this time it was complete; she was seeing Gabriel as he truly was, as Huntmaster. And it was monstrous. He hissed a challenge at the feral in their own tongue and his fury raised a line of storm grey spikes from his spine. Similar shards of bone prickled down his forearms and Gemma saw how the feral had once been the same race.

All of the feral except one bowed back from his challenge. The one which had been eating his companion had sidled off to explore the rest of the body, but the largest of them remained. He eased his rotten bones straight until he was standing, matching Gabriel for height, the muscles beneath his creased and moss speckled skin bunched for a pounce. He lept, and Gabriel caught him. For a moment it almost seemed they were embracing, and then the feral fell to its knees. Gabriel didn't move, but in his clenched fist he still held the creature's heart.

"Let's go," said Owain.

189

14.
DEVIL

"Tonight we shall have a new Huntmaster." Asterra refilled her glass with wine and raised it to the unconscious form propped in a high backed chair. Fian's eyes rolled weakly beneath the purple lids. The air of the room was thick with a sickly sweet smoke that smelt of warm days and carrion and honey. She drained the glass in one, smudging the red dye on her lips as she wiped a rivulet of spilt liquid from her mouth.

"Tonight my brother shall pay for abandoning me for his mortal harlot." She leaned close to Fian, her wine soft breath in his ear and her long pale fingers resting on his scarred throat. The tip of each pointed nail had been dyed red to match her lips. "Tonight you shall raise the hounds for me." Her fingers wandered up over his chin and traced the angular line of his young cheek, then slipped over the beads of sweat gathering on his forehead and raked back his dark hair.

A knock rang against the chamber door. Asterra hissed between her teeth and ripped a pinch of hair from Fian's head.

"Who is it?" she asked.

"Your brother would see you Mistress."

Asterra swallowed a snarl and measured her tone.

"He may see me tomorrow." Swirls of incense snaked and collapsed in the thick air, the movement accentuated by the flickering of countless candles.

"He would see you now, but will wait a short while if you are indisposed."

She clenched her fists, the red tips of her nails

pressing into her palms.

"Then he will wait."

"Not too long Mistress."

She listened to the footsteps of the messenger fade away and emptied the last of the wine into her glass.

"Why now?" she asked the unconscious Fian, "why this hour after all these years?" She paced the slate floor of the room, her long blue dress dragging up the splinters of bone and stale herbs that littered the floor. She stopped behind a wooden table, piled untidily with leather pouches and glass vessels filled with barks and berries and the dried carcasses of animals. "Have I told you why I hate him?" Asterra didn't look at Fian as she spoke to him, her gaze was on a bundle of rags knotted tight with plaited strands of hair. With the points of her nails she picked the knots undone, folding aside the crumpled cloth, stiff with dried blood. She smiled at Morgana's gift and stroked a tentative finger along it in the candlelight. "Old bone," she purred, "taken from one of the hounds before my brother was Huntmaster, before the Master who taught him and from the Master before who exchanged it for the key to Morgana's chamber. Sated with his blood, bound with his hair, it will bestow his will and his power over the pack." She dropped it into a stone bowl and began to grind it into dust.

Fian moaned quietly at the sound of the bone splintering, but Asterra didn't hear. She was rhythmically grinding the bone into pieces, then into shards, then into powder. "I hate Gabriel." She spat on the floor and then drank the last of her wine to wash the taste of his name from her mouth. "Because once there was a girl of our Clan that he was infatuated with. But the little wretch took no heed of him because she was too busy wandering the moors like one of the feral looking for mortals to spy on. But he persisted, against all of my advice, and eventually she made a deal with him. He told me this with his own mouth, he brazenly came and told me that she had asked to spend a lifetime as a mortal, and if he granted her that then she would bind herself to him with the vows. Of course that magic was beyond his knowledge, so he begged me to tell him what to do, and like a fool I told him. In truth, I hoped that he would fail and disappoint her enough that she would hate him. But it worked. She left for the town and the Clan disowned her."

Asterra paused to rifle through a few of the skin and hide pouches, tossing unwanted ones onto the filthy floor until she found what she was looking for. She smiled and threw the wormwood into her bowl. "After that my brother became distant. We had been close, sharing all things as a brother and sister should, but I began to notice his absence. Often he should have been at my side and he was not there. At first, when I was questioned on this, I lied and said that he was spending extra time with the Huntmaster. I made him sound like the perfect apprentice. But as the years passed I grew tired of lying, and lonely, and unable to watch him slip out towards town to watch his mortal woman. He shamed me. Humans are less than animals and he chose her over me."

In the bowl, the bone and wormwood had been reduced to the finest of powders. Next Asterra poured in boiled water with honey; the whole mixture must be swallowed without gagging and the sweetness would hide the taste. "She died the year he was raised to Huntmaster. He came to me and I turned him away."

A single tear slid down Fian's cheek as Asterra poured the mixture into a bottle and corked the top. She

193

reapplied the red dye to her lips and strode to the bolted door.

Gemma didn't remember the journey back to the car, only the fact that Owain left his knife on the dashboard. He drove just as fast as before, and sent up clouds of dust as he skidded to a halt on the dry gravel of the car park.

"Hound Tor," mumbled Gemma, "why are we here?"

"So I can buy you a bacon sandwich," said Owain.

It was ridiculous. It was the most absurd thing Gemma had ever heard. The stone had told them that Adrian was at Grimspound. Why weren't they still there? Why weren't they keeping the feral away from him? She grabbed Owain's arm across the car seat.

"You don't understand. Adrian is still there."

"I know."

"Then why the hell aren't we looking for him?"

"I'm going to buy you a bacon sandwich. You are going to eat it. Then I am going to explain." Owain's voice didn't carry the power of Gabriel's, but he was very definite about the plan.

Gemma got out of the car and leaned on it as she slammed the door.

Owain was greeted as a regular by the owner of the snack van, and minutes later he had deposited two hot bacon sandwiches on one of the faded plastic tables

"So why are we leaving Adrian to die?" Gemma asked him as soon as he sat down.

"Eat your bacon."

Gemma shoved a tasteless corner into her mouth and raised her eyebrows.

"Thank you. Gabriel will be furious with me if you

black out again." The glint in his eye was faint; he wasn't joking. "No one is leaving Adrian to die. You saw it wasn't safe."

"I've seen Gabriel chase off the feral before. Why didn't they obey him up there?" She took another exaggerated bite of sandwich.

Owain's forehead creased as he chose his words.

"The feral there weren't acting as they usually do. You're right, it is unheard of that one of them would confront a Huntmaster like that. Usually they're pretty much a joke, a scary story to tell young ones, but those had something driving them beyond hunger."

"I thought they were nothing like you. But Gabriel looked-"

"Inhuman?" Owain was wiping his mouth with a paper napkin after finishing his bacon sandwich.

"Evil. Like a monster."

"He is Huntmaster." Owain shrugged like this explained everything.

"Would you go all like that too?"

"Yes."

"And the hound that nearly killed a pub full of people. That was his as well."

"He told me Fen fought it off."

"Yeah while he did nothing except a little bit of his freak show transformation. I thought that was bad until today."

For the first time, the twinkle disappeared from Owain's eyes completely.

Gemma chewed the last doughy mouthful of sandwich, aware that she'd crossed the line.

"Gabriel's duty is to the pack, and through that to the Clan. He is our protector, which in this time means a

195

life of walking the moor saving dim witted humans from themselves, spreading rumours that any sightings of the beast are hoaxes in pubs and just every so often fighting off murderous feral or scouts from less amicable clans. Not only is he protecting our secrecy and our way of life, but he is protecting all of you by making sure that you are oblivious to us. He didn't choose to be Huntmaster, and he was raised to the position after the last Huntmaster killed himself. It takes a very hard life to push someone technically capable of immortality to instruct their own hounds to devour them."

The tables around them were empty, but on the breeze Gemma could hear the sound of children yelling with glee as they played 'It' round the lower rocks of the tor. A car rumbled past on the nearby road and pulled in so a lady with a camera could take a quick picture of the view.

Gemma hung her head.

"If he had completed his 'freak show transformation' as you call it, he could have hurt the humans around him. He was lending strength to his loyal hound without giving in to the power, which is no easy task." Owain said.

Gemma inspected the crumbs on her fingers.

"He promised to find Adrian for me." When Gabriel hugged her after Fen died he had been a man. He had promised to help her like a friend would. He had watched over her mother and her mother's mother through the years. "I think I'm being an idiot again."

Owain looked a little placated.

"Nothing in this world or any other will stop him fulfilling that promise to you." He caught her in the gaze of his steel grey eyes and in them for that moment she saw a glimpse of the man, and the Huntmaster, that he would one day become. "Even if instead he should have been binding the hounds afresh at Houndain this morning. Instead I merely checked they were sleeping. But there is a traitor in our midst and they would have the hounds for their own devices."

"I thought only the Huntmaster could control the hounds?"

"Anyone with the skill may raise them, if they are strong enough. But Gabriel and I should be the only two capable of doing that alive."

"You said there were other Clans. Could someone have come from one of them?"

"Their customs will be the same. One apprentice and one Master. To interfere with the pack of another Clan would be an act of war."

Gemma shuddered at the thought of a clash between two groups of people who not only were naturally very hard to kill, but that also had a pack of animals taken directly from the worst kind of nightmare at their command.

"So the hounds are out of control."

"One was out of control. But whoever it is isn't strong; their will can't even sustain their wakefulness for long."

"Long enough to potentially kill a lot of people. How do you know that it hasn't killed people out on the moor?"

"I don't. That's what I'm trying to tell you. That's why we couldn't stay and dig up Adrian-"

"Dig him up?" Gemma clenched the edge of the table until her knuckles turned white.

"He is trapped in the barrow mound above the

ruined village. He's alive."

Gemma opened her mouth to speak again but Owain cut across her.

"Someone is influencing the feral. Someone is tampering with the hounds. Whoever this individual, or group, are there is no doubt that they're extremely dangerous; too dangerous to take on while you are with us and too dangerous to anger if there is any doubt about the fitness of the hounds to respond to their Master's call. The Master and the pack are one, if they're weakened so is he."

"What does this someone want with Adrian?"

"I'd like to know the answer to that myself."

Gemma slumped back in her chair, deflated. Adrian was trapped underground, goodness knows in what kind of pain, just like the boy in his dream. She had doubted him and humoured him and finally half believed him, but all too late, and now it was all terribly true.

"Then what do I do?"

"Wait."

Asterra inclined her head slightly as Gabriel rose from the log bench to meet her. Faintly she caught the scent of petrol on him, and on another breath the air told her that he had been close to humans recently.

"To what do I owe the pleasure?" Her lips curled unpleasantly around the last word.

"I know we have been strange to each other, but I hoped to give you the time and space to understand."

"What more could I understand?"

"I know you have loved!"

"We do not love outside our race. Never"

Gabriel pushed his hair back in frustration, loosing

it from the leather band and letting it settle about his shoulders. As they stood the likeness between them was obvious; the same fine cheek bones and proud eyes, except Gabriel's face was shaded by sadness and Asterra's was twisted with righteous hatred.

"So you command love? You bottle it up and sprinkle it with your powders and potions?" his low laughter was grim.

Asterra blushed, remembering how he had seen her play at such things as a child.

"Love potions are for infants. I have grown strong without you holding me back. Now I could bottle lust, or hatred or obsession if I chose."

Gabriel clasped the empty air and then let his hands fall to his sides.

"I held you back only so you could learn to think of the effects of your actions, and perhaps when not to act."

She scowled, her hand clasping the knife hung from the back of her belt.

"What do you want?"

"I am calling Court. Stand with me."

The request hit Asterra like a wave and stirred the memories buried deep down below the sediment of bitterness and hatred. She would have cut her finger on the knife if it hadn't been sheathed. Gabriel raised his hand and held it out to her. It would be such a small step, just to take it and lay all of the years since they had last stood together to rest, and be as they once were when neither of them were tainted by mortality.

Asterra spat on the ground. "I stand alone."

"Try to sleep." Owain looked at Gemma from the driver's seat through the open passenger door of the truck.

"Of course. No chance of nightmares for me."

"Gabriel is doing everything he can."

"Remind me again what happens if we simply dig Adrian up?"

"Well there is the obvious possibility of death for all of us, potentially via being eaten by the hounds. Alongside that there is the potential of war between my Clan and another if that is what this traitor wants, the chance of our existence being exposed by their actions and, of course, the small detail that attempting to rescue Adrian unprepared is likely to result in our defeat and his certain unpleasant demise."

"Yeah that's an issue," Gemma sighed.

"If Gabriel wins over the Court we will have an army to take your Adrian back, and crush the individual responsible."

A tired smile flickered on Gemma's lips.

"Rescuing in style. What's the Court?"

"The Court is our council who decide on a course on action on behalf of the Clan."

"And Gabriel is asking them to send their army out to save Adrian?"

"And destroy a threat to the Clan."

"But I thought you, I mean, I thought the general consensus in your Clan was that humans weren't in the good books?"

Owain crossed his wrists on the steering wheel and looked at the reflection of the moor in his wing mirror. The sleepy shadows of the clouds crawled slowly across the brown green grass, blurring at their edges with the first shadows of evening. The last of the sun was

200

honey thick and the soil by the roadside was cracked with thirst.

"The Council will be given a reason they believe in. Gabriel will see to Adrian."

"But-"

"I must be at Court."

The slam of the door was firm. Gemma waved Owain off half heartedly and turned to the gate at the back of Fox Tor Café that led to the bunkhouse. So much had happened since she was last there looking for Adrian. Too much.

Her feet turned her around and led her away from the door, back out towards the moor and the dry stone wall where she had sat just a few days ago. In the unpleasant knowledge of the truth, her days and years of disbelief seemed somehow quaint and precious; as if she could tuck her head back under the covers and make the bogeymen disappear if she simply told herself that they weren't real enough times. But they were real. All the myths and legends and stories and warnings. *Elaine*.

The air in the bunk room was cooler than outside. The other guest, whoever they were, had come and gone, remaining a stranger. They had left behind a creased newspaper. No one else had opted for twelve pounds worth of privacy since, and Gemma was glad she could sit there alone. Her back was against the wall and her hand lay palm upwards on the bed, Adrian's phone resting across her fingers. She had listened to the message another three times without discovering any extra useful information.

Tell her to stay away, tell her to run if she sees it. I've never been wrong but it isn't an angel. Tell her to run…

201

She typed 'angel' into the search engine on her laptop. A cold cup of tea was balanced on her duvet next to another empty cup. The screen filled with bright lights, aura photos and overweight babies. She clicked the back button. Gabriel was no angel, although he'd never claimed to be; it was her mother who had labelled him the night he had murdered another driver to save her life. Apparently the white light people claimed to see during near death experience was just an effect of the cells in the eyes shutting down and glowing was no sign of divinity.

Her fingers hesitated over the key pad. Then she typed in 'huntmaster'. A lot of well fed men in scarlet jackets popped up, alongside a few images of mutilated foxes, which she was too wearied to even feel shocked by, and finally a smattering of anti-hunt protestors. She scrolled listlessly down through the images, uninterested in politics or class, until a small thumbnail image at the very bottom caught her eye. She zoomed in and the screen blazed with an image that raised the hairs on her arms and neck. A figure all in black astride a furious white horse, galloping blindly through the torn clouds of an unearthly storm. Her shaking finger clicked again and she scanned the description under the image. All at once the air tightened and the room around her seemed to stretch away into nothing, leaving her in a barren blur with only the words 'Dark Huntsman' and 'Devil'.

The laptop slid from her knees as she clenched in on herself, hugging her knees to her chest and feeling the pounding of her heart echo through them. Faintly she could still hear the infrequent passing of cars on the road outside and the fragmented chatter of friends discussing meeting at the pub. Hadn't Mike warned her of the

202

'Devil's dog' in the Plume of Feathers? And the woman had stood up and called the beast a hellhound. Hadn't it all been glaring her in the face? She counted her breaths until her heart finally slowed and her eyes had cleared enough to let her look back at the screen.

"*The Devil rides*," she mumbled, "*across desolate places on his enormous steed, gathering spirits and living souls alike, cutting down all in his path. His terrible entourage are called the Wild Hunt; monstrous hounds, half human abominations and demons dragged up with him from Hell.*"

The ludicrous hyperbole calmed her a little, but it was difficult to dismiss the Devil when your mother believed in angels and Adrian was in the hands of who-the-hell-knows. She sniffed back a delirious laugh. Perhaps Hell does know, and her deal was with the Devil.

15.
COURT

Owain was not known for his punctuality, but he left the pickup steaming and took off towards Wistmans Wood at a sprint with ten minutes to spare. The moor was empty, tourists and locals alike having retired to the pub or their homes for an evening meal now that the heat was subsiding. It was only the third time Court had been called in his memory and it wasn't something to be done lightly. As Huntmaster Gabriel's word carried a lot of weight, but the elders would be expecting to hear about something vitally important, or deeply dangerous, for all of the Clan. They would question why he had allowed the hounds to be tampered with; what had distracted him from his endless watch over their safety, and human lives were of no concern. He would focus on the threat to the Clan, explain that he suspected that there was a more far reaching plan afoot, but would that be enough? The Clan had dwindled and it would take a grave threat for the Council to risk any lives, let alone those of their diminutive army. It was all a risk; and there was Asterra of course.

Late sunlight settled on the leaves of the stunted oaks and seeped through the newer growth, dripping into the glade as green gold light. The forest was solemn and the first bite of evening chill was chasing the heels of the day. All of the Clan was waiting as Owain skidded to his place at Gabriel's side.

"Draw the wards. The Court is assembled." The Herald of the King brought his staff down onto stone.

Owain had seen it done before, but it still set a

shiver in his spine and clenched his stomach tight to see, and feel, the wards being drawn. It felt like a net, each word, each symbol scratched into the trees, felt like another rope thrown across his shoulders, and all of the Clan felt the same; when Court was called they were bound as one to the verdict. Fresh sap oozed from each new line carved into the bark, cutting open old scar tissue where the wards had been drawn in countless years past.

The masked figure stopped to draw the final ward in the gnarled oak behind Owain, and he couldn't resist turning his head to watch. Her slim figure was displayed to her advantage by the clinging blue dress that fell in ripples from the silver belt at her waist like the midnight sea. But there was a sharpness to her grace, a keenness with which she sank her blade into the scarred flesh of the tree that was not wholesome or womanly. Her pale fingers sheathed the knife as she whispered the last words to pull the wards tight and lock all those assembled together until a decision was made. Then she pulled off the mask and nodded towards the stone dais where the King stood. Owain glanced back at Gabriel beside him, but his eyes were fixed straight ahead and his lips were set in a thin line.

"Begin," said the Herald of the King.

It was a moment before Gabriel spoke. Owain sensed the hollowness of the unoccupied space at his left hand; they were two with no one else in the Clan to vouch for their word, and to risk a Clan life for a human one was treason.

"This is good earth," Gabriel said, "between the rocks the roots of the trees run deep. The rivers team with fish and at night the high tors whistle with the winds music. This is our earth and we are strong here."

There were murmurs of agreement from the crowd, and Owain returned a few smiles. No contentious topics so far.

"You may not always see me, but you know that I am tasked to patrol our borders, watch over our lands and protect what is ours and good. I am your Huntmaster and in autumn when the nights grow long and dark I ride out to remind mortals that we own the seasons, and the night and the dawn and the dusk and the day."

A few spat the taste from their mouth at the mention of mortals, but more laughed quietly to themselves, or knowingly shared a look with their neighbour, remembering a time when they had seen a human flee from their Devil.

"You know that I lead the hounds, and that in order to lead them I made a blood sacrifice at Houndain to bind them to my will alone. It is with these hounds that I protect our borders and keep our lands safe from any intruders who may seek to enter with quarrelsome intention. I am your safeguard and you trust in me."

The response was muted this time. Traditionally the Clan would assemble to watch the spectacle that was the binding of the pack to their new Master, but there was a number who saw it as an unsavoury necessity rather than a tradition to be proud of. They were happy to leave the mysteries of the pack to the Huntmaster. Mostly. That, and the fact that by now most must have guessed that there was something unpleasant coming; Court wasn't called to brag about how well protected their lands were.

Owain saw that Asterra had taken up a position on the right hand side of the stone dais, and that her face was currently twisted into a vision of hatred. There was no more time for candied words or drawing on pride from the past; it was time to speak fear and harness it.

"Someone else is trying to raise my hounds," said Gabriel.

The effect was immediate. Owain shut his eyes and felt the wards strain under the burgeoning bubble of panic. The hounds were sacred; old magic in blood and bone. It took serious power to redirect their loyalty.

"They succeeded in raising only one, and that was for a short amount of time. But it was long enough for the rogue hound to be seen by humans, not that they remember the encounter now."

Owain's keen ears dredged through and intensified the whispers rippling around the clearing.

"More interaction with humans. Are we protecting them now?"

"To take a hound is an act of war."

"Who would do this? The Clan in Avalon are allies."

"If he can't control the hounds, are our borders safe?"

"If he can't control the hounds, why is he Huntmaster?" Asterra's voice rang clear and cold above the hubbub.

The Herald of the King brought his staff down on the stone of the natural dais again and considered her sternly. She dipped her head in the most minimal bow of apology and he conceded to pass her his staff, giving her permission to be heard. The chatter thinned to whispers and then a heavy silence.

"The title of Huntmaster is both a responsibility and a privilege. Only the strongest are raised to the role. How many of you have given up a son as meat for the hounds?"

Couples quietly clasped hands. It was merciless and her words cut to the bone.

Owain watched her without making eye contact; the fury in her gaze was too stinging and he needed to think. Hurt alone wouldn't sway the Clan to her view, but she knew the scabs to pick and she wasn't afraid to draw blood. Her knuckles were bone white on the hand that clasped the oak staff and she gripped it like a weapon. Each time Court is called a new staff is carved from the living wood of one of the ancient oak trees; as the still green leaves wilt they are supposed to remind all there that whatever discord or danger is being discussed has the potential to weaken them as a Clan. Spend too long squabbling and, like the cut oak, we will wither and die.

"Tell me, are we rushing our sons to their deaths for an incapable and impotent Huntmaster who cannot even keep control of his pack?" Asterra snarled.

The assembled crowd were restless. To dare question the Huntmaster was uncommonly bold, and it was akin to questioning the core values of society as they knew it. If their Huntmaster was fallible, then who could they trust to keep them and their children safe?

Gabriel waited for the swell of talk to pass.

The Herald of the King took the staff from Asterra, his tread for a moment seeming weary, and motioned to Gabriel that he should speak.

Wordlessly, Gabriel unlaced the black doublet he wore and pushed up the sleeves of the grey shirt beneath.

"I speak to you as I am. As I have been made." The glamour cracked and peeled away, washing him clean of humanity and leaving him as Gemma had seen him at Grimspound. No one there was shocked by the pale skin drawn tight across sharp cheekbones, the dark eyes or the vicious spikes that poured down his spine and bristled from his forearms. "There is a terrorist tampering with our pack. Fae blood stains the stone at Houndain. Their plans, whatever they are, extend to using the feral as an organised attack force. They are risking our exposure to nearby humans and sending out a message to other Clans that we are weak. But this is not the case. They are not yet aware of how much we know, which leaves them vulnerable to our attack. The main evidence of their activities lies at Grimspound. I say join me as I remake my bond with the hounds and send out our best fighters beside me as I bring our fury to this traitor."

The hush trembled but held. On the dais, the Herald of the King leaned heavily on his staff.

"Do you know the nature of this traitor that you say we are dealing with?" He asked.

"He knows our ways," said Gabriel, "and to play at leading the hounds he must be of our kind."

"But what is it that he wants from these actions?"

Gabriel looked down at the trampled wildflowers and moss. Already the thin grass was turning brown after being crushed underfoot.

"I don't know."

"What evidence did you find at Grimspound?"

"Disturbed earth. The feral attacked us. It was clear that we were not wanted there."

"You say the feral attacked you? They did not run when you challenged them?"

Owain took half a step forward.

"I've never seen anything like it. I know most of you see them as wretches too foul to look upon, or as a night tale to scare young ones, and I would have agreed with you. But they acted in a way that I've never seen before; they were focused on killing us, outmatched as they were."

Gabriel put the back of his hand to Owain's chest, and the apprentice was immediately aware of what he had done. The Herald of the King was eyeing him with a creased forehead.

"My apologies, I should have asked to speak." Owain dropped to one knee and hung his head.

"You may rise apprentice," said the Herald of the King, "your words were hasty but important to hear. Are these feral destroyed?"

"The leader and one other."

"The feral have no leader!"

"Is this not proof?" cried Asterra, her hand grasping eagerly for the staff. "Even the feral see his weakness. What Huntmaster has ever been unable to turn back those senseless beasts?"

A shrivelled oak leaf fell from the staff and slowly spiralled to the ground.

"Silence," said the King.

The small corner of newsprint was still crushed in Gemma's palm as she threw the bunkhouse door shut behind her. The air outside was cool and smelt of baked earth and dry grass; the last breath of the day. Mike had never mentioned where he lived but she knew it was in Princetown. She turned left past the Fox Tor Café and strode towards the dull frontage of the Plume of Feathers. If anyone knew where he was they'd be there.

"Mike," she told the young man at the bar, "he drinks in here all the time. I really need to speak to him. Do you know where he lives?"

The man redoubled his concentration on the glass

he was polishing.

"I can't say I know who you mean," he said.

"Come on. Older guy, drinks a lot, covered in tattoos of keys."

The barman shook his head.

"Have you tried calling him?"

"No. Do you have his number?"

"Can't say I do."

Gemma balled both hands into fists, clenching them shut until her nails bit into her palms and the black letters of the newspaper were printed onto her skin. The man couldn't be oblivious to the pubs best customer, unless he'd been sampling some of the special brew they were doling out to customers after the hellhound attacked.

"This is important. Please," she said.

"Ryan, we're out of Baskerville. Change the barrel would you?" It was the landlord that Gemma had last seen ushering drinkers to safety out back.

"Is he new?" Gemma asked after Ryan had retreated towards the cellar.

"We have a high staff turnover," said the landlord grimly.

"My name's Gemma, and I was wondering if-"

"I know. Luke." He offered a large calloused hand, the knuckles reddened from years of working with cleaning products. Gemma shook it. "Mike's tough enough you know."

"I know, I just, really need to ask him something." A thought struck her. "It's about one of his stories." That sounded better than explaining her demonic predicament and the fact that her best friend was buried alive.

"Here." Luke was drawing a crude map on a

beermat. "It's maybe five minutes walk."

She smoothed out the creased article over the beer mat as she walked. The family of walkers were still missing. Search and Rescue had flown over the area of the moor where they were last seen, and on the ground rescue workers and volunteers had swept the heather and hills. The search area was being widened, but it seemed likely they were looking for bodies now. *Or bits of them*. How much would a monstrous undead hound waste after all?

The house number was missing, but reading those on the properties either side Gemma guessed that she was standing outside Mike's house. The front garden was overgrown, with evidence of a vegetable patch that had been planted and forgotten, containing a few stringy potato plants being choked by weeds. The path leading up to the door was cracked, with wiry grass pushing up through gaps in the paving, although a line worn bare down the middle suggested that it was still used. She knocked twice, rattling brittle panes of glass in the dry wood. Shadows deepened in the corners of the garden, a slight breeze rustled the dry seed heads of weeds and wild poppies. There was no answer and the house was suddenly uninviting. She shuffled back and felt something cold against her foot. Before she could think, a squeak had whistled though her teeth and she had thrown herself sideways into a woody buddleia bush. A few gardens down a fox called to its mate and on the path in front of her the horseshoe settled face down after being knocked from its perch on the step.

The sweet scent of the purple flowers clung to Gemma's clothes as she dredged the larger twigs from her hair. She picked up the horseshoe, transferring a dusting of red rust onto her fingers. The placing seemed deliberate and further convinced her that Mike wasn't in. But why leave a rusty old horseshoe there? She twirled it quickly in her fingers, shaking gritty flakes from the weathered iron.

"Iron," she said aloud. A roosting bird clucked at her from a nearby tree and the fox called again impatiently. It was a paragraph that she had skim read on the internet; fairies hated iron and you could protect your house from them with a horseshoe. She laughed aloud, sending the bird flapping indignantly away to find a quieter tree. *Fairies in the garden are the least of our concerns*.

Without Mike to guide her she felt less sure about the idea. But his absence worried her further; she couldn't just sit in the dark on a bunk bed and do nothing. She gripped Adrian's car keys like a promise.

Every head in the clearing turned with rapt attention to the King. He took the oak staff from his bowing servant and stepped to the very front of the dais, where the natural stone was worn flat and low. His black hair hung long and straight about his shoulders, a crown of woven oak branches tangled into it. He wore a fitted tunic, edged with gold and belted at the waist, and his feet were wrapped in soft leather boots that came to the knee. Compared to his masked runewriter and the leaf cloaked servant who spoke his wishes his attire was plain, be he needed no ornament to display his power. Gabriel dipped to one knee and the crowd mirrored his gesture.

The King indicated that all could rise.

"The behaviour of the feral surprises me, and the matter of the hound is of great concern. But this individual has not challenged us outright, who knows if they even still live? To raise a hound without adequate control over it is to risk being consumed by it. Have you seen the individual you believe to be responsible?" he directed the question at Gabriel.

"I have not."

"Then take your apprentice and renew your bond with the pack, whoever may wish to observe can join you. As for the feral, they are a ruined race that should rightfully have been culled generations ago. Reducing their numbers will no doubt put to rest any delusions of equality." The King turned to retake his seat on the stone throne, the movement dislodging another curled leaf from the staff.

"My King," pressed Gabriel, "but what of the disturbed earth at Grimspound? There is more to this than can be seen on the surface, I know it. Something foul is unfolding in our midst, before our very eyes. Let us not be blind to it."

The King turned sharply, the base of the staff dragging a circle on the dry stone.

"We were bold once, but these are not our years. This Clan is kept safest by courting peace, not war. I will not risk our exposure by sending out my guard to scare off some nomadic dabbler digging for treasure. We will halve the feral; that is a gesture of strength enough. If anyone meddles with our hounds again Huntmaster, then kill them."

"But there are other lives at stake if this lunatic is loose on the moor," cried Owain.

"Let me be clear apprentice, human lives should never have been our concern, and never will be again. To risk any Clan life for a mortal is treason." He struck the staff to the floor and there was no more to be said.

Asterra left as soon as the wards were lifted, her long dress pulling the petals from wildflowers as she stalked off through the woods. Weakness disgusted her and she was surrounded by it; the talking husks of a once imperious race, reduced to hiding in the forest like fawns. She stood at the edge of the woods, watching the moonlit Dart race along below, catching up the occasional dry stem of gorse and dragging it along in the flow. When her brother and his apprentice were dead she would turn her attention to the King. Tonight Fian would raise the hounds. She examined her long fingernails lazily; the red dye on the tips had been partially rubbed away after scrubbing off the sticky tree sap. But fresh stain was easy enough to find. Her eyes narrowed.

Gemma stumbled once and caught her fingers in vicious spikes of gorse, but as soon as she was out on the open moor the path was easy enough to follow if she kept her eyes on the ground. It seemed further, moving between a walk and a run, balancing on boulders scattered across dry stream beds and gurgling natural springs. But the moon was near full and the dark splodge on the rise ahead was where it said it should be on the map. She climbed the final stile, catching the faint murmur of the Dart on the night breeze and looked ahead towards Wistmans Wood.

In the velvet shadows caught up round the edge of the wood Asterra drew a slow breath. On the air she tasted limestone and earth, distant decay, and swirling nightcooled water. Through her bare feet she felt the pull of deep unseen tributaries, patient and slow beneath the earth. She emptied her lungs in a single note, and her voice was the crystal cry of the Dart. She sung as she walked; sculpting the high tors with her voice, singing of spring and the greening of the earth. She sung of the heat of summer, the searing days and long dry evenings where the soil shrank and gaped with thirst. She sung of the clinging autumn and the first crisp dry frost that burns off too soon.

The woods were near, but Gemma realised she had forgotten to bring any water. The walk had been further than the map suggested and she was unpleasantly reminded that she had allowed her tea to go cold untouched. The busy water of the Dart sounded so soothing and fresh, becoming louder with each step she took closer to the woods. It probably wasn't good to drink, but if she could just dip her hands in and perhaps splash some on her face. That would be refreshing. Then she could start looking for the fenced off section of the woods.

She turned left and began walking easily downhill. The nearer she got, the more the running water sounded like an actual melody. It made her think of long summer days and sleeping on dry grass in the sun, but most of all it made her thirsty. Maybe she could cool her toes in the shallows for a second.

Asterra let the water close around her feet, then creep up her thighs to her waist. It was crisp and cold, and deep below the surface she could feel the current swirl fast and strong. A wicked smile pulled her mouth wide and turned up the corners of her lips as she turned to the bank with open arms.

Gemma pulled off her shoes without undoing them and tossed her socks aside. She didn't bother rolling up her jeans, and as she stepped into the water she felt them grow heavy as the fibres swelled. Lapping at her

217

knees the water was soothing and clear. It was singing to her about how it hurt to be dammed and blocked and bridged and turned, about how wearing it was to turn the heavy spokes of a waterwheel. It told her how in some places stone caged it and in others banks had been built high to hold it in. But why were people afraid? When it was so pure and beautiful and good. Gemma felt the water close over her head. It was refreshing and really she deserved it, after all that people had done to the river. She was ready to just float away when a hand roughly grabbed her by the throat and pulled her back to the surface. Her lungs were suddenly burning and she choked on air, stretching her stilled chest and spitting water.

"Dart, Dart, cruel Dart, every year thou claim'st a heart," sang Asterra, "and the river shall have your heart child. But first I want to tell you a story. Don't worry, it isn't a long rambling one like Michael tells; I will get straight to the point. Gabriel wears a red coat when he leads the hounds. This is unusual, as it is a tradition held by your human huntmasters. But he always did have a fascination with humans. So much so, in fact, that when the time came for him to be raised from apprentice to Master he decided to do it with a certain flair. A sacrifice must be made to the hounds. It could be a full antlered deer or a fine russet fox, but these were not to Gabriel's taste. He laid a scent from the moor down to Houndain and he waited for your mortal hunt to ride out. And ride they did, and their hounds followed the trail down, down, down and their hunt master followed them in his scarlet jacket with his silver horn. And his horse crashed through the thorns and reared wild eyed in the hollow. And we looked on as Gabriel set the Wisht Hounds upon him and he took the scarlet jacket from his back while the hounds

218

still prowled for scraps."

Gemma was shivering in her wet clothes. Images in red swum before her and bile burnt at the back of her throat.

"That would have been your fate too child, if I hadn't spared you for the river."

The grip was loosening. Gemma's hand closed around metal in her pocket. She was falling, but at the same she was lifting the old horseshoe and slamming it as hard as she could against the moon pale face. She felt it make contact. And then there was the water.

16.
RISE

"But why were you carrying a horseshoe?"

Gabriel pushed Owain's eager face aside and looked down at Gemma. She coughed again and sat up to retch the last of the water from her lungs.

"Get her the spare cloak from the safe house," Gabriel told Owain.

The coughing subsided, leaving Gemma's teeth chattering violently, her wet clothes clinging and chilling her in the night air. Gabriel watched Owain sprint rapidly in the direction of the hidden shelter and then turned back to Gemma, taking her hands and rubbing each one between his until they felt warm. Then, having no coat or jacket to put over her he sat beside her and wrapped his arms around her until the shivering slowed. They were a strange pair, sitting there by the bank of the Dart in the moonlight.

Owain returned minutes later, and Gabriel took the cloak and tucked it around Gemma's shoulders.

"I mean, where did you get it?" Owain continued.

Gemma chattered a half laugh. "It was in Mike's front garden. I just put it in my pocket. It's meant to deter fairies."

"It would deter most things when applied directly to the face," Owain said.

"We heard the cry of the Dart, and we were nearly too late."

"The river," said Gemma, springing upright, "it was speaking to me."

Owain nodded. "The Dart requires the sacrifice of

one life each year. It's cry is the song that lures the victim in."

"But there was a woman."

Gabriel snapped to his feet and strode a pace away.

"My sister."

"That was your sister trying to kill me?"

"She is a wytch. She has the right to call the cry of the Dart on a lone mortal wandering the moors in the night."

Gemma's mouth fell open. Clearly a spot of light murder was of no consequence between siblings. Everything she had read, everything Elaine had told her, even the display in the Visitor Centre was warning her to stay the hell away. But Gabriel had promised to save Adrian, and in the moonlight his skin was warm and it smelt of woodsmoke and honey.

"Owain left you safely in town." Gabriel's eyes blazed as he turned back around.

"I did," said Owain.

"So why have we just dredged you out of the river?"

Gemma hung her head and pulled the cloak tighter about herself.

"I thought that if I could find Mike we could come here together and make people understand what's at stake. He wasn't at home, but I looked online and Legendary Dartmoor told me that the Wild Hunt rode out from Wistmans Wood, so it made sense to look here first."

"Gemma," said Gabriel softly, "you are the only *person* here. My Clan do not share your ways and would have no time for your reason. It is a lack on their part, but I can no more change them than I can reverse the flow of the river."

She looked down at the tight knit fibres of the soft wool cloak and knew that the same deft fingers that had made it would be just as nimble around her neck.

"Then why not kill me yourself?" With blank eyes she let the cloak fall from her shoulders. Her top hung off below one collarbone and the dark blotches on her neck promised blossoming bruises in the shape of fingers. "Why am I a mortal to be saved?"

"I have protected your bloodline for many years."

"But why? What am I worth to you?"

"An unbroken vow." Gabriel caught Gemma by the arm and pulled her to her feet.

Shaking his hand off, she bent to grab the cloak from the damp grass. Clearly he was in the mood to keep his motives to himself, and why shouldn't he be? If his kind had the right to kill as they chose what more right did she have to ask why than the fox had the right to ask the hound?

"Can we save Adrian now?" She only had to keep Gabriel's attention long enough to get Adrian dug up safely, and then they could drive home in his old Beetle and forget the moor and all of its mysteries and go back to the comforting belief that none of this stuff was real.

Owain fell into step beside her as they walked back along the path that led off of the moor. The grass was trodden flat and the earth worn away by the hundreds of tourists and travellers that walked it, lured by the beauty of the woods and curious about the quaint legends. She wondered how many had laid back on a sun warmed boulder, wiggled their toes in the light, leafy earth and dreamt of being in their own adventure. She wondered how many had wandered alone and not returned.

"The King agreed that the behaviour of the feral and the incident with the hound was very concerning, "Owain told Gemma awkwardly.

If she didn't catch herself, it was too easy to forget he was a cold blooded killer and talk to him like she might to Adrian. But he would lead the hounds one day.

"So he'll help?"

Owain carefully refolded the cuff of his shirt.

"No."

Gemma stopped walking.

"So this is it? He just says no. I thought it was an issue for your security as well? I thought someone messing with the hounds was serious for your, whatever they are, as well? In fact, just what are you if you aren't people?"

"Fae," said Owain.

"Fae. You're bloody fairies. Is that why Mike had an iron horseshoe set up in front of his house? Was it to keep you out?"

"Iron burns our skin," explained Owain helpfully, "It doesn't technically keep us out."

"Then why might he want to burn your skin?"

"Why might I be stupid enough to pick it up?" said Owain.

Gemma kicked a small stone on the path and sent it skittering out into the darkness. She imagined what it might be like buried inside that mound; complete darkness without the moon or stars, and no voice to tell you that it would be ok.

"Well I'm still going to rescue him. If you could just not let your friends kill me until I've done that."

"We're still going to rescue him," said Gabriel

from ahead.

"But we have no army. You said it would be too dangerous."

"It is. But I told you I would save your Adrian, so I will."

Tears were running down Gemma's face as Owain patted her gently on the back.

"You seemed ready enough to die earlier." Gabriel said grimly.

They walked to Houndain. The damp hollow pooled shadow, darkness lapping at the twisted trunks of the trees, deep green leaves glinting wetly between the thorns. Above them the moon was still bright. Owain set Gemma down on her feet and she realized that at some point on the journey she must have fallen asleep as she walked and he had carried her.

"Fetch our sacrifice," Gabriel told Owain.

He dipped his head and turned heel out towards the swathes of sun crisped bracken.

"There should be more," said Gabriel, rolling up the sleeves of his shirt, "when I bound myself to the hounds before all of the Clan were around me. Their strength was with me also, and it helped me to complete my task."

"But you have grown stronger," Owain reappeared with an antlered roe deer thrown across his shoulder.

"But I despise them. I despise myself, and if they see that in me they will eat me alive. What wishes to be shackled to something so broken?"

Gemma reached out and touched Gabriel's hand; she did it without thinking and grabbed her hand back when he shied away, as if it were an electric shock.

"I'm not made of iron," she said.

"No." He looked at her very intensely for a moment, the moonlight dancing over stormy blue of his eyes and the dark pupil searching and searching... for something he did not find. He turned away, disappointed.

"Your sister told me about the first time you raised the hounds," Gemma said. She saw Gabriel's shoulders slump further and rushed on. "I don't think you're a monster. I think you're just very good at being who you need to be. Your Clan needed that then, and you needed to show them that you had the strength to do what you had to do. And if they believed that you had the strength, then just maybe you could have it, and you have had it, all of these years."

Owain had laid the buck down and was listening thoughtfully.

Gabriel turned slowly back to face Gemma. She was lightly breathless from speaking so fast and her heart was pounding against the bars of her chest like a battle drum.

"Is your belief truly that strong?" he asked her.

None of it was lying. She hadn't had the chance to mull over her moral opinion on sacrificing a human hunt whilst being strangled in the river. But as she had spoken the words that came out somehow made sense, as if they had bypassed her questioning mind and arrived pure from somewhere else.

"Yes," she said.

"And I have every faith in you too," said Owain, hoisting the deer back into position.

"Then we begin," purred Gabriel. A predatory smile curled up the corners of his pale lips and when he moved it was with a deadly grace. He glanced briefly at

Gemma, instructing her to not be afraid, and that glimpse of hair shining like spun silver and bottomless darkling eyes seared into her and set something boiling inside.

"Wait," hissed Owain.

In a moment they had retreated back into the tall bracken and huddled crouched in the shadows. Owain had one finger pressed to his lips, and with the other he was tapping his ear. Gemma felt a touch light as spidersilk on her skin, and guessed that Gabriel had used glamour to hide them further.

It was perhaps a minute until a small figure came slowly into view. They moved stiffly, every third step limping, and as the moonlight lit the small, pale face Gemma stifled a gasp. It was a child; a young boy.

Asterra had worn her finest gown, as this would be a night to remember. It was white, with an alternating pattern of bird skulls sewn round the neckline and a trail of mistfine silk that she had made Fian carry across the moor. When he had stumbled she had taken her bone handled whip to his scarred back, and the result was only one minor snag in the material, which she was pleased with. But now that Houndain was in sight he walked ahead of her. Tradition must be obeyed here, and she dare not walk ahead of a soon to be Huntmaster.

"You have the meat?" she asked him.

He checked for the hard lump that was a hare, already dead this time, in the leather bag by his waist.

"Yes Mistress."

"Then see this done. Call each hound by name, we need the whole pack."

If he hadn't been beyond worrying, Fian would have been concerned about the legitimacy of the list he had been given; names transcribed from the slurred speech of a weary Huntmaster, now dead by his own devices. But the potion Asterra had forced down his throat burned hot in his veins, and for once he couldn't feel the aches of his battered body and his mind was the sharpest it had been since she took him. She didn't need to tell him that the power he felt surging within him was borrowed, but tonight he would use it and he felt comforted by the certainty that channelling it would burn him to ash from the inside out. Then Asterra would be left for the pack. He smiled a genuine smile and pushed aside the hawthorn to step into the hollow.

The stone altar was the only spot that caught a shaft of moonlight, piercing the canopy of leaves and lighting the still stained stone. Asterra paced the outside of the circle, blowing handfuls of white fire into the trees, where they sat and twinkled like fallen stars, banishing the deeper of the shadows. Fian descended the sloping bank, his feet sinking slightly into the soft earth, perpetually waterlogged even through the driest of summers. His step raised a rich smell of fertile soil, fed by countless sacrifices, and the potion thrummed in his flesh, drawing him to the altar, unsheathing the knife in his hands. All else was forgotten. He needed no prompting as he stretched the hare across the stone and opened it up so the stilled blood flowed again, out into the waiting basin. As it filled, he dragged the same knife through the latticework of scar tissue on his arm and raised a rivulet of thin liquid, which he let drip onto the earth as he paced a circle around the altar.

"Rise," he said, and the stone basin overflowed. A red line ran down the side of the altar and onto the earth.

"No!" Asterra was screaming but the sound was

distant to Fian. Beneath him the earth contracted, tearing open cracks in the grass and spewing up blackened water that smelt of old death and recent death and the promise of death yet to come.

"Fenrir, come to your Master."

A skull bobbed to the surface, dipped under and returned clothed in flesh. Fian watched as black fur crept across the muscle and two amber eyes blinked from sockets empty a moment ago. The first hound scrambled out from the earth and shook itself.

Somebody else screamed and Fian raised his hand vaguely as if to bat the sound away. The hound sniffed the air, hungry for more of the blood it had tasted in the earth. It stepped tentatively toward the altar and Fian welcomed it with open arms. But it didn't approach him. Instead, it turned and trotted up the side of the hollow. Fian spun round in confusion, his borrowed power ebbing and admitting a cold wave of terror.

Owain was holding a thrashing Asterra, her white dress smeared with mud. Fenrir sat obediently beside Gabriel, whilst a human girl made a fuss of her.

Asterra stretched out a hand and cried his name. Her lips curled round it strangely, unused to the feel. For a moment the scene was too absurd to make sense of, and then a wonderful knowledge crept over Fian. Asterra had been stopped. All of this was over. The others were gesturing to him and yelling words he couldn't make out somehow. A pleasant tiredness was washing over him and all he wanted was to sleep like he hadn't slept in years. The coolness of the earth was a wonderful relief.

Gemma stopped yelling because she thought her throat would bleed and it wasn't helping. The second hound prowled close once, twice and then made a dash

229

for the frail figure, which crumpled in its jaws.

"Do something," she begged Gabriel hoarsely.

"That is our rogue," he said, laying his hand on Fen's silky head.

"Please," Gemma said.

Owain half stepped forward and Asterra took the opportunity to elbow him in the face, twisting out of his grasp as he recoiled in pain. She thrashed against the thorn bushes, her dress snagging her like a net. Owain moved to grab her but Gabriel held an arm across him.

"Let her go," Gabriel said.

Asterra threw him a last venomous look and tore herself free, racing off and disappearing like a ghost into the moor.

"But she-" Owain began.

"Will have her fate decided at Court."

Gemma turned back to the hollow, where she caught the last glimpse of curling fingers before they disappeared below the earth.

"The boy," she whispered. Adrian's dream came back to her in a dizzying blast; again she saw darkness and close cloying soil, but now with the addition of the child being dragged down through the swilling mud gripped in ravenous jaws. And alive. Still alive.

"Now you see the true nature of the hounds," Gabriel said.

Gemma looked down at the patient Fen, and ran her hand over the hound's soft fur, looking into the amber eyes for any trace of the monster she had just seen take the child. Then she fell to her knees and hugged her, feeling the warmth of the skin under the fur and counting the beats of a convincing living heart. It was a believable mirage. But Fen was alive. Or alive in the only way that

230

she could be.

"But you make Fen like this," she said.

Gabriel looked at the ground.

"It's a weakness." He laid his hand on Fen's head and the glossy fur crackled and peeled back. Gemma forced herself not to move as oozing flesh stretched apart to reveal the pitted bone beneath, and along the jaw two rows of cracked and jagged teeth. Beneath her hands she felt the fur turn matted then slick as the skin pushed against ribs and split, and inches from her face amber eyes blinked shut to open again as searing red slits. Fen twisted to sniff her hair, leaking reddish froth from rotten gums, and the next thing Gemma knew was the rich scent of summer grass as she pressed her face onto the earth and gasped for air.

Gabriel said nothing and Fen followed him down into the hollow.

Owain had dragged the roe deer out from the bracken and was now sitting cross legged beside it.

"It's almost a waste," he said wistfully, "there's a few good meals on this."

"Small meals for all those hounds," said Gemma. Adrenalin had numbed her. She sat down beside Owain. "What happens now?"

"Isn't that enough excitement for one night?"

Gemma dropped her head into her hands. "I just want to save Adrian. That's all."

Owain wiped all humour from his face.

"I know. We have plenty of night left for that."

"But everything takes so long," she looked up at Owain, his red hair slicked back except for a few strands that had worked loose after his encounter with Asterra.

He smiled and she remembered the awkward

teenager who had scared her with the hound mask in the Visitor centre. That felt like a lifetime ago.

"Not so long ago I thought I should be allowed to raise the hounds quicker. I took Gabriel's hunt coat and I played at it like a child with carved toys. It was too soon and I looked like a fool. I imagine that you find Adrian's life more important than my dignity, so let's get it right rather than rush this time." Owain said.

Gemma gave him a watery smile.

"Hit me with our pre quest then."

"Gabriel is trying to find out how much his bond with the hounds has been damaged. No hound crossed the circle of blood that was cast, so technically no new allegiance has been made, but at least one hound is rogue already and answering to no Master."

"That's definitely a problem."

"It is. The rogue hound took the boy, but it could just as easily have gone after one of us."

"But why did he do it, why try to raise the hounds?"

"I doubt it was any of his choosing. Asterra is behind all of this."

"That's Gabriel's sister?"

Owain nodded.

"She's a bitch," said Gemma.

Owain barked a short laugh, leaning his back against the cold bulk of the deer.

"She has overstepped her mark this time, that's beyond doubt," he said.

"Wait," said Gemma, "I'm sure you told me that anyone else other than you who was born able to lead the hunt was fed to the hounds anyway. How did he manage to stay alive?"

Owain sighed, reclining on his grisly throne. He had plucked a long stem of grass and was peeling it layer by layer back to the stem.

"I know what you must think of us. I've watched humans for long enough to have some understanding of how you feel. Our ways are not your ways, and as much as I might sometimes wish that it were different it is right that each of us is unique to ourselves. But greed is a human trait. That boy would have been kept to be caged and sold to the highest bidder as a weapon. And a wasteful, ineffective one at that." Owain stood suddenly, his eyes darting to the hollow below. "We begin."

He threw the deer back onto his shoulder and strode down the slope towards Gabriel and the altar. Gemma followed hesitantly. The horror wasn't new now but the knowledge of what was to come already turned her stomach. Success would be monstrous, but failure deadly.

"Wait on the edge of the hollow," commanded Gabriel, "if it looks like I will fail, run and warn the Clan."

Owain nodded quickly and laid the stocky deer across the altar, still glistening with the blood of the previous sacrifice. Then Gemma felt his hand on her shoulder, steering her back up the slope and away from the blackened grass and the suffocating sweet smell that she knew would haunt her senses for years. Next Owain had left her and he was dressing Gabriel in a tattered old hunt coat, snagged and stained and looking as if it had spent some years buried in the earth. For a moment Gabriel's shoulders seemed to sag under the weight of the threadbare wool, but then he was transformed.

Owain was back beside her as Gabriel pulled the knife from his belt, raised it high, and neatly slit the

233

carcass from throat to stomach, spilling entrails and blood alike. Already overflowing, the shallow basin disgorged its gory contents, shooting rivulets down each side of the altar until the whole stone seemed to be a seeping, flowing mass of red. Gemma felt the soil shift beneath her feet and gripped a rough trunk of hawthorn to steady herself. Gabriel laughed and it was the wind whipping through the trees on a winters night and the rattle of icebound twigs on the glass when you've locked all your doors at night and you're praying the darkness can't get in.

Gabriel laced the heaving earth with his own blood, nimbly stepping across the widening black pools and casting a circle wider than Fian's. The first hound was already sniffing at the blood as Gabriel completed the circle, and soon it was joined by a second and third. It was hard to tell Fen apart from them now, except that she was already inside the circle, prowling restlessly in wait for her command to begin the feast.

"Gelert," called Gabriel. The air was still and stifling. In the summer heat the smell of rotting carcasses was thick and clinging. One of the hounds pricked up its ears.

Gemma felt Owain's grip tighten on her shoulder and she held her breath as Gelert sniffed the thin line of blood one last time, then raised a paw and stepped inside the circle. At Gabriel's nod he tore the liver from the deer and settled to eat his prize. Another hound yipped and whined as two more dragged themselves from the earth to line the outside of the circle.

"Skriker, Valefor," Gabriel called the hounds by name and they accepted his blood right in exchange for the meat.

"Guinefort, Barghest, Shuck," he called and they came, slick fur dripping pus and earth, slack jaws hanging open in expectation.

"Gytrash, Sirius."

Gemma counted the hounds and there were only eight.

"Sirius," Gabriel called. Fen pawed impatiently at the earth, then turned sharply, tufts of fur prickling up along her spine. The night was filled with the squelch and crunch of the hounds eating, but Gemma was tense and straining her ears for another sound. The earth inside the circle seemed to breathe, and then a small section fell in on itself, just large enough to be a grave.

"There!" she screamed.

Fen had already dipped her head, the visible muscles of her legs tensed to pounce. The final hound climbed out of the earth and shook itself. Gemma gasped. It was pure white. She stared as the gore slid slowly off its fur. Not pure white after all. Its ears were both stained a deep red at the tips.

Gemma felt Owain slowly pulling her backwards.

"It has not crossed the line," he hissed, "there is no pact made here."

Wordlessly, Gabriel had gathered all the other hounds behind him.

"Sirius," he called again, "join your pack, or be devoured by them."

The white hound whined low and shook his head as if something was irritating him, then took a clumsy step forward. He made a sudden rush up the slope and Fen sprang at him, her jaws closing around his neck. He seemed to ignore her, more intent on rubbing his red ears against the yielding grass.

"Something's wrong," said Owain.

The white hound was limp in Fen's grip, as if exhausted. The others waited, and the night crept on.

"Fian," Gemma whispered. Asterra had called him that.

"What did you say?" said Owain.

"Fian!" She yelled it as loudly as her stinging throat would allow.

The hound struggled feebly and Gabriel gestured for Fen to let it go. Pricking up its strange red ears, it looked up towards Gemma.

"Fian," she called again, pulling loose from the startled Owain and meeting the hound at the bottom of the slope.

"It's still rogue!" Owain yelled.

"But it needs no Master now," she said, reaching out to let the hound sniff her hand.

"There is no hound without a Master. End it," Gabriel commanded. The hounds turned as one and Gemma moved without thinking. She stood in front of the white animal and glared back at the eight pairs of red eyes.

"No," she said.

17.
TREASURE

Dusk was creeping over Grimspound. In a dark green Range Rover, a father and daughter were drinking tea from a flask. Next to them the road snaked away into the rising mist, exhaled as the moor cooled for the night. There was space for another car in the small pull-in but camera clutching tourists and seasoned walkers alike had left with the sun.

"It's getting dark," said the girl.

"Not dark enough," her father replied. He drummed impatiently on the leather steering wheel while she poured out the last small cup of Earl Grey from the flask.

"I imagined it would be more interesting." She dipped a small silver spoon back into a pot of sugar and tried to balance the most heaped mound possible.

"You haven't seen them yet."

"They're all the same though aren't they? It's all the same after a while."

"This will be different. The collector who wants this piece is willing to pay. A lot. We can have a house again. You can have a horse." He plucked at the cuff of his tweed jacket in agitation. The wool was thin between his fingers and he could feel a chill where the garment was threadbare at the elbows. The girl stirred the huge spoonfull of suger into her tea and dipped the wet spoon back into the pot to get some more.

"I don't want a horse," she said.

"Well you can have whatever you want Evangeline." His concentration had skipped briefly over the travel worn suitcases and unwashed clothes on the back seats and then settled outside the car, monitoring the thickness of the progressing night.

"That's not true." She knew better than to sound angry, but her words would have made midnight seem balmy. If her father heard, he chose to ignore her.

"It can be like old times again," his voice had turned dreamy.

Eva pulled a book from the doorcard and purposefully hid her face behind 'Dartmoor Air Crashes'. She had stolen it from the National Trust shop in Widecombe-in-the-Moor the day before and was looking forward to reminding herself that yes, life could certainly be worse. She was about to find out just what had caused a Spitfire to crash in Widecombe when a rush of cool air told her that her door was open.

"It's dark enough," said her father. He had his black wax trenchcoat on and his old hunting rifle was slung across his back in its case. Just past full, the moon was brightening , but he also gripped a camping lamp in case. Eva poured the last of her tea onto the gravel and pulled her brown riding coat from the back of the car.

"I hate walking," she told his disappearing back. Then she thrust her hands in her coat pockets, kicked the car door shut, and followed.

The outer wall of Grimspound soon came into sight. Eva slowed her pace. Another ancient momument. Another precious artefact to dig up. There had been an endless parade of saints armour, magic swords, sacred knives and other scrap metal; dead treasures to decorate the libraries of men who would soon be dead themselves. Perhaps they thought that if they could amass enough of these priceless finds they could somehow absorb their importance and transcend history. But the swords were just rusty and the collectors just died. Time rolled on.

A hand caught her arm. "Yeah I'm coming," she said. The grip grew tighter, threatening a bruise, and she looked up to yell at her father. But instead of tired blue eyes she looked into two dark pits set in a shrivelled stonegrey skull. And not far beneath them was a wide, thin lipped mouth bristling with rows of flintsharp teeth. The feral was starving. It pushed her to the ground and made a lunge for her neck, the unpleasant teeth shutting with a grim click millimetres from her skin. She could smell its breath, stinking like something rotten in water, as she bunched up her legs and drove her knee upwards as hard as she could. It felt like running hard into a dirty leather armchair. Pain blossomed in her knee and the night peeled back. The smell of her mother on the riding jacket was overwhelming. She breathed the sweet dusty hay and the warm horsehair that were the scents of home. She felt the shiny coat of the mare that her father would brush to perfection but never, ever ride, and the ache that had been part of her since she was born stretched open until she felt sure it would eat her alive.

"Leave her!" Benjamin Maker chanelled all the authority he could command into the words. It was effective. He was transformed. The feral cowered back from him.

"You take no payment until the dagger is delivered into my hand. And she is not to be touched. Ever."

The feral lowered its head and gurgled a low noise that may have meant yes. It was a particularly poor specimen; clearly starving with each sharp rib pushed tight against graveyard skin. It had grown too frightened of the light to hunt in the day, and people were wise

239

enough to stay home at night. The necromancer's offer of a meal was half of a necessary bargain. And it wasn't much effort to guard the stone hut circles at night. It would find patience, for now.

"Eva, are you hurt?" Benjamin fell down beside her, catching up her shoulders so her head could lean back against his chest. She was taking deep measured breaths, but her skin had no blood left in it. "Did it happen again?" he asked. Eva twitched a nod. It wasn't always the same, but there was always her mother, the stables and the terrible gravity that tugged her down to somewhere dark.

"It's your gift. It's getting stronger."

"I don't want it." The blackouts were a disability that had struck ocasionally as a child, an inevitable end to long evenings of her father using whisky and the rifle to help himself forget that her mother was dead. They had got more frequent through her teenage years and now seemed to be triggered by any kind of shock. When the bailiffs came for the house, there wasn't an item left intact.

"I shouldn't have brought you up here, I'm sorry."

"No," Eva pushed him away and swayed to her feet, " like I said, it's all the same. I should be used to it by now."

"If you push yourself, if you try to use it..."

The words dissolved under an acid glare.

"If it all works this time, if your creeps can actually find this dagger, if whatever arthritic toothless collector it is that wants this junk actually pays up; if all of those unlikely things actually happen, I don't want a horse. I can even live without a house; it's been long enough. But I would really, really like to just be bloody normal."

Benjamin watched her walk off towards the ruined village. It would work this time, he told himself, it would work.

He stepped over the fallen stones where the Victorians had punched a hole in the outer wall for their convenience, and noticed a few feral slinking around the hut circles. Eva sat on the stone remains of the chiefs hut, holding her book close to her face as she tried to read it by moonlight. Benjamin reached into the inner pocket of his jacket and produced a small silver hipflask which he quickly upturned into his mouth.

"Let's begin," he told no one.

It was hard for Adrian to tell if his eyes were open or not. His arms and legs were tied, and the darkness around him felt like it could go on for inches, or miles. But the air smelt stale and peaty, so he guessed he was underground.

"Hello," he whispered. His mouth was dry and sore.

"You're awake too. Must mean it's nearly dark," a female voice replied. They knock you out enough to sleep through the day."

"Is there-"

"No. Just us. But they'll be looking; I'm running low." She coughed a small laugh.

"How long have you been here?"

"This will be the third night."

Adrian fought a wave of nausea and clenched his teeth.

"I'll get us out of here. Somehow."

"Oh it's not the in here that we need to worry about. They'll be here to dig us up soon. But all the same, don't put that pressure on yourself. I have no fear of moving on. I sent my John on trustful enough and I hope to see him soon."

In the absoulte darkness, the wet heat on Adrian's cheeks told him that he was crying.

"I'll hold your hand then, when the time comes. If you like."

"That'd be nice enough. Thank you."

There was no spade, but that didn't hinder the undead. Fresh from the earth themself, they laboured to peel back the cut turf and remove the loose soil infilling the tunnel. That had been Benjamin's strict instruction; cut the turf and replace it to keep the digging secret. The undead didn't think about things like that. The summoning process left them with little more than control over their ragged limbs and an awful need to stay in that lesser state of dead. They drained the life force from living people to do this, and they could sense the two prisoners. It drove them to a frenzy as they dug, throwing earth behind them with skeleton fingers. The necromancer would make them clear it all later, but that was later, and for now there was life within reach.

"Stop," Benjamin's voice sliced the night air. They stilled their arms reluctantly, fists clenched with anticipation. "The feral can take this from here. You start digging the circles. I want this dagger found tonight!" Stiffly, the undead backed away, their loose jaws hanging open as they gulped the air for a taste of their denied meal. Benjamin didn't trust them, each night they got a little bolder and he didn't need that. They were no use to him gorged on life and still active in the day. The boy had been a blessing, but he still needed to make the fuel last long enough for the dagger to be found. "Tonight," he told himself with whisky breath.

"Drag them out," he told the gathered feral. "If I see so much as a scratch from a stone on one I'll feed you all to them!" he pointed a finger back towards the shambling corpses. The feral understood.

With amazing care, the two bodies were carried out into the moonlight and laid on the nightchilled grass. As Mary had instructed, Adrian stayed completely still, barely even flinching when he felt a sharp fingernail brush his cheek.

"Is the other site prepared?" Benjamin asked the slightly better fed of the feral who served as a spokesperson for the others, if not quite a leader.

"Almost. There was a lot of earth. It was difficult to make secret for the day," it replied.

Adrian nearly opened his eyes, but checked himself. The voice of the feral was dry from disuse, but beyond that not greatly different to Gabriels. It was out of place on those leather lips. Gabriel. The name burnt on his tongue. He had fed those horrible ideas to Gemma! But the heat quickly subsided. It was he, Adrian, who had dragged her here, following a stupid dream that he had been told to ignore. It was him who needed to prove that he was something different, something better. And here he was, waiting to be a meal.

The night dragged on. At one point the undead were allowed to feed and Adrian braced himself for the icy needles again. His hands hadn't been unbound and he regretted not being able to reach out to Mary, but he felt her hand on his arm; the lightest of touches. When the meal was over he whispered her name and felt a slight squeeze in answer. Still there.

He began to brave allowing his eyes to slide the

slightest bit open. There wasn't a great deal to be seen from the angle he was at, but he heard the man in tweed barking orders at the undead in an increasingly agitated manner. The word dagger was repeated often, but no progress seemed to be being made in locating it. With everyones attention elsewhere, Adrian began to very slowly roll his head to one side to get a better view of potential routes out. What he did see was a pair of boots. Involuntarily, he looked up and into the face of a young woman. For what seemed like a long time, they both stared.

"Run," Adrian said.

"Why?" Asked the woman. Her blonde hair caught the moonlight as she pushed it back behind an ear.

"This place is full of things that will eat you. Untie us then, quickly."

She stepped back. "I can't."

Adrian rolled onto his side. "Look there's a crazy guy who can bring the dead -"

"-to life. My father."

Adrian dropped his cheek onto the grass. The undead must have felt the drumming of his heart through the ground. He was surprised not to feel cold hands grabbing him immediately. There was no shouting, no teeth, no being torn limb from limb. Just the stillness of the moor and the scrape and thud of digging.

"Does it hurt when they feed?" asked the necromancer's daughter.

"Yes," said Adrian.

The girl's lips were beginning to form a word when there was a sudden commotion near one of the hut circles. She turned to go. "Wait," said Adrian. Her head turned back, hesitating. "Could you just untie my hands. I still won't be able to get anywhere but the lady here with me hasn't got long and I promised to hold her hand." It was very matter of fact, he was pleased about that.

She looked back over towards the noise. A few of the feral were clustered round her father. Then, very quickly, she pulled open a penknife from her pocket and cut the rope wrapping Adrian's wrists.

"Thank you," he said. But she was already gone. He rolled back to face his companion. "Mary," he whispered, "my hands are free." He took her right hand in both of his. It was soft and cold. "I'll get the rope off my ankles and we can run," he told her, rubbing her hand to wake up the blood. "I saw the road last night, it isn't far and we could get a lift to a hospital" The tears were coming now, dropping with pathetic thuds onto the flattened grass. "We could make it." he lied.

Mary closed her fingers slightly round his.

"Kill me John," she said.

There was no doubt it was monstrous. Gabriel's pale fingers were smeared red where the knife had turned up flecks of blood from the carcass. The blade was still gripped in his clenched fist and the ripped hunt coat hung stiff with dried on gore. It was a grotesque trophy, torn from the back of the human huntmaster that he had lured to his death.

"Get out of the way," yelled Owain.

Time slowed. In the thick darkness Gemma saw the car crash again, she saw the figure on a white horse rear up and the other driver swerve off the road. Their pain flared through her and faded, replaced by the faintest whisper as her mother told her it was an angel. A burning angel who will kill to keep a vow.

"I came here to set a spirit free. There is freedom here. Adrian would have wanted this," Gemma said. She placed her hand on the head of the docile hound and stepped towards Gabriel.

"You don't understand!" Owain was scrambling down the slope behind her, his boots squelching into the damp base of the hollow.

Gabriel's hounds formed an arc around him, still licking the taste of meat from their rotten teeth.

"The hounds are the borrowed bones of a thousand sacrifices: human, fae and animal alike. To them there is either meat or Master and nothing in between," Owain was reaching out to Gemma, gesturing for her to step back, his eyes wide and shining, "don't throw your chance to rescue Adrian away."

"This is my vow," said Gemma, "nothing else good dies if I can prevent it."

"That doesn't help us on numerous levels. Let's go," begged Owain.

Gabriel reached out to the deer carcass, deftly reached inside the ribcage and tore out the bloody heart. Without taking his gaze from Gemma, he raised it chest high and gripped tightly, crushing the stilled chambers in his fist and forcing the last of the red liquid out in a thin stream.

"There is no goodness," he said. Tossing the heart aside, he punched his bloody fist into the ground and dragged up a slimy loop of black leather. He tugged again sharply and stepped back as the other end of the strapping emerged, still lashed round a skull too large to be a hound. Nostrils flared where there had been only bone a moment ago, then a hoof still shod with a rusty shoe scraped for purchase on the soft earth and dragged a heaving empty ribcage from the soil. Then with one swift movement Gabriel had vaulted onto the horse's back and he and the hounds were gone.

Gemma turned to Owain. A second half skeletal horse was standing next to him.

"One of us is getting on that?" she asked.

"We both are." Owain pulled her onto the horse behind him and urged it forward into a canter, bursting through the narrow gap in the hawthorn and building to a drumming gallop across the moor. Fian came racing behind them like a white dart.

"The hunt is on," Owain said.

The night bled past them in a blur, Owain skilfully navigating the treacherous ground without losing any speed. They leapt across narrow gulleys and skidded down and up larger ditches, the undead horse losing chunks of peeling flesh to gorse bushes and scattered stones. Ahead of them the baying of the hounds rumbled across the moor, ringing in abandoned mine shafts, echoing off the tors and sending night creatures to their holes. Gemma had locked her arms round Owains waist, then closed her eyes to stop them streaming. The rhythm of the horse was steady beneath her but in the quiet of her head Mike's stories were screaming loudly. *There is no goodness left. Tell her to run...*

"We're coming Adrian." The wind whipped her words away.

They stopped on the low ground ahead of the first of the twin tors, rising now between them and Grimspound. Gabriel had already dismounted, and the hounds waited obediently around him. Owain gratefully peeled himself from the horse and helped Gemma down, steadying her as her legs buckled at the unfamiliar

247

sensation of solid ground. The horse crumpled immediately, folding in on itself as the invisible bonds that held bone to bone dissolved away.

Gabriel took a step forward and half raised a hand to Owain.

Gemma pushed Fian carefully behind her.

"Guard her," Gabriel said. He let his hand fall back without completing the gesture.

"What are you doing?" Owain asked.

"Scouting the perimeter. No doubt there will be feral, but the hounds will mow them down." His jaw was tight as if each word caused him pain and his fingers opened and shut impulsively on the knife now sheathed at his waist.

"And then?" pressed Owain

"Dig. When everything is dead." Gabriel turned abruptly and caught up the reins of his horse, leading it a short distance away before leaping back on and setting off at an easy trot. The hounds padded silently now, slipping through the shrub like passing shadows.

"Is this normal when he's gone all Huntmaster?"

"No," said Owain, "normally you'd be dead."

"Lucky me. Why does he go all white?"

Owain raised an eyebrow. "The pale skin is a mark of his power."

"And the-" Gemma spread her fingers into points, "spines?"

"We all have those. The feral were not so different to us once."

"You know, I can believe that. What are we going to do while Gabriel kills them all?"

"Wait here."

"Fine." Gemma eased herself down and crossed

her aching legs beneath her. The night was still and quiet, flavoured now by the faint sweet smell of bruised heather. Fian lay stretched out nearby, his paws crossed over in front of him and his head tilted towards her. The moonlight lent his white fur a soft lustre, blurring him towards the ghosts of lonely walks and drunken stories. What would Mike say now, wherever he was? If he had met the rogue hound then he wouldn't be getting the chance to tell his greatest tale. *Take that and think yourself lucky.*

"So how do the hounds work?" she asked Owain.

He lay back on the grass and gazed up at the star prickled sky.

"You said they were borrowed bones," she prompted, "is that why the child is one now?"

"That is not how it works. It's impossible."

"I'm getting used to impossible things."

Fian crept over on his belly and pushed his slender snout under her hand. She stroked his head without thinking and it was comforting. Beyond the tor a shrill screech was cut short. The feral had started dying.

"The pack is an ancient thing," said Owain softly, "no one remembers a new one being made, and as you know it takes us a long time to die. Clans fade and their packs sleep, never to return. Their fates are utterly tied; the Master uses the hounds to protect the Clan, and the Clan offer the Master any sons born with the gift; either to be trained or to give their power back to the protection of the Clan. The boy is said to be houndmarked and either fate is an honour. Their bones go on to build part of the hounds. That way they live on forever.

"Then it makes perfect sense." Gemma patted Fians strong neck and looked down into his beetleblack eyes.

"Their bones," said Owain, "not their thoughts. Not their memories. Not their name."

Fian rumbled a low growl and Gemma felt the fur rise along the back of his neck. Owain was on his feet before she thought to move.

The feral hadn't seen them. It was too preoccupied with a small bundle gripped tight to its chest. Another feral approached, its thin armspines raised aggressively.

"I found it. I present it to the Death Man."

"I dug it. He will have this gift from me." The second feral swiped at the bundle and was hit away with a growl.

"I found the tin bird. The prize will feed us both. That or I eat your corpse meat now."

Gemma mouthed "They can speak?"

Owain nodded.

She noticed the faint tingle of his glamour, thrown out to hide them.

"You trust men to keep promises? Who says he has meat; who says he will give it to us?" The feral who had failed to steal the bundle spat at the ground. He was the thinner of the two, which was saying something as they were both emaciated. The other one had some muscle wrapping his bones and seemed to have no qualms about eating his companion, which were enough qualifications for dominance.

"He has meat. One dead. Two still alive. He can't use the dead ones."

Gemma leaned on Owain's arm to steady herself. She felt the pressure of Fian's head on her thigh, holding her up. *Two alive*, she she repeated in her head. She let her mouth silently shape the words, willing them to be true; willing one of the to be Adrian. *Two alive, two alive*.

The feral were out of earshot now, and nearly out of sight, their greydappled skin blending with the stones and shadows. They had made it to the outer wall of Grimspound without being spotted by Gabriels stalking hounds. The glamour evaporated and Owain took a gulp of air.

"I'm not as good as Gabriel at that," he said, "still practising."

Gemma spared him a distracted smile.

"How will we know when?"

"When everything's dead he will send a hound."

"Then we dig," said Gemma.

"Then we dig."

18.
FATE

There had only been two feral set to watch the outer wall, and the returning scouts thought little of stepping over the body of one of them. A broken neck could happen for any number of reasons on the moor, and it was one less share of the meat.

Benjamin was sitting on one of the large stones of the chiefs hut, but stood as the feral approached.

"Well?" he snapped. There was dirt under his fingernails and smeared on the sleeves of his jacket. The undead were too slow, and he kept having to remind them about digging.

"I have your prize-"

"-We have your prize," said the two feral.

Benjamin leaned on the porch stone to steady himself and tried to conceal the surprise from his face. Sending the feral to dig nearby crash sites had mainly been something to keep them out of his way at night; they gave him the heebie jeebies. Secondly a small part of him had hoped for some extra income if they did find anything, but this was completely unexpected. Why would an ancient dagger be buried with the remains of a plane? Where was it being flown and why? Yes, his divination skills were rusty but the rods had crossed over the settlement, he was sure of it. He resolved to ask his client a few more questions before money and artefact changed hands.

"Here, shiny gold, very pretty," said the feral holding the dagger, unwrapping the wet leather rag ensnaring it.

He would need to take a look at this crash site too.

"Could you take me to where you found this?"

The thinner of the two feral looked panicked. Was it not the right item? Would payment be denied?

"I will take you to the tin bird. After a small meal..." it said. Best to please the Death Man.

"Thank you, a job well done." Benjamin held his hand out for the dagger. There was absolutely no movement. "The body of the man is in the barrow, help yourselves," he added. The dagger was dropped at his feet and the two feral were gone. He shuddered, then glanced round to check that no one had seen. He was getting too old for this.

The dagger lay on the ground, half the wrapping thrown off carelessly like so much rubbish. It was larger than he thought; perhaps the length and width of a forearm, and the middle was sheathed somewhat crudely in gold. If there had once been a handle, that had long since rotted away and only metal remained. It was ugly really. But who was he to question the interests of a collector? He plucked it from the ground and held it, feeling the weight. A clumsy weapon, he thought. Heavy. Heavy enough for some fuel for the car, heavy enough for a proper meal, heavy enough for a house. He began to smile, then he grinned, and in the peatdeep darkness of the moor he raised the dagger and laughed.

The two feral who had just left didn't hear him. One, because it was dead, and the other because it was leaping the boundary wall with all the strength its thin legs could provide. The hound had come silently; all the fleeing feral saw was a flash of burning eyes as fierce jaws snapped its companion out of sight. It wasn't upset by the loss, but it was very keen to choose a different fate. With all the practice that comes from being last in the pecking order, it waded into a thin stream and then sloshed for a way against the current to hide its scent. Once it slipped, but ignored the pain until it was curled up beneath a large fallen stone that bridged the stream.

With no feral remaining, the hounds shed their secrecy and grew from the shadows, bristling and wolven. One howled and the others joined in chorus. Ancient and enchanting, their song rose up and carried over the twin tors and bled out onto the moor, promising death and grace. Nearby, Fian tipped up his milky head to the moon and melded his voice with the pack.

"We are the fire at night," whispered Owain.

Gemma turned to him and saw he was shaking. The howling had her shivering too; it inspired a primal fear that no progress could extingush.

"We are the first born sons. We are the flame that cannot die," Owain said.

There was the hollow beat of hooves on turf and then Gabriels horse cleared the outer ring of stones. It landed and cantered on without slowing, directly towards the undead.

"We are the stewards of the ways. We are the cleansing blaze." said Owain.

Gabriel spurred on his mount, loosening a little more flesh from its ribs and extended a clawed hand. The spines that ran along his forearms showed through the ragged sleeves of the red hunt coat and they were raised in anger. As the first of the undead looked up he caught the remains of its face in his hand. The creature that had one been a man buckled and fell. The Huntmaster rode on, the head raised as a prize. The other undead were slow to react and Benjamin's commands came too late. Aimlessly they bumbled about and Gabriel cut them down.

Benjamin clutched the dagger to his chest and yelled for Evangeline, but the howling of the hounds was thick in the air. If she heard she didn't answer. He slipped on a pile of dug earth and landed hard on his ankle. Cursing, he pushed himself up, and looked into the burning eyes of a hound. Slavering jaws stretched wide and he crawled backwards until he hit something else. His eyes on the first hound, he reached back to feel what was stopping him. The feel of matted fur sent him scrambling in a fresh direction. But the hounds were all around him.

Fian whined and strained his head up towards Grimspound.

"The noise has stopped," said Gemma, "everything must be dead."

Owain reached out to pull her back, but she dodged him.

"Wait," he said.

"Adrian needs me."

"Gabriel is not himself." Owain's voice cracked. For a moment Gemma saw him as any other teenage boy and understood his horror at what he must become; at what he would do as Huntmaster one day. She hugged him briefly, and ran for the wall. The white hound followed her.

"I don't fear death, Huntmaster," said Benjamin, wincing as he forced himself to his feet. The pain in his right ankle told him that it was probably broken.

The circle of hounds parted as Gabriel dismounted and strode through, carelessly letting his horse crumble to a pile of bones behind him.

"You all fear death. You even more so necromancer. You know the truth of it."

"Come then, let me welcome it as an old enemy." Benjamin produced his reserve hipflask from an inner pocket, kept for very special or extreme ocassions only, and drained it in one.

Gabriel laughed. It was a sound empty of mirth or happiness.

"We only hunt. Fight. Or run."

Benjamin wilted.

"There's little sport in me," he said. The Wild Hunt had come up in all of his research and he wished now he had spent a little more time on the topic. All he knew was that the hunt collected souls of the dead, and they were happy to help anyone or anything in their path get that way.

"Which will it be?" Gabriel said.

Gemma steadied herself against the cool stones and watched through a small gap. She felt Fian at her side, every muscle taut beneath his fur. There seemed to be just one left alive. She squinted her eyes. He looked human and appeared to be wearing quite an expensive tweed jacket.

Benjamin gritted his teeth. He had always imagined his death involving more whisky. There were no lies left about death being a long sleep for him. But there was his wife Lauren with her soft hands, and their son without a name.

"I'm sorry Eva," he told the grass. Then he clenched his jaw and ran.

The nearest hound caught him easily and tossed him back into the middle. He landed hard on a stone and felt the pain thrum through his chest. He ran again without looking up, almost immediately feeling another set of jaws catch his arm and throw him backwards. The ground took the wind out of him and for a moment he lay snatching gulps of air. But the hounds were impatient. He felt a bony snout thrust under his stomach and roll him to the other side of the tightening circle. Another hound bit into the back of his leg and he scrambled away on his knees. Then Gabriel was behind him, with sharp fingers thrust in his back, dragging him to his feet.

The Huntmaster's lips were close to his cheek. His voice was soft in his ear; "Run."

Benjamin shut his eyes.

The sound of the hunting rifle sliced the air. Two shots.

And the Necromancer died.

Gabriel dropped the body with a growl. As one, the hounds turned their yellow teeth in the direction the shots had come from.

"Wait," yelled Gemma, climbing over the stone wall. Owain had followed her. She felt him try to catch her arm again but shook him off. "You promised to dig for Adrian."

"Adrian," said Gabriel. His cold smile bared two rows of sharp teeth.

"Take me to him now."

"As you wish." He turned without waiting. The hounds followed, some melting off to slink through the shadows, only their red eyes to be seen.

Gemma ran after him, Fian at her side.

There were two bodies. Gemma sprinted the last steps and dropped to her knees. Her hands were thrown out but something held her back from touching. Adrian

258

lay slumped over an older woman, his back shielding her from some terror that was now gone. Fian nosed Adrian's shoulder and his body rolled back face up. He was still holding the womans hand.

"Are they dead?" Gemma asked the night. The silence was enough answer. She stood and spun round to face Gabriel. He was close; she could smell his scent of honeysuckle and woodsmoke faintly, but more strongly he smelt of blood and earth. "Bring him back." Tears burned the edges of her eyes. There was no room for fear left. There was nothing more monstrous than the thought of Adrian not being alive.

"You have no need for him now, Elyn," Gabriel purred. His pale hand was held out to her. Blood had dried round each of the knifesharp nails. "Remember who you are."

Gemma clenched her fists, concentrating on the pain in her palms until she could calm her breath enough to speak. There wasn't time for this.

"I have no idea what you're talking about."

He moved too fast for her to hit him away. But he would have been too strong to fight. His hand dragged her back from Adrian's body and pulled her into his arms. He pressed her close and the smell of rotting flesh overwhelmed her; his jacket was wet with blood on blood; the sad detritus of so many small lives. Her stomach heaved and he let her fall with a laugh.

"I see that I repulse you. I smell it on your human skin. Isn't it time you shed that baggage? Have you not had fun enough?" His lips curled the last words into a snarl .

An angel. Stalking her through generations. Fat chance. Anger flared within her, pushing up through her veins like lava rising to the surface. Scorching away fear and pain; expanding like the granite tors beneath the earth when they were born as liquid rock.

"The blood doesn't repulse me. Your skin and your spines don't repulse me. The mud and the rot and the gore don't repulse me. I feel for you for all that. But all this crap about an unbroken vow? You wouldn't understand a promise if the broken shards of it were shoved in both your eyes."

Silence flooded Grimspound. The whole moor drew a breath and held it as the young woman faced the Huntmaster. "And I have no idea who Elyn is. But she probably hates you too." Gemma added. A small part of her appraised the spines and the claws and the teeth and wondered if that was a step too far. A far larger part of her didn't care. She wanted every word to be a knife. And Adrian was dead.

Gabriel diminished. A hound slunk to his side and it was Fen, amber eyed and sleek, doing her best impression of being alive.

"Four human generations I've waited. I watched you grow old and die. But you promised you would be reborn; daughter of your daughters daughter."

Gemma almost felt sorry for him. Almost.

"Bring Adrian back for me."

"You misunderstand my powers. It cannot be done."

"Bring him back."

He reached towards her and she didn't flinch; not when his cold finger touched her cheek; not when his claw brushed her skin and trembled lightly through her hair. She even reached round and lay a hand on his back as he kissed her. But all she thought was *Adrian is dead*.

A slight breeze carried the cry of an owl, and further away a stallion called to his mare at the first quickening of dawn. Passing the outer wall of the settlement, a slow stream sang softly between the rocks. At the highest point of one of the twin tors a crow woke and began to call up the sun.

"There will come a time," said Gabriel softly, "when I will ask something of you in return. You must not refuse." His hands lingered on her shoulders, framing her for a moment longer. His eyes were the colour of murky water, black with the blue bleeding back in. Then he let go.

Owain steadied her. She leaned on him and they watched Gabriel summon back his horse and lift Adrian's body easily, laying it gently over the saddle. Then, without looking back, he took up the reins and walked out onto the moor.

Gemma went to follow, but Owain held her. She looked back, wide eyed.

"Where's he going?"

"To Houndain, I would imagine."

"We should go with him."

"No."

"But Adrian-"

"Listen," Owain took both her hands. She could feel his thumbs pressing into her palms. "There is no rite for this. No spectacle. To drag life back is an abomination."

"But the hounds- that horse-"

"Puppets. With the lifeforce of the Huntmaster inside."

"But they were themselves once."

"Yes, before they died. But what they left behind is just chemicals and earth, which is no more them than your wool coat is the sheep it was shorn from. But you are asking for more than that. You are asking for Adrian to be alive. You are asking for the coat to once again become a lamb."

Gemma began sobbing and Owain hugged her, a little awkwardly.

"Can he do it?" she asked.

"I don't doubt it."

Evangeline sat with her back to the rock and stared. She watched dawn trickle in, the sky growing a little paler with each rasp from the crows at the top of the tor. She watched small figures moving around Grimspound below, piling the bodies into the open barrow. She cried out as they took the body of her father by both arms and dragged it to join the others. The rifle lay across her lap, and for a moment she thought to shoot them, but of course the cartridges were with her father. It was humiliating, piling him up like meat. But what could she have done better? Carried him into town, dug him a grave on the moor, sat him in the Range Rover and set it alight? Town would mean all the ineviatable and unanswerable questions. She had nothing to dig with and the ground was full of stones. The car; the car might have worked, like a modern ship burial burning on the earth waves of the moor. But there was no fuel in it. It'd be a macabre barbeque.

She watched them push earth back into the barrow and lay the turf back over the surface. It was a ready made tomb, and heathen kings were buried with their slaves. Perhaps it was best after all; better than she could do anyway. The rifle slipped off her knees as she stood, and she left it there as she walked down from the tor. Archeology for the future.

Grimspound was deserted and dawn was breaking itself upon it, wreathed in a fine mist as the land breathed the warming air. She was the only murderer left. The porch stone of the chiefs hut took her weight as she leaned against it. Her father was dead. She had killed him. But the others- what had they been? Huge dogs with rabies and a man dressed to go fox hunting. Had no one told him that was illegal? But robbing historical sites using undead monsters fed with dead strangers was hardly above board. Benjamin couldn't ever have gone in a car crash or in his sleep. It was all very him really.

Very softly she began to cry.

What was it all for? Another huge house where they could only heat one room, filled to the roof with the absence of her mother. Another cellar filled with whisky and grounds where the grass grew waist high for the want of mowing? No dagger could buy away that emptiness. And there was no sodding dagger anyway. She turned and kicked the standing stone hard. It wasn't the bloom of pain she was hoping for, as she had aimed clumsily and mostly kicked the grass. She looked at her foot and the creased turf.

Why was it creased?

She knelt and caught a tuft of short grass between her fingers. This stone had come down during the digging and been set in place again. The turf was still loose. She pulled it back and the pink and yellow dawn lent lustre to something gold. Part gold, and shaped roughly like a dagger.

"He found it," she mouthed.

"This, you old bugger," she yelled, waving the dagger towards the barrow mound, "this is it?"

The moor answered her with a comfortable silence.

It felt heavy in her hands as she looked at it more closely. Around the gold wrapping on the middle of the blade it was intricately bound with sections of wire that seemed to hold the metal together. It was potentially the least practical dagger ever. She gripped it nonetheless. Screw this collector.

"I'm sorry," she told the barrow.

The feral watched her from the damp beneath the rock. Cold spring water rushed over its feet, cooling the blood beneath its scarred skin. It felt slow and hungry. Too hungry. But she was with the Death Man, and he was in posession of the meat. If he had survived the hounds. If he had not...

"Lady," it called.

The young woman spun round sharply, her heel carving a circle in the grass.

"Evangeline," she corrected. The feral had been useful enough servants to her father, but they couldn't be trusted for a second. They had been starving for so long that it was all that compelled them.

"Evening," it hissed, garbling her name and creeping closer, "did you kill the hounds?"

It was testing her, checking if her father was still alive.

"Yes," she lied, "my father is torturing the Huntmaster as we speak." She lingered on those words, enjoying them. The feral stooped low and bent itself into an awkward bow. To tame the Wild Hunt was unknown; it was like chaining down a thunderstorm or turning back the torrent of a snowfed river.

"Remember how I have served the Death Man,

how I have found him his dagger." The feral reached out its long fingers for Evangeline's hand. She snatched it away. "He said I must show him where I found it, so I will show you Death Lady. Come." The creature beckoned, limping off ahead.

She swayed on her feet. There had only been tea for dinner and she had been up all night. But without the rifle she had no easy way to kill the feral, and to go back to Grimspound would be suicide. It musn't know that her father was dead. Only good acting would keep her alive.

"Quickly then, he will be waiting," she said with arrogant disinterest. Or she hoped she did. In her ears her voice was shaking.

19.
DYING ARTS

The turf was rolled back, dissected from the peat beneath it. The small pool had been picked open like a scab and glistened wet with mud.

"Move back," Evangeline told the wounded feral. The dawn air was chill but she was sweating in her wool jacket with the effort of keeping her voice sharp. One slip, and there was no doubt it would eat her. "Did the Death Ma- , my father, tell you what he would do with the plane?" This was pushing it, she knew.

"No Evening. Maybe the tin bird would fly and carry him and the dagger away. I have never seen a dead bird fly again," the feral attempted a grin, showcasing a mouth full of sharp and broken teeth. It was padding a slow circle around the mire, flexing its bone thin fingers.

"We are necromancers. We control the dead."

The finger flexing stopped. It would be wary of striking until there was no doubt she was powerless. She had bought some time. Now it was a simple case of doing what she said she could. Bile was churning in her stomach. She had never raised the dead; she had spent a lifetime trying to avoid that weirdness. The gibberish that her father spoke when he reanimated corpses was nonsense she had pushed from her mind, and now, when she begged herself for it, the knowledge was nowhere to be dragged back from. That was the problem with dying arts; soon enough they were dead. She had seen her father kneel, but mud had been splattered everywhere by the feral digging, so she crouched. Then she placed both palms flat on the earth and closed her eyes. It was risky,

267

but she hoped that the ceremonial stance would discourage thoughts of her edibility.

Under her fingers, the grass felt smooth and cool. Small patches felt damp, where the rotted plants and soil had been turned up from the pool. She breathed in the sulphur scent of vegetation decayed in water and forced herself to fill her lungs. In this most unlikely of places, she fought herself to relax. She pushed her hunched shoulders down and stretched out the creases on her forehead. It was time to let all the barriers down.

It hit her immediately; like a dam bursting and reclaiming the channels and valleys it has been denied.

Her mother was pale in the hospital light. Her father was wearing his sport backed hunting jacket and smelt of mud and pheasants.

"A son," she was saying, "a son." Her voice was quiet, but it felt loud in the white walled visiting room. Benjamin held her hand, where a gold wedding ring betrayed the fact that she had not always been so thin.

"You will get well. Then maybe-"

"Our son." The delicate hand gripped his tight. It was a plea for something unspeakable.

"I can't do it," he said, "I won't."

"But it's such a gift. A cure for death." Her cornflower eyes were shining.

"It doesn't work like that, and I'm still learning to use it. I'm not ready."

The pale hand fell limp on the white bedcover and the woman beneath it seemed to shrink away, recoil back into the thin body as if all the fight in her was defeated.

"There is nothing for me here. My son," she turned and sobbed the words into her pillow, "my son, my son, my son..."

She was shutting the door on life; refusing it, and Evangeline felt the pull through her fingers. Vaguely she felt the mud seeping through the knees of her jeans as the dark gravity sucked at her, an irrestistable comfort that promised rest and an endless velvet peace. To rest. The bliss.

"Dead enough. Perhaps."

The voice was a painful intrusion and flickered open her eyes. The feral sat very close now, patiently spilling a fistful of earth into its open palm like a crude hourglass. When the earth ran out, it would eat her. This made her very angry. It was completely incompatible with her elegant vision of death. Rage burned through her and the gravity dimmed, washing back. An easy death? It was all a lie. *Do not go gentle into that good night. Fight, Fight.*She pushed back at the gravity and it shied away, creeping back down into the earth. But that wasn't enough. She pushed harder; she hurled every embarassing black out, every evening spent watching her father cry and every ridiculing look at it. And the gravity reversed. And it wasn't dark; it burned.

The grass beneath her hands blackened and smouldered. Ahead of her, the pool rippled and began to bubble. The water was boiling. Evangeline laughed. The liberation was overwhelming; her senses expanded, piercing the earth like a great tap root. Things came to her. The soil was made of a billion tiny dead things that were suddenly bursting with the electric of life, and the living earth pushed the metal out of its skin; every shard in place, reforged in the heat.

But the reaction wasn't slowing. Her hands were welded to the earth and it was too hot. The bounds of herself had travelled so far, so deep, that she was forgetting where her edges were. The great busyness of the earth overwhelmed her and she was lost in remembering the tiny lives of the creatures that had died to create the rocks before the lava came.

A gunshot broke her concentration.

The gravity snapped and she slumped face down on the grass. She felt a hand on her forehead and crawled backwards, sharp nails dragging at her scalp. But there was no further attack. She scraped her hair out of her eyes and saw the feral laying still in the dawnlight. She had fallen on the body.

She looked up. On the other side of the bog there was a plane. And a man.

"*Scheisse*," he said.

The plane wasn't English.

The man was still pointing a gun in her direction. It was a long time since German lessons at school.

"Mein freund hat blonde haare," Gemma volunteered, wildly trying to remember something more useful. The man was wearing a greygreen uniform with black shiny boots and a little eagle embriodered on the chest. "Ich habe keine haustiere," she added. The pistol looked very efficient and he had just used it once. "Werden sie in die Disco?" she ended clunkily. She was all out pf phrases and the dagger wasn't even sharp.

"Your German is very bad," said the soldier.

Evangeline released the breath she was holding in a gust.

"You speak English!"

"I am not going to the disco. I'm sorry that you have no pets and I hope your friend is satisfied with her blonde hair. Who are you? And what was that?"

"Evangeline Maker. Eva. That was one of my

fathers servants. They're not very loyal."

"You are dressed strangely Eva Maker."

"It's a hacking jacket. And you can't talk."

The man glanced down at his jacket but kept the gun level.

"You will tell me what happened. Where is my pilot?"

"No idea on the pilot I'm afraid. But what happened is that I'm a necromancer and and I raised your plane from that bog." she gestured at the muddy pool between them. "And I brought you back from the dead. I think."

He let the hand with the gun in fall to his side.

"We also need to leave right now. Can you fly that plane?"

"I understand the principle."

"Close enough."

The earth around the bog had been baked hard by the summer sun and the Messerschmitt trundled over it awkwardly, listing side to side like a wounded bird of prey. A few sheep had wandered over, drawn by the strange sight, but they scattered as the plane rolled towards them. Dawn was rapidly becoming daylight and they were too exposed. Would bullets work on the terrible hounds or their Master?

"We need to go faster," she yelled up to the cockpit.

"The ground is too uneven. We need a long straight stretch without stones to take off."

Eva scanned ahead and smiled.

"Ok."

A car drove across the moor. The road crossed the rolling

271

heather clad hills and damp brackenthick hollows in almost a straight line, stretching away into the early morning haze. The driver, Mr. Young, was hoping to beat the crowds to Grimspound and get in a morning of painting in the open air. He glanced down to adjust his radio, narrowing his eyes as he skipped through frequencies to get rid of the interference. Where was that cursed whirring noise come from? When he looked up it was too late to brake. But he did just have time to take in the black and white cross on the side of the plane as the wheels passed inches above his sunroof.

"Bloody hell!" he said and after a moment, quite decisively, threw his hip flask out the window.

The buzzard watched the plane climb laboriously, propeller scything the sky into a million tiny pieces. The morning thermal roiled beneath it, pushing up towards the gods, carrying the faint sweet scent of heather and grass to the invisible stars. But the buzzard had turned its eyes to the earth. The rabbit had no attention for the stars, and soon it had attention for nothing at all.

Mike watched the buzzard drop, took note of where it had landed, and then began walking across the scrub. A lady rode sidesaddle on a white horse beside him, its bit and bridle chained with silver reins. Little silver bells hung from its harness, and its hocks ran red with bloody thornpricks from the gorse.

"She flies well," said the lady. Her voice was soft and tuneful, pleasant like the breeze on a hot day that stops you noticing how much your skin burns.

"Yes m'lady, said Mike.

She spurred the horse forward through a low tangle of gorse.

272

"Have the dreams ceased now?" she asked.

"I don't dream m'lady."

"Of course not," she purred, let's drink to that." From a leather case strapped to the saddle she brought out a crystal flask. Unscrewing the silver lid, she offered it to Mike.

"Thank you m'lady, but I think I won't."

"Nonsense!" She put the flask to her rosebud lips and tipped it upwards sharply, then offered it again. "Old friends must share a drink, and we are old friends aren't we?"

Mike caught sight of the buzzard ahead. It was eating the rabbit's eyes.

"Yes m'lady."

"Good." She turned her horse around and held the flask out to him. He took it and raised it to his mouth. "The cure to all ills."

"All ills," he repeated, draining it.

Morgana smiled.

Dawn had bled into day, breathing warm and golden across the moor, casting the first shadows from lone windstunted hawthorns and standing stones. Flies buzzed lazily, attracted by the carcass of the rabbit. Mike gutted it quickly, leaving the organs on the grass for whichever scavengers came first. The buzzard had its eyes on the meat, but he called it back to his wrist.

"Not that Pandora," he chided, taking the leg of a chick from the bag slung over his shoulder. Pandora took it from his bare hand and swallowed it in one, then readjusted herself on his wrist and began to preen her feathers. He had never bothered with the leather gloves for his birds; the scars on each wrist had built up thick enough to be protection from talons in their own right.

They criss-crossed the tattooed keys that covered his arms and his chest beneath the shirt. Some had faded in the sun where he had rolled up his sleeves, others were partially raised where they covered old scars that had swelled again for the summer. Each one was a different design, some depicting ornate keys with swirls in the handle, others a basic outline blurred into the surrounding skin and a few were crisp and new with white ink added to give them a realistic lustre. The meaning of them was lost on Mike as he studied them. But they distracted the eye from the scars. That was good.

"Will you eat rabbit m'lady?"

"Not today. Take the bird home."

"Yes m'lady."

"We will see each other again."

"Until then, m'lady." He pinched the peak of his flat cap and pulled it off.

"Until then Michael." Morgana pulled her horse around and set off at an easy trot. Mike watched until she passed out of view and then settled his hat back on his head. The contents of the flask had been strong and he could feel it burning in his stomach. But his feet felt light and the walk ahead was not daunting.

"Home then girl," he said, and turned his steps to Princetown.

Gemma sat opposite Owain in the Princes Tea Rooms. It hadn't seemed right to sit in the Fox Tor Cafe somehow, but he was insisting that she ate again. She had also showered, on his advice, and lent him a hoodie of Adrian's to wear while he was in town. The tea rooms had only just opened and were empty except for them, although the warming scent of bacon and eggs was beginning to creep

274

out from the kitchen.

"How much longer?" Gemma asked.

Owain looked out the large windows and counted one, two, three cars as they passed. The sun glinted on paintwork, glass and tarmac alike, smoothing out the world into postcard scenes and memories.

"I wouldn't know," he said.

Gemma followed his gaze out the window, watching the car park fill with the days quota of tourists. She saw the snooty woman step out of the Visitor Centre as she opened the doors. She was wearing a very flowery blouse with a pencil skirt that was at least a size too small, meaning that she could only take very small steps. Gemma almost smiled. For a moment she felt a glow of affection for the woman; it was wonderful, her normality.

The pavement was slowly becoming busier too, and a few people had stopped to peer in through the tearoom window, before thinking better of it. Gemma wondered vaguely if Owain was doing anything to keep them out. One figure outside caught her interest. He was walking a little unsteadily, a brown wax jacket half zipped up, despite the increasing heat, and a flat cap pulled low over his eyes. There was also a large brown bird of prey dozing on his shoulder. Gemma stood up so fast that she knocked her chair over backwards.

"Mike!" She yelled through the glass.

The man slowed and looked around in confusion. Gemma rapped on the glass and waved. He turned round and looked at her, but somewhow his gaze seemed to slide past, leaving his face blank. Gemma dodged between tables and pulled open the tearoom door, jogging out onto the grey pavement. "Mike," she called again. His confusion seemed to have rooted him to the spot and he

275

stared back, his mouth very slightly open. The buzzard cocked its head to one side and slowly stretched out one hefty wing. "Are you alright?" She slowed as she got closer to him, losing momentum a few strides away.

His sturdy boots were even more scratched up than before, the steel of the toes showing through slits in the leather. His jacket was dusty and his chin bristled with stubble a few days old. There was also a definite aroma of gin. But the look on his face, that was the worst.

"Yes m'lady," he said vaguely.

"No need to lady me."

"Yes, m'lady."

"Mike!" She wanted to grab his shoulders and shake him, but the amber gaze of the bird suggested that she refrained. "It's Gemma, do you remember?"

Mike fiddled with something in his pocket. It was awkward. Gemma glanced back and saw that Owain had followed her to the door and stopped, leaning against the frame. She widened her eyes at him for some help, but he turned down the corners of his mouth and very slightly shook his head.

"Mike, we ate bacon sandwiches at Hound of the Basket Meals."

Nothing.

"We climbed Hound Tor and got turned back by Ga- a stranger on the moor."

Whatever bit of fluff had been residing in his pockets must be pulverised.

Gemma clenched her fists in frustration. "You told us stories in the pub when it was dark and there were candles burning inside."

A flicker. The ghost of something.

"The stories," said Gemma, desperate not to lose

it, "the moor in the evening. A farmer was riding home from Widecombe Fair. He had done well and he had been drinking. He heard a noise in the wind and he was afraid. A rider on a huge white horse approached, wearing a red jacket stained with mud and more. 'Huntsman give us some of your game' said the man. The Huntsman laughed and threw a bundle down. It was too small to be a deer and too big to be a rabbit. Then he was gone into the darkness, his hounds howling around him. The farmer rushed home, eager to take a look at his prize. He called his wife out with a lantern and they unwrapped the bundle." She was struggling. She knew some of the details were wrong; the huntsman's jacket and horse should be black. And somehow she couldn't tell the end of the story and she was crying.

"In the lantern light the woman began to wail," continued Owain, "wrapped up in the bundle was nothing other than the body of her own child."

Around them the sun shone, people chose personalised fudge for their neighbour who was cat sitting at home and tourists decided if it was too early to get a cream tea. But where Gemma stood it was freezing cold.

"The story was probably made up to warn people about the evils of drinking and greed. Plus some priests used the well known figure of the Dark Huntsman as another guise of the Devil, hence the hunting and killing of unbaptised children. It's a symolic death of the soul." Owains voice was measured and factual and somehow, beneath that, endlessly tired.

"But he's not the Devil," said Mike.

Gemma stared at him and he shrugged,embarrassed.

"Did you say something about bacon?" he added.

277

"Yes," she said, wiping her face with the back of her sleeve, "come inside."

At his nod, the buzzard stirred and flapped up from his shoulder. Seconds later it was continuing its snooze on the tearoom roof.

Two plates had appeared on the table in their absence.

"Another breakfast please," said Owain, pushing his plate towards Mike.

"I can wait."

"No need. You should drink as well."

Mike was fiddling in his pockets again, lingering still standing by his chair. His cheeks were red from the walk and years in the weather anyway, but shame had turned them a deeper crimson.

"I was off it, you know," he said.

Owain smiled; patience and sadness.

"Eat and you'll feel better."

Gemma ate slowly. She was hungry, but her mind was whirring so fast she felt dizzy. It was over, the quest. Adrain was saved. He was dead. But he would be alive again. The meal tasted like dirt in her mouth; gritty and thick like the earth piled over the barrow at Grimspound. Gabriel was bringing him back to life. But the cost- *you must not refuse*- there was the cost. And Gabriel was a monster.

Opposite her the clicking of cultery on china stopped, signalling that Mike had finished eating. He placed his knife and fork together and reached for the glass of water beside him, draining it in one. Gemma half smiled as he clinked it back down on the wooden table, remembering Adrian plying him with beer in the Plume of Feathers to hear more about the mysterious moor.

"You said the Huntsman isn't the Devil," the words were out of Gemma's mouth before she had fully decided if she wanted to speak them or not. But they were thrashing around in her skull so much that it was difficult to say or think anything else. "Why?" She heard Owain put his knife and fork down.

Mike tilted his head a little to one side, his gaze wandering out of the window. There was no view of the moor but in the electric lights of the tearoom Mike's eyes were somehow still filled with it; a touch of the wilderness that might be mistaken for madness.

"The Devil and the Huntsman share some things," he chose each word carefully, testing it on his tongue before releasing it, "but not a body. They are not the same."

Gemma prodded her fried egg with a fork and watched it bleed yolk over her plate. What had she been expecting? A grand explanation that would somehow redeem the horror of her pact? A list of ten things that might actually be great about making a blind promise to a murderous fairy?

"They both have a duty; a jagged hole that must be filled, and which they have been so many times cut and snagged by that they have come to fit it perfectly. The Huntsman cannot turn his back on the hounds any more than the Devil can return to being a shining angel in Heaven, as much as I'd wager he wants to."

"The hounds protect the Clan, I know that. But why the cruelty? Why the torture?"

"That's old magic. Blood spilt in terror. The ground remembers. Those who tread on the ground remember."

"Has anyone around here considered a simple keep out sign? No blood, no rituals, everyone involved gets to stay alive?" Gemma was tired. She knew she was rambling, but she didn't seem to have the energy to keep the words in. "Tell me why you're covered in keys, Mike."

Mike glanced at the back of his hand, taking it in as if it was the first time he had laid eyes on it. "The keys." He narrowed his eyes and tried to focus. The patterns were swimming on his skin, impossible to pin down. "They help me-" each word was an effort, but the pressure behind his eyes was the weight of the answer trying to push its way out; push past the memory of the woman on the white horse and the eyeless rabbit and the burning of the gin. "-remember," he finished, wiping the sheen of sweat from his forehead.

"Remember what?" asked Gemma.

Mike shook his head. "I have no idea."

20.
Messerschmitt

"I'm sure Mike would like to get home." Owain snapped to his feet

"Yes," Mike said, standing and knocking his cutlery to the floor. He stooped to pick it up, cheeks burning. "I think I'll just, ah, cool my face quickly first." He shuffled towards the toilets.

"You will walk him home."

"But I-" Gemma protested. Owain spoke over her.

"You will take care of him. He doesn't have anyone else." He lay a pale hand on her shoulder. "As soon as I have news I'll know exactly where to find you. Drink tea. Save your questions for another day."

She nodded sullenly. Of course.

"And wait-" Owain pushed a hand down one of his boots and retrieved a very crinkled fifty pound note. Gemma stared. What had she been expecting him to use? Enchanted gold? "There's a shop next door. Fill his cupboards please."

Miles sped by beneath the plane. Whatever had rolled on in the rest of the world, the sky was still the same. The Messerschmitt had been converted to a two seater training plane towards the end of the war, and the current pilot was flying without an instructor for the first time. But it was going well. Except for one small snag.

"We are low on fuel," he told Eva. She was sitting behind him, her teeth chattering violently.

"How low?" she managed to stutter.

"In English? *Bloody low*."

281

"You seem a little too relaxed about it! How long do we have?"

"Five minutes."

"Great. Any suggestions on what to do?"

"Well you say that you can bring back the dead-"

"Yes well not if I'm dead too. Plan B?"

"Land in the next four and a half minutes."

Below them, the fields and houses seemed very small; fragile like the figures on a miniature railway. The radio coughed up some static and a stern voice filled the plane.

"Come in unidentified aircraft. You are in British airspace. Please identify yourself."

"Do you think I should speak to them?" said Eva.

"This is RAF Flight Lieutenant White of North Weald Airfield. I repeat, you are in British Airspace. Please identify yourself immediately to avoid defensive action." The last crackle of the transmission faded out and the cockpit gathered silence. Seconds stretched out uncomfortably.

"This is Second Lieutenant Franz Schell of the Luftwaffe. I request emergency landing."

The radio stayed silent. The plane lurched, dropping a few feet before stabilising. It was heavy in the air as it turned to circle the runway.

"Just land!" urged Eva. The plane pitched again and for a moment the roar of the engine spluttered and cut out.

"I repeat, we request emergency landing. We are out of fuel."

The propeller coughed back into action but it was labouring badly. They were losing height and the ground pressed closer. The numbers painted on the runways were clearly visible and getting closer.

"You have permssion to land," said a voice over the radio. It was different to the previous one. "Runway number nine is clear."

"Received," said Franz. He turned the plane and Eva felt a slight jolt beneath her as the landing gear was lowered.

Flight Lietenant David White watched the Messerschmitt roll to a halt on the runway. He was in his twelfth year of leading the local wing of Air Cadets, and he had enjoyed it so much that he had chosen to take the uniform route and become a comissioned Officer. He was extremely proud of his achievements and he was a brilliant Cadet leader. But today he had experienced the misfortune of being the highest ranked Officer at the Airfield during a breach of security. He was more than relieved when one of the civilian pilots who rented a hangar at the runway explained the situation. Disorientation and a nearby reenactment event. It made perfect sense. He nodded thanks to his informant again and headed back to the café to see if his all day breakfast could be saved.

Eva and Franz were met on the runway by a man with floppy blonde hair and a small moustache.

"Are you hurt?" he asked.

"No. Thank you," said Eva. She watched the man's skyblue eyes flicker over Franz's uniform, lingering for a split second above the breast pocket. How were they going to explain? "We were-" she began.

"Part of a reenactment display. I know," said the man.

Franz opened his mouth and Eva trod on his very shiny boot.

"Yes," she said, "we lost our way somehow and ran low on fuel."

There was a twinkle in the mans eyes now.

"It's easily done. On a short preplanned flight," he winked conspiratorially.

Eva decided that she didn't like him.

"Now where are my manners? My name is Edward Blake." He held out a hand.

"Eva." She took his hand and shook it briefly. One of his eyebrows had travelled slightly higher up his face.

"Maker," she added.

"Eva Maker," he repeated, testing out the name in a way that made her feel uncomfortable. And Franz Schell." He turned and offered his hand again. Franz took it.

"Thank you," he said politely.

"Just perfect!" Blake exclaimed, seemingly to himself. Then, with a striking turn of speed, he pivoted on one heel and landed a hard slap across Franz's back. "Come with me." he strode off, his brown leather shoes clicking on the tarmac.

Eva peeled Franz's fingers off his pistol with a wide forced smile.

"It's probably a traditonal greeting in the, ah, aviation circle. Shooting people however," she pushed his now empty hand back to his side, "is never a traditional greeting."

"What year is it?" Franz asked.

"Does it really matter?"

Franz touched his breast pocket, and for a moment let his hand linger there. Then he dropped it again.

"No," he said.

Blake was leaning against the hangar building as the huge metal door rolled upwards. It was immaculately tidy inside, a small selection of tools hung from a rack on one wall, and beside them a wooden work bench. Next to it were two large brown leather arm chairs, which would have looked more in place in a Victorian study. Between them was a spindly legged coffee table with a lace placemat in the middle.

"Please sit," he said as Franz and Eva approached the door. The crunch, crunch of the metal studs on the soles of Franz's boots grew louder in the cavernous hangar building. Eva heard the slight hesitation in his step as he walked inside. The chairs were a little too low to be comfortable, and the old leather felt chilly and hard. "Coffee?" Blake asked, "you must forgive me if it's too sweet." He poured from a flask into two bone china cups without waiting for an answer, and placed them on the lacy table.

"Thanks," said Eva, squirming in the horrible chair.

"Your plane really is spectacular."

"Yes. Thank you," she said.

Franz was looking over her left shoulder at a wall mounted display cabinet.

"Iron Cross, First Class," said Blake, following his gaze. Picked that one up at a bootsale." Eva noticed the colour draining from the knuckles of Franz's clasped hands.

"You have a large collection," he said.

"Well," said Blake, waving a hand in the air, "I pick them up here and there. I don't think of myself as a collector, the term's so stuffy, you know? But when I see something I like, I just have to have it." He encompassed the further reaches of the hangar with an expansive arm gesture. "Those are my girls."

Eva and Franz looked. There were two planes stored there, one almost identical to theirs and both bearing the same black and white cross logo.

"Do you fly both of them?" Eva asked.

"Oh no, not myself. But there are plenty of young pilots who would do almost anything to get up in one. It's so nice to leave the steering to someone else." He smiled, showing his very white teeth. "Of course it took years to restore them. But look-" he flipped open the leather case of a tablet and swiped a few times across the screen, "-I managed to find original pictures of both to work from." He passed the tablet to Franz. "See the damage? The pictures were taken after the war."

Franz handed the tablet to Eva. He was getting paler by the moment.

"Well you have done a fantastic job," she said. She picked up her teacup and drained the tepid coffee as a signal that she was keen to leave. But Blake was having none of it.

"It's so interesting," he pressed on, "what you can find out with a little bit of research. Your plane, for example, did you know that it is recorded as having crashed over Dartmoor?"

"Is it?" she said, her face suddenly matching Franz for pallour, "well that's not right."

Blake leaned back on the workbench, his hands in the pockets of his spotless tan trousers, and smiled like a little boy with all the sweeties.

"Of course, the internet can be so unreliable," he said, still smiling.

"Yes," said Eva, trying to slow her breathing.

"So tell me the truth. How did you two come to be

286

flying a vintage, low on fuel, German aircraft over Essex?"

Eva had been dreading this. Telling the truth had never been further from her mind, and suddenly she was too hot sunk awkwardly in the armchair with her jacket still on. But she could feel the dagger pressed against her back beneath the wool and she knew she couldn't remove a layer.

"It's my fathers," she lied.

"I see. And does your father know you have it?"

"No."

"Will he not notice that it's missing?"

"No. He's dead." Her bluntness bought her a second or so to think. "He left it to me in his will. My brother has been learning to fly it. We never meant to come this far."

Franz looked at her sideways.

"Where did you fly from?" Blake asked.

Eva wracked her brain for place names that she and her father had driven past on the road.

"Wiltshire," she settled on.

"And that's the truth?" Blake pushed himself away from the work bench with one foot and circled to the back of Franz's chair.

"Yes," said Eva.

Blake continued his circuit, pulling a small eye glass from his pocket.

"May I?" he said to Franz, and didn't wait for an answer before leaning in to inspect the embroidered badge on his uniform jacket. "Quite remarkable," he concluded after a moment.

"He does reenactment," Eva added.

"Yes," said Blake vaguely, "that is quite the most perfect replica world war two German uniform I have ever

287

seen. Where did you get it?"

"In Berlin," said Franz curtly.

"How much would you take for it?"

"It is not for sale."

"But the plane is," said Eva.

"You see I already have two," said Blake, suddenly losing interest. "But I know a collector who may be interested. He would want to meet you though. He likes the story."

Eva glanced around the hangar. She struggled to guess what the contents might be worth. She had nothing and the plane was the only thing of any value that she could swap for money. Other than the dagger perhaps, but she wasn't parting with that. "Alright," she said at last.

"You may leave the plane with me."

"I don't think-" Eva began, but he interrupted.

"Where else would you store it?"

She conceded with a frown. He was right, she could hardly park it on the street.

"Don't worry *mein kinder,* I won't steal your plane."

"Don't you want to change your clothes?" Eva asked Franz as they walked away from the hangar. "I think he would have swapped you." She had a piece of paper with Blakes phone number folded in her pocket and instructions to call in the afternoon.

"No. Thank you," he said.

"Well," Eva turned to walk backwards in front of him, "I guess you'll be doing a lot of reenactment then. Plus his trousers were hideous."

The corners of Franz's mouth twitched into a smile.

"He reminded me of the time I had to borrow my brothers leiderhosen for a school play. My *younger* brother!"

Eva sniggered.

"What a creep."

They sat with their backs against a seemingly little used hangar building near the edge of the runway. To their right, stalky elder trees and a dark green holly were forcing their thin fingers through the razor topped fence. The wind had deposited enough dust in this tucked away corner that grass had managed to take hold in a few clumps, and amongst that the odd rattling seed head marked where poppies had flowered earlier in the year.

"You said I was your brother."

"Yes, well, undead stranger doesn't have quite the same *it's fine to let us go* vibe to it."

Franz looked suddenly out over the runway, empty except for a father and son flying a model biplane. He began distractedly spinning a silver ring on his right hand.

"That was really out of order, I'm sorry," said Eva.

"I am also sorry," said Franz, "I was too proud to change clothes. This is not very good cover."

"These losers are the least of our worries. The really awful stuff was back there. Thank you for flying."

"What is the really awful stuff?"

Eva turned her body to face him, resting her weight on her left hand. "I'll tell you all of it if you promise to believe me. I'm only sorry I haven't got any money to buy us some food." Her stomach rumbled accusingly. "It's quite a story."

"Wait," said Franz, unbuttoning his jacket and reaching into an inside pocket, "I have money." He was on his feet and striding towards the café, his boots click, clicking determinedly.

Eva opened her mouth to try and stop him, but fell short of any words. She didn't have the heart, and with adrenalin subsiding the emptiness of her stomach was painful.

He returned quickly, walking carefully with an entire armful of food. Sausage butties on paper plates were piled on top of each other, sandwiches in wrappers were wedged between eccles cakes and cans of drink. Eva's eyes widened at the amount. Franz lay it at her feet.

"I-", she said.

"I got a lot. I didn't know what you liked."

"What did you pay with?"

Franz sat back down on the ground and opened his palm. Nestled on it was a large and very shiny gold coin.

From the markings on it Eva guessed it was Roman. "Shouldn't that be in a museum?"

"It was." He already had a cheese and pickle sandwich in his hand.

She followed his example and reached for a sausage roll. For a while they ate in silence, working their way through the feast on the concrete in front of them. Eva threw a crust to a robin that had appeared to assess the threat of the newcomers in his territory. High in the weedy holly tree another bird began to sing and the summer breeze carried the fresh scent of a nearby crop of mint. Their corner of the airfield was an entire world away from the horror of the moor and the hounds. Here the concrete had pushed the earth back and the wildness had grown soft; it's harshest aspect being the little robin's righteous fury.

290

"Am I undead?" asked Franz, staring at the half eaten cake in his hand.

"What do you feel like?" Eva asked.

"I feel... the same."

"That's good," said Eva. She wanted to say something more, something reassuring. But the truth was that she didn't know the answer herself. She had never raised the dead before and Franz was nothing like the awful, rotten minions that she had seen her father use to search for the dagger. They needed to be fed additional energy from a living source constantly, and even with that they were slow moving and slow thinking monsters. The young soldier next to her was complete in flesh and mind; recreated true to the body that had first climbed into that plane on a distant airfield all those years ago. "You don't look undead."

"Thank you. Tell me this unbelievable story."

So she did. She started at the beginning with all the old books that her father would keep about the house. She relived the hospital visits, perfectly described the scent of stale whisky and shot and she explained the vast wilderness of the moor with Grimspound, their stranded Range Rover and the dagger within it. Tears rolled down her cheeks as she told of the hounds and the spectre that rode before them. She stumbled over her awkwardness holding the hunting rifle and the painful recoil that she had not been prepared for. But her blood fizzed as she described the raising of the plane, the memory of the power and the fear searing through her afresh. Through the heat and the water they had both been reborn.

"So we are brother and sister," she said. The memory of the lava and the deep earth was in her eyes.

291

Franz had dropped his cake.

"There were some who believed it was possible; the reanimation of the dead. But we tried many times and never had any success," he said. "In 1945 I was both the last to join and the last man left of the Division of Mysteries. Before the war began I had wanted to study folklore, so when that was no longer possible I continued my own education in the evenings. A fellow youth leader mentioned my fascination and after a brief interview I was appointed in an advisory role. It was not a choice."

"I never wanted anything to do with what my father did. I thought it was so weird."

"But here you are."

"Here we are," said Eva.

Franz smiled.

Gabriel sat with his back against the stone altar. Adrian lay on the ground in front of him, breathing shallowly in his sleep.

"You know it's an abomination," said a silky voice.

"Yes Morgana. And the Clan would what? Banish me?" Gabriel was tired. Raising the hounds, raising the dead; it was exhausting. That and he lost something every time he led the hunt. Each time he was a little but more Huntmaster and a little bit less himself.

"Your Clan," she tinkled a laugh, "not mine. My Clan were not afraid of their power. Or themselves."

"And now there is only you. So how well did that serve them?"

"Better to live a little time than merely exist for all the ages." Her lips caressed the words as she crossed the flat base of the hollow towards the altar. Her red gown was darker at the hem where it had dragged on the ever damp earth, growing heavy and pulling the material tight around her thighs. Her feet were bare on the soft grass. She knelt in front of Gabriel.

"I know you helped my sister," he said.

"Oh all of that?" her tone brushed it aside as if the enslavement of Fian and the forbidden raising of the hounds was the mischief of a child. "I gave her a small trinket, nothing more."

"You knew what she was planning."

"Just as I knew your mind when you bid me to touch the dreams of the human boy. Do you now wish that I had not brought her to you? Now that she has spurned you all over again?"

Gabriel tilted his head back against the stone, allowing his eyelids to close. His red hunt coat lay beside him, crumpled awkwardly where the wool was so thick with gore. The air was hot even in the shaded hollow and his will was ebbing, far overstretched these past days.

"What she did was wrong. I will enforce whatever punishment is decided at Court," he said.

Morgana leaned closer, one slim white calf uncovered amidst the folds of dress that blossomed around her.

"Right and wrong. Heroes and villains. They are all such human labels. They are mud in our mouths; we must discard them." She breathed in the scent of woodsmoke and honey, her lips hovering over Gabriel's neck as she spoke.

He opened his mouth to speak, but only managed a sigh as Morgana ran her tongue from his collarbone up to his chin.

"You taste of death," she said.

"I am death." His right hand found the space

293

between her shoulderblades and pulled her close. Beneath the skin his blood still ran hot with the chase, and in the heat he let his glamour melt away. A great weight lifted; the human form he tried to wear, the mask he used to hide his power and his shame.

  "Magnificent," whispered Morgana.

21.
VOWS

"I'm sorry," said Mike. He looked down sadly at the shattered cup on the floor. His workworn hands were still shaking.

"Don't worry at all. Sit down and I'll make us both some tea." Gemma pulled out one of the wooden chairs around the square kitchen table. Mike sat down gratefully.

They had carried four bags of provisions back from the small local shop. It was a wise suggestion from Owain and Gemma wondered how he might have guessed, or known, that all of the cupboards were bare. She turned to Mike. "Do you have sugar?"

A minute later they were both sitting with steaming, and intact, mugs. Mike cradled his with both hands even though it was far too hot to drink. A fresh newspaper lay on the table. Pandora the buzzard had been returned to her large aviary in the garden, and immediately begun a comfortable nap in the sun.

"I almost forgot," said Mike suddenly, rising and nearly sending a second mug to the floor. It stopped an inch from the table edge, but he didn't notice. He was busy opening up the leather satchel, from which he produced the rabbit he had gutted on the moor. "This needs skinning."

Gemma wrinkled up her nose.

"Tea yes. Skinning; no idea."

"Shall I show you?"

Before Gemma could object, Mike had laid the rabbit out on the kitchen table between their mugs of tea. Its stomach was already slit open and the fur and meat had an unfamiliar musky odour. Gemma swallowed, forcing back down her disgust. She had watched the hounds crawl out of the earth. She had ridden to Grimspound on a skeletal horse. *She had seen Gabriel torturing a man who raised corpses*. She shuddered. Things were not ok. But here, in the small sparse cottage, pride made her watch Mike prepare the rabbit.

His hands worked quickly, with help from a sharp penknife that appeared from his pocket.

"Of course it's quicker if you don't want to save the skin," he said, handing the rolled pelt to Gemma. The skin was rolled inwards so her fingers felt only the soft of the fur.

"Thanks," she said, "what do I do with it?"

Mike explained stretching, salting and tanning. He was comfortable now; the shake in his hands and voice had disappeared as the influence of the gin receded. But he spoke fast, unwilling to let the air empty of words, as if that space might allow something else to creep in. He was still afraid.

"Where have you been?" Gemma asked. Owain had told her to save her questions but the significance of the horseshoe still puzzled her, and a flutter in her stomach told her that if something had Mike scared then everyone else should be very scared indeed. The question halted Mike mid word and a now familiar blank expression bled back onto his face.

"Did you leave the horseshoe out for a reason?" she prompted.

"Iron," he muttered, "forged iron."

"To keep away the fae?"

"The fae," Mike's expression darkened. He stood, lifting the skinned carcass by the hind legs, and crossed the room to a large white chest freezer. He dropped the rabbit inside carelessly. "Best stay away from them my girl."

"Why?" Of course she knew why. They would kill you as soon as look at you and humans were pretty much a disgusting plague as far as they were concerned. But he hadn't denied their existence and that was promising.

"Their rules aren't the same." He washed his hands in the large white sink by the window which looked out onto the untidy front garden.

"Have you met them?"

"You don't meet them. Nobody meets them. But they do find you, if they want something." He dried his hands on a well worn teatowel that may once have been printed with popular places to visit on the moor.

"What would they want from a human?" she let the question hang in the air, suddenly worried there was too much weight behind it. And Owain had told her not to ask.

Mike snapped back around, his face fading through stages of confusion back to the familiar blank.

"I'm sorry?" he said

"What would the fae want?" Gemma repeated.

Mike shook his head, distractedly wiping his already dry hands on his trousers.

"I'm sorry, I don't understand," he said. Whatever was causing the blank expression was back in control and it was not to be shifted.

"Don't worry." She forced her face into a smile. Something had happened to Mike while he was gone, and she suspected that Owain might know more about it than he was letting on. Why else would he suddenly want to be so helpful? Was it guilt that had driven him to restock

Mike's cupboards? She struggled to imagine Owain as being purposefully cruel, even after seeing Gabriels transformation and knowing that the boy was Huntmaster in training. He had scared her in the Visitor Centre when she first arrived, but that was just messing around and he had already said sorry. *Their rules aren't the same*. Maybe she was going wrong by putting human expectations on things that were so far from being human.

She jumped at the knock on the door. Mike stood to get it but she felt suddenly protective. *Us humans best stick together*.

The door opened to Owain. His pale face was flushed red and there was no doubt he had rushed straight back as promised.

"Adrian?" Gemma pressed.

"Is very tired," said Owain "he needs to rest." He stepped aside and Gemma saw Gabriel carrying a familiar body up the drive. The Huntmaster carried Adrian with ease, cradled like a child tired out by a long day. She couldn't stop herself crying.

Mike jogged up the stairs ahead of them, opening windows to air out the bedroom and turning back a neatly made, but threadbare, quilt. Gabriel lay Adrian down gently. He stirred slightly, a momentary frown on his face, but then settled back into sleep. Gemma lay the quilt over him and smiled down at his face. It was dark with stubble, flecked with mud and a brown stain that she guessed was blood, but he was alive. Breathing quietly and alive.

"Thank you," she said, turning back around. The room was empty. It was a relief. "Listen Adrian," she said, "when you wake up we are going to have the most amazing breakfast ever. You can have whatever you want. Then we can go home and we can watch something bad on TV; something with nothing scary in." The tears rolled down her cheeks, releasing the pain and the fear. But the guilt was harder to shift. "I should never have said those things. I can't even blame any weird supernatural forces because those horrible thoughts were there in my head. But I don't think you need to do anything to make yourself special. You already are." She turned her head to a quiet knock.

Owain leaned in the doorway, his face half smiling.

"Sorry," said Gemma, embarassed that he might have heard her speech. His face turned serious.

"I don't blame you from wanting to get away from this-" he made an expansive gesture with his hands which included himself, "-weirdness."

Gemma blushed.

"But you will have to hold out just a little bit longer. Adrian won't be back to himself in an instant. He may not be... quite the same."

"What do you mean?"

Owain stepped closer and lowered his voice. "He has been with the dead. It is not usual to return."

Gemma glanced back towards the bed. He didn't look any different. It felt so much better to pretend that nothlng had changed. *It is an abomination*. That's how he had described bringing Adrian back when they were at Grimspound.

"Will he remember?"

"Snatches, perhaps. Like a bad dream."

Gemma sighed. She'd had quite enough of dreams, bad or otherwise. She realised that she should probably call Elaine. The painting and even her voice message seemed like a lifetime ago.

"I'll be here when he wakes up."

Owain nodded. The conversation had petered out, but he still lingered in the doorway, one foot over the threshold.

"You made a promise," he said eventually.

Gemma swallowed. For a second she felt like she was falling.

"Yes."

"It is not a light thing, a binding vow."

Simultaneously she could see him both as the boy who had mocked her in the Visitor Centre and the Huntmaster that he must one day become. The same heaviness she had seen in Gabriel was in his eyes. He was already growing weary and there were centuries yet to come. She realised that he knew all too well the weight of a binding vow; as apprentice he had not been given even the illusion of a choice. At least her debt was chosen.

"But it means I might well be seeing you again, Owain." She smiled and it was genuine.

Owain smiled back, his pale cheeks maybe just a shade brighter, and pushed back a strand of his red hair.

"See you Gemma." With a comforting lack of grace he spun round and clomped down the stairs.

In the kitchen, Gabriel was waiting to leave. His eyes flicked up to Owain as he walked in and then he turned to Mike.

"Look after them both," Gabriel said.

"Of course," said Mike, "they won't want for anything here."

Without meeting Mike's gaze, Gabriel handed him a package wrapped in cloth. Mike took it wordlessly and Gabriel immediately turned heel, leaving Owain to shut the door behind him.

"Get whatever you need from the shop," Owain told Mike, "they won't charge you."

Then, before Mike could object, he was also gone and the door was shut with a firm thud. Only Fian was left behind, rejected from the rest of the pack, but happy to sleep on the sofa.

Mike looked down at the bundle in his hands and for some reason the story Gemma had been telling outside the tearooms came to mind. The cloth was light coloured wool and sat as a square just larger than his palm. Too small for a rabbit. Too small for a child. He shook the story from his head and unwrapped a freshly forged iron horseshoe. As if following an old habit, he stepped out of his door and felt for the empty nail in the timber above it. Then he hung the shoe up, the two ends pointing downwards, so that the luck was pouring out.

Eva was asleep in the late afternoon sun. The shadows of the treecrowded fenceline and the hangar building stretched out across the airfield. Franz was awake, watching the sky out of habit. He didn't feel altered in any way, but he knew that he had been down in the bog with the plane. How much of him had been left before Eva dragged him out? And what held him together now? He picked at the stitching that bound the eagle above his pocket. The world was changed and he wasn't entirely sure if he had a place left in it.

Eva stirred, her face troubled by whatever was in her dreams. She looked small and fragile, curled up into herself with her back to the hangar, her riding jacket unbuttoned in the heat. It was a curse, Franz thought, raising the dead. There would always be people who wanted to use that power for their own ends, and they

301

wouldn't all be planning on asking her nicely. He understood that better than most.

She woke up, her eyelids fluttering in the sun. Franz smiled and she returned the gesture, the expression chasing some of the worry from her face.

"Best call Blake then," she said, stretching.

He answered after one ring, as if he had been waiting. If they could meet back at his hangar, he would drive.

Franz helped Eva up. Her legs tingled where she had slept awkwardly and she leaned on his arm until they were able to support her again. She felt lazy in the late sun that spread heavy and golden across the tarmac like spilt honey. Their feast had been the most she had eaten in weeks. If she could just close her eyes again she could believe it was no more than a nightmare and she would wake early, uncomfortable in the back seat of the Range Rover.

"Ready?" asked Franz.

They had both been inwardly wondering what kind of car a man who owns two vintage planes might drive, and they weren't disappointed. A gleaming cream Aston Martin was parked outside the hangar, top down and flaunting tan leather seats and steering wheel. Blake was polishing a small mark out of one of the sweeping wheelarches with a handkerchief. He stood as they approched, stuffing the cloth back into his pocket.

"Excellent," he said, seemingly as a comment on the world in general. His eyes flicked up and down Franz again but he didn't make any further comment. Instead he swept open the car door and theatrically beckoned them to sit inside. "You don't mind the top down do you?" he winked.

"No," said Eva, stepping up onto the sideskirt of the car and then shuffling along the back seat.

"This is a beautiful car," said Franz.

"Yes," said Blake, "I couldn't quite resist her. We're not going far and I thought she could do with the run."

They pulled away smoothly, purring across the airfield, and then turned left past the control building and out onto a small road. Blake's silk scarf caught in the breeze and danced around his shoulders. *Pretentious prick* Eva thought half heartedly, but she was enjoying the steady rhythm of the car and the air between her fingers as she dangled her arm over the door.

As promised, it was a short drive before they turned up a narrow lane that ended with grand wrought iron gates. Some hidden technology sensed their arrival and swung the heavy gates open noiselessly almost as soon as they had rolled to a halt. Blake drove on slowly, easing his precious car along the gravel driveway. Eva watched the mature beech trees that lined the track march past in perfect rows and realised that she had no idea how much money to ask for the plane.

Blake knocked on the grand front door and was answered by an elderly gentleman in a suit. The gentleman ushered them all in down a hallway lined with ornately carved wooden panels and medieval paintings, then on into a large reception room with bay windows looking out over golden fields and green hedgerows. Eva couldn't help standing and spinning slowly on the spot to take in the wonder of the room. She recognised the mounted head of a huge red deer, antlers spreading out in many tines, but there were other more exotic animals that she didn't know the name of as well. Between these trophies were great swords and crossed guns, resplendent in their shine or fascinating in their decay. On a side table a woman cast in bronze supported a glowing orb whilst simultaneoulsy twirling out her delicate layers of skirts.

The manservant reappeared silently.

"Mr. Early will see you now."

Blake started forward but the man held out a wrinkled hand. "The sellers only," he said. This seemed to come as an unwelcome surprise. Blake brushed the floppy front of his hair out of his eyes with agitation.

"Now see here-" he began, but the old servant had already beckoned Eva and Franz to follow and begun to walk away. They followed without hesitation, Eva feeling a little smug as they left Blake behind, wringing his hands and insignificant in the grand parlour.

The manservant led them to a dark wood panelled door and knocked sharply. From inside the room Eva could hear the swell of classical music. They waited; there was no answer. Unperturbed, the servant turned the ornate brass doorhandle and gestured that they should go inside. They music was immediately louder, crackling tunefully from a gramophone in the corner of the room. An unoccupied writing desk stood immediately in front of them, carved from the same glossy dark wood as the door, and topped with green leather. To the left was a large fireplace, ornately decorated but looking a little dismal unlit. To the right the walls were lined ceiling high with books, and at the base of the shelves there were two leather armchairs and a low table crowded with crystal decanters. It was from here that the voice came.

"This piece was recorded over sixty years ago," it said, "and it never ceases to amaze me how it still sounds unchanged. How is it that I feel I know them so well; the slightly missed beat, the breath before the chorus, each individual voice, when I have only heard the musicians after they've died?" The man rose from his chair and turned to extend a hand. "Maximillian Early."

"Nice to meet you," said Eva.

"Miss Maker, I presume, and Mr. Schell, bedazzaled of course." He kissed Eva's hand and shook Franz's, utterly unfazed by his attire.

Eva glanced to her left and gave Franz a small smile. His grey eyes were glassy and she arrived at the conclusion that he was familar with the music.

"Will you take a drink?" Maximillian asked, already pouring himself a brandy.

"Yes," said Franz.

They sat in the two deep green armchairs, arms resting on the padded wings, and watching their host as he paced enthusiastically between them. He had insisted on standing as Eva narrated the story of why they had the plane and how they had come to make an emergency landing at North Weald Airfield. She had used their waiting time to pad out the tale considerably and she was pleased overall with the result.

"Your father sounds like some man, I would very much have liked to meet him," Maximillian concluded.

"Yes," said Eva truthfully, "he was."

"And I can understand why you would wish to sell the plane at this point, what with all the matters that you must now attend to."

Eva thought of her father, buried in the barrow with rotting monsters, and vowed to return one day to give him the proper send off he deserved.

"He would be pleased to see it go to a collector," she said, thinking back to the many he had attempted to supply, and the final one left somewhere waiting for his prize. She felt for the dagger impulsively, glad to feel the metal pressed against her skin.

"Well, that's me," said Maximillian cheerfully, "and please don't worry, I'm not here to drive a hard bargain. Shall we say one and a half and shake on it?"

Eva reached out to take his hand slowly.

"One and a half what?"

"Million," he said.

They were about to leave, when Maximillian called them back.

"Are you interested in history?"

"Yes," said Eva cautiously.

"Take a look at this." For the second time that day, a tablet with an image on was thrust into her hands. She recognised what it was immediately. A clammy film began to form on her palms. It took all of her willpower to stop her hands shaking; Maximillian had a hand on the tablet also and there was no doubt he'd feel it.

"The spear of Longinus, said to have pierced the side of Christ," Franz said, over her shoulder.

"Precisely. Called by some the Spear of Destiny."

Eva relased the device slowly, fiercely taking in the detail of Maximillian's cufflink, which was a nine spoked wheel. Anything to not look at the dagger.

"It looks interesting."

"Extremely interesting. I've seen it on display in Vienna of course, but they say that is merely a replica, and that the true lance was smuggled out of Germany near the end of the war." He nodded conspiritorially at Franz. Eva wondered who 'they' were.

"I'd do anything to get my hands on that." Maximillian said.

There was a strained sort of silence and then Eva faked a lengthy yawn, the cold metal of the dagger pressing into her back.

"Of course you've had a full day," said Maximillian, "so sorry to be boring you with my stale old fancies."

"I hope you like the plane," Eva said.

"Eh- oh yes, of course. With your situation, would you object if I put it on a pre paid credit card for you? Difficult to carry around that much cash and all that."

"Um, ok."

"Splendid. I'll have my driver bring you to the nearest hotel. He will return with the card before you check out."

"Thank you."

"Yes, yes, of course." Maximillian's concentration had released them and was on the tablet in his hand. The manservant opened the door by some invisible communication, or perhaps he had been standing outside listening.

"Well?" asked Blake, as they walked back into the parlour.

"Sold," said Eva.

"Ha! Thought as much. He'd best remember me for this." Blake waggled a finger at the impassive manservant.

"Mr. Early will have his pilot collect the Messerschmitt tomorrow morning. Please arrange for all necessary clearances," said the old gentleman. It was clearly a dismissal.

Blake curled his lip and half turned, expecting Eva and Franz to follow.

"Mr. Early has made arrangements for his guests." Blake bowed sarcastically.

"We may cross paths again, *mein kinder.*" Then he was gone and there was the sound of a large engine outside, which quickly dwindled to nothing.

Eva let her head fall back against the soft headrest of the black Mercedes, and thought how she had never before travelled in such a range of expensive cars. The image of a real bed with soft pillows had taken over her mind. She reached out and patted Franz's hand sleepily.

"We're rich," she said.

Epilogue

Three days later, Adrian woke up. He had no memory of anything beyond being lost on the moor, except at night, when he would scream in his sleep until Gemma came in to comfort him. But he was alive. And slowly, he began to smile and laugh again. He helped Mike to tidy up the front garden. Between them they pruned the roses, dug out the vegetable patch and cut the lawn to a length that could be deemed respectable. They even cut wood to make a little rustic border to edge the path. Owain retrieved Adrian's car from the moor.

Gemma stretched and tanned her rabbit pelt under Mike's supervision, and in the evenings they cooked meals together or one time drove out to the Warren House Inn for a pub dinner. Mike drank ginger beer and Adrian mocked him because he was so impressed.

Two weeks passed like this, until one morning Gemma got a call on her phone. It was Elaine. Wanting to speak privately, she pushed open the front door, scattering a small pile of bones. She glanced around, surprised she hadn't noticed that there was a cat about, and thought no more about it. Elaine was relieved to hear that everything was alright now, although Gemma heard her breath catch down the phone when she told her how Adrian had been missing. The worst details she held back.

The next morning Gemma went out to get some milk, and dislodged a slightly larger pile of bones. The day after it was the skeleton of a fox. Then a badger. That night Gemma decided she would stay up.

Around two in the morning she heard Adrian stir. Sitting motionless in the shadows, keen to move her legs from the position she had been dozing in but not daring,

309

she watched his bedroom door swing open. He walked past confidently and Gemma crept behind him, noticing Fian slip out of his basket to shadow her. She followed Adrian out the front door, down the garden path and onto the pavement. He walked briskly, heading past the Plume of Feathers pub on his right and on towards the moor.

He stopped near a gully than ran along the moorside of the hedging and fencing that followed the road. Gemma climbed the low fence ungainly, pushing herself through a small gap in the hawthorn and cursing under her breath. She was sure she had torn her trousers. Adrian was very still, his head tilted upwards and his face bleached by the moonlight. The skin of his eyelids was stretched taut and his eyes rolled behind them. There was a tingle in the air and an earthy taste on Gemma's tongue which made her shiver despite her jumper. It was familar. She remembered it from Grimspound and Owain's words were a shout in her head; *he may not be quite the same*.

She flung a hand across her mouth as the skull bobbed up from the ground, tossing off the earth like treacle. Her arm was stretched out towards Adrian, undecided if it was warding him off or wanting to slap him free of what flowed through him. The pony caught purchase on the ground with its front hooves and lurched forward, shaking itself to clear clods of earth from its smaller bones. On one side the ribs were shattered and Gemma guessed it must have been hit on the road. Adrian reached out. The pony dipped its head and stilled as he lay a flat palm on its shoulder. For a few stretched out seconds the boy and the skeletal pony did nothing except collect moonlight, falling full and thick on pale skin and pale bone alike. Then Adrian turned and began striding back towards town. The pony followed, clearing the hedge in one leap and clattering down on the other side. Gemma ground her teeth and headed after them.

There was no traffic but she winced each time the pony broke into a jaunty trot, the clank of hooves echoing loudly round the sleeping town. But it was not an unusual sound and no one ran out screaming. Adrian's pace was slowing as they neared the cottage and Gemma was able to nip ahead of him and push open the front door for him to shuffle through. She closed it, quite decisively, on the pony.

Adrian scaled the stairs wearily and climbed back into bed. Gemma watched him turn over fitfully a few times before exhaustion claimed him. From outside there was a tinkling crash as whatever held the pony bones together released them.

Gemma frowned.

"I see."

Acknowledgements

I am indebted to Karen Hamilton-Viall,
Gordon Newstead and Carole Newstead
for their attentive proof reading.

Thanks are also due to an army of people who have offered
encouragement, support and inspiration when it was most
needed.

This book has been completed with help from the
'Graeme Cook Young People's Writing Challenge'.

facebook/heatofthehunt

The tale continues in 'Lie of the Land'.